Praise for

Alice At Heart

Book One: WaterLilies

Awards

- *Romantic Times* BOOKclub magazine's Reviewer's Choice Award for Best Fantasy Novel, 2002

- Winner of the prestigious 2003 Maggie Award for Paranormal Romance, presented by the Georgia Romance Writers of America

- Finalist, Dorothy Parker Award for Paranormal Romance, presented by the Reviewers International Organization (RIO)

Reviews

"Readers of Alice Hoffman will enjoy Smith's surprisingly convincing blend of romance and magical realism."

— *Booklist*

"Old secrets, revenge, and passion fuel this compelling, intricately plotted story of love, trust, and acceptance, which successfully straddles the line between romance and fantasy and should appeal to fans of both genres."

— *Library Journal*

"Absolutely magical and, in my mind, a real masterpiece. Kudos to D.S. for producing something so fresh and so perfect."

—*Susan Elizabeth Phillips,*
New York Times *bestselling author*

"Wonderfully original and different — brava!"

— *Susan Wiggs, bestselling author*

Alice At Heart is available in trade paperback direct from BelleBooks at *www.bellebooks.com* and at fine bookstores everywhere.

Praise for the novels of

Deborah Smith

"When this generous book [Charming Grace] throws its arms open to assemble a family with Boone and Grace at its center, the reader rejoices. Romance is about the future, and everyone gets a new one in this big-hearted Southern tale."

— *Washington Post*

"Deborah Smith is one romance novelist who just keeps getting better."

— *Publishers Weekly*

"Nobody can create strong, interesting and intelligent female lead characters the way Ms. Smith does."

— *www.readertoreader.com*

"A spellbinding storyteller."

— *Booklist*

"For sheer storytelling virtuosity, Ms. Smith has few equals."

— *Richmond Times-Dispatch*

"One of the best romantic writers in the business today."

— *Woman Magazine*

"A great Southern novelist."

— *The Romance Reader*

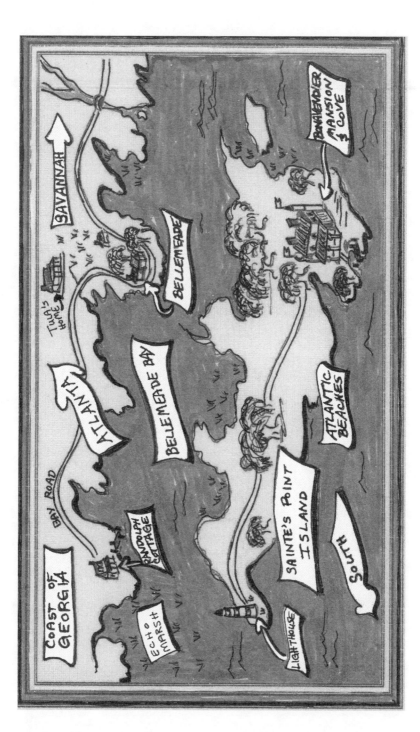

The books of
Deborah Smith

Beloved Woman

Blue Willow

Silk and Stone

A Place to Call Home

When Venus Fell

On Bear Mountain

The Stone Flower Garden

Sweet Hush

Charming Grace

Alice at Heart (WaterLilies, Book One)

Diary of a Radical Mermaid (WaterLilies, Book Two)

Deborah Smith

Deborah Smith is the award-winning, nationally bestselling author of 35 novels, including the *New York Times* bestseller, A Place to Call Home. Film rights to her 2003 novel, *Sweet Hush*, have been bought by Disney. Her WaterLilies series for BelleBooks will continue in 2005 with *The Radical Mermaid Gets Rude*.

Learn more about the books of Deborah Smith at
www.deborahsmith.com

www.bellebooks.com

www.deborahsmith-solomonseal.com

POPULI AQUARUM

Diary of a Radical Mermaid

Deborah Smith

Smyrna, Georgia

BelleBooks, Inc.

ISBN 0-9673035-7-5

Diary of a Radical Mermaid

Published by:
BelleBooks, Inc. • P.O. Box 67 • Smyrna, GA 30081
We at BelleBooks enjoy hearing from readers. You can contact us at the address above or at BelleBooks@BelleBooks.com

Visit our website— www.BelleBooks.com

First Edition July 2004

10 9 8 7 6 5 4 3 2 1

Cover art: Sheila Aldridge
Cover design: Martha Shields
Map: Deborah Smith

Hidden between Earth and Water Await Miracles

— *from the Bonavendier family crest*

❧ ❧

Diary of a Radical Mermaid

❧ ❧

"Most of the world is covered in oceans. Ninety-five percent of the world beneath those oceans has not yet been explored. We can only imagine what may exist beyond our shores."

— *Marine biologist, a Lander*

"*What* may exist? How about *who*?"

— *Marine biologist, a Mer*

Donald and Me

∽ ∽ ∽ ∽ ∽ ∽ ∽ **1** ∽ ∽ ∽ ∽ ∽ ∽ ∽

I was herding Paris Hilton and her shopping entourage down a Manhattan boulevard when I broke the biggest rule of mermaid life: Don't show your tail in public. It seemed like such an innocent joke, dissing Donald Trump. But a Merbabe of real class does not, simply does not, shout across Fifth Avenue, "Bad hair is *not* a symbol of self-confidence! Donald, I don't care how big a hit *The Apprentice* was last season, the seventies are *over*. Stop with the comb-over, already! Or shave your head and get some transplants!"

Doing a bitch slap on a man's hair is never a good thing, especially if a loud, beautiful redhead (me) yells at his (Donald's) hair in the company of a famous heiress (Paris, who asked for my fashion guidance after recent public fiascoes) while a crew from *Entertainment Tonight* happens to be filming his (Donald's) Manhattan stroll.

Because then they started filming Donald's *hair*.

Donald's a charming and rich man, but like most ordinary, plain-footed people on the planet he thinks he rules the whole globe when, in fact, he only rules the dry parts. The rest, which is covered in sweet, deep water, belongs to us — the Merfolk, aka Water People, aka People of Water, if you want to be politically correct about it.

Landers, one fourth. Mers, three fourths. Who's more important? Donald or me? *You* do the math.

Still, I shouldn't have pissed him off when he was on the verge of signing a huge New York real estate deal with

Riyad bin Mahadeen, who is my great aunt Lilith's lover, one of the world's richest men, and a senior member of the world-wide Mer Council. Not that Donald knows he does business with Mers. Like all Landers, he never suspects. His hair would probably stand on end. What a mental image.

"Juna Lee Poinfax," Donald told Riyad, "needs to be locked in a room somewhere and forced to look at pictures of my hair until she apologizes to me."

Horrors. I refused.

So Donald pulled out on the multi-million-dollar deal, and Riyad banished me from polite Mer society for costing him a small fortune, and, thus, here I am, just another Mer rebel without a cause, sentenced to community service in the boondocks. Jane Austen could have written my woeful tale of class and privilege purloined, it's so sad. She was a mermaid three times removed on her father's side, you know.

Anyway, here I sit. Serving time on the beautiful but bucolic Georgia coast. What am I to do? How can I possibly preserve my *Je ne sais quoi de mermaid*?

I know. I'll start a diary. A really hell-raising one.

Be warned. Mermaid at work.

Sainte's Point Island, Georgia

ॐ ॐ ॐ ॐ ॐ ॐ ॐ **2** ॐ ॐ ॐ ॐ ॐ ॐ ॐ

Dear Diary:

All right, first, you ordinary people (Landers) need to know why my name is Juna Lee Poinfax. Yes, I know how it sounds.

Juna Lee. I might as well buy a beauty parlor and a house trailer.

Juna Lee is a very Southern name in the sense of being melodramatic and a little fey, thanks to a streak of pomposity among Mers, who love classical names, and a streak of humor in the Poinfax family tree, which is rooted in the Southern mint julep waters of Charleston, South Carolina. Juna is from the Roman goddess Juno, queen of just about everything. Lee is from my mother's family, who claim to be related to Confederate General Robert E. (Lee).

I say claim because Mers are related by blood or marriage to just about every Lander of any consequence, or, should I say, more accurately, Mers believe every Lander of any consequence is related to a Mer.

We Poinfaxes are proud to be Southern Mer gentry. We always believe in gilding the lily. If we had a motto on our family crest, it would probably be this:

We're Better Than Everyone Else, And We Know It

That motto has become my *cri de couer* since I've decided to write this subversive little journal. Where to start, hmmm, where to dive in? What do you Landers need to know first about us Mer people? Well, the obvious:

Mermaids are real.

Do I mean that half-naked, flipper-bottomed people are hiding in your local lake? Absolutely not! How tacky! But, as with most worldwide mythology with ancient and abiding roots, there's always a pearl of truth in the middle of the oyster of folklore.

Mers are that pearl.

I am a "person of water." One of the Water People. merfolk, if that makes you happy. I don't have fins, I don't live in an underwater condo, I don't shapeshift between a pouty Darryl Hannah clone and a half-fish cartoon figure. I have two legs, I *always* have two legs, and I look more or less like anyone else. Only better. And with webbed toes.

Mers are real, yes. Very real. Thanks to certain psychic gifts and endless charisma, we live among you discreetly, though often in control of local and, indeed, worldwide events. If not for a hapless inability to reproduce like Landers, aka horny rabbits, we'd no doubt rule the planet.

Mers are diverse. You have your purists, your anarchists, your outcasts, and your middle-of-the-streamers. But in general, we share the following:

- Gorgeous good looks
- Very long hair that tends to grow six inches per day (this is true for both men and women)
- Ability to see very well under water, aided by a highly developed sonar talent
- Ability to remain under water for long periods of time, up to several hours in rare cases
- Incredible swimming ability (I mean, that's a given, right?)
- Beautifully webbed toes
- Psychic abilities, including a "singing" type of thing among ourselves, plus a fair amount of mind control over you ordinary Landers

You don't believe a word I'm telling you, do you? No way will you admit that some of the mysteries that go bump in the night (or in our case, splash in the water) might be real. But, trust me, there's a whole different world out there beyond your safe little shores. Hang in there with me, sweeties, and I'll tell you about it.

Even if I'm not supposed to.

Ali Bonavendier, my cousin by virtue of being Lilith's long-lost baby half-sister (don't ask), wrote this little tidbit in her private journal when she came to Sainte's Point. Her name was Alice Riley then. She'd been raised up in the boonies of the Appalachian mountains without knowing her father or his Mer heritage. She was practically a hillbilly. She had no clue that she was a superior human being. Poor baby. But she's fine now.

How did I get a peek at her private journal? Well, we're both living at the island's mansion right now, and we're the best of friends, and she trusts me so much she shares her most intimate writings with me.

Okay, okay. I swiped it when she wasn't looking. Here's what she wrote:

"The Bonavendier sisters own Sainte's Point Island and everything of importance in the town of Bellemeade, just across the bay. Lilith and her two sisters play with the village as if it were their pretty toy: the shops are exquisite, the bay front inn, WaterLilies, is a place of internationally renowned charm, and the marina along Main Street is a perfect combination of hardworking fishing boats and exotic little yachts. People swear a kind of enchantment comes over them when they visit the town. They gaze across Bellemeade Bay with wistful envy at the secretive island, which looks like a magical, wooded kingdom floating on the horizon. Look *toward the other side of the world*, people say, *and you'll see Bonavendiers*.

"Sainte's Point Island, enclave of the Bonavendier family since Revolutionary War times, is glamorous, notorious, alluring, and haunted by gossip. It is said every Bonavendier for two centuries has been born with webbed feet, always swims naked, can seduce anyone at will, is beloved by dolphins, and drinks like a fish. Vodka, preferably.

"Those rumors, as I'm coming to learn, are quite true."

Isn't that perfect, how Ali put it? Glamorous? Notorious? Yum. Drinks like a fish? Double yum. Your vices are our virtues. Delicious.

As Ali said, Bellemeade is a tiny, quaint, exceedingly rich little village perched on the Georgia coast near Savannah. If you look at a map of Georgia you'll see that the coastline resembles the nubby fringe of a frayed scarf. There are hundreds of little coves, bays, inlets, and waterways — it's a remarkable and sultry subtropical world of ancient history — Indians and pirates and brave Africans escaping slavery and bell-like Southern belles! — all sheltered by enormous maritime oaks dripping moss. If you know the right people you'll be invited to the hidden mansions, the shaded lanes of the fishing villages, and the coves where some of the world's richest Mers discreetly moor small yachts.

But you'll rarely be invited to the private islands. A pretty string of them dot the waters off the Georgia coast, some no bigger than a glorified hummock, others vast enough to harbor all sorts of fascinating lives. Follow them up the continental coast and you'll glide among the Outer Banks of the Carolinas, then on up into the cold beauties of the northeast, Long Island, Cape Cod, and the like. Only a few of the Georgia islands are public, and even the public ones are charming in their own way — St. Simon's and the teensy islands around its gilded shores, and Jekyll, where we Mers have quite a history among the Rockefellers and other rich Lander clans who turned the whole island into their private play-ground during the early 1900s.

But the most amazing islands are privately owned, and the most amazing of them all is, naturally, Sainte's Point, which is owned by Mers. The Bonavendier mansion is a marvel of antiques and acquired treasures. I say *acquired*, because, quite frankly, Mers have never been immune to a certain love for piracy, although the modern Bonavendiers eschew such crude and graspy behavior. Besides, with so much inherited money to spend, why bother with any con-temporary yo-ho-ho-ing on the open seas? What fun is it to waylay some ugly modern ship chugging along with all the challenge of a floating metal box? What fabulous treasure would one steal? A Toyota?

As I am somewhat persona non grata in many of my usual world ports at the moment, Sainte's Point is a lovely place to, well, let one say, it's a lovely sanctuary where my, hmmm, controversial reputation for partying and meddling can take a little hiatus from deeper scrutiny of recent activi-ties.

Or some shit like that.

☞ ☞ ☞

Dear Diary:

Okay, so much for discretion. Today I waltzed into my cousin's fabulous jewelry shop in Bellemeade, and I an-nounced, "I have a blog."

To which my cousin replied, "Juna Lee, I believe plastic surgery will remove that kind of thing."

Very funny. Tula Bonavendier is a wry snit, more smug than even the typical Mer, since she's established herself as quite the high-end jewelry designer. Most Mers are content to live off the fortunes their families have amassed over the centuries, and most are players and wanderers, to say the least. But not Tula.

She's as industrious as a crab in a garbage dump. You'll see ads for her designs in almost every issue of *Vogue* and *Vanity Fair*, the stunning arrays of pearls and diamonds draped around the sleek necks of barely clothed models whose pouty cheeks are so sunken I wonder if they've had some molars pulled to achieve the look.

Mers are magnificently built but not skeletal. We not only love spending inordinate amounts of time underwater, we aren't much affected by even the iciest water temps. That kind of talent requires a lovely, softly dense layer of fat beneath our perfect skin — it's quite the scientific marvel, not that we ever allow Landers to cop a peek at the cell structure under their microscopes. At any rate, we are lusciously endowed in more ways than one, and while we may pout to dangerous excess, we never look gaunt when we do it.

But back to Tula. She's a tall, svelte redhead, a few years older than moi, though she'll never admit it. I gauge her at about fifty, but of course, that means nothing in mer-person years. She looks thirty and is always adorned with the latest designer fashions and the wry grimace of a self-righteous nerd.

Tula spends a lot of her time trying to understand Landers, so she can sell them high-end trinkets. I think she's been tainted by Lander attitudes, which are boringly anxious. Tula has never quite gotten over some Lander love affair from a few years back. Since I'm an expert on love and sex, let me say right now, with all fairness, that no Mer has any business diddling a Lander.

It only ruins the poor Lander, who becomes totally obsessed with the mer-person (a given), and it puts the Mer in a watery pickle since Landers, well, like *land*. They tend to want to move far from the oceans and live in high places where the altitude is atrocious. (Did I mention most Mers can't tolerate heights?) Also, Landers are sweet but fragile. They keel over at young ages, compared to us. Who wants to be in her prime at only 70 or 80 and care for some decrepit old Lander whose hunky Lander appeal long ago disappeared behind hearing aids, skinny legs, and a subscription to the large-print edition of *Reader's Digest?*

At any rate, don't pay any attention to Tula.

On my blog-announcement day she was dressed in one of those coy, retro, Lily Pulitzer shifts, looking like a cartoon daisy with breasts. Only Tula could pull off a look like that with a straight face. Leaning on one of the polished display counters at her shop, she crossed one perfectly tanned webbed foot over the other perfectly tanned webbed foot — both feet clad in strappy little yellow sandals with tiny ruby anklets — and she eyed me as if I'd lost my mind.

"What do you intend to write about in this on-line diary, Juna Lee? All you do is shop and chase Eurotrash and throw parties."

"Why, those credentials alone qualify me to write a trashy gossip column pretending to be social commentary. I could be a columnist for *Vanity Fair.*" (Always hit Tula where her ads live.) "I have a masters in writing from some university. I forget the name."

Tula sniffed. "You got your degree by seducing professors."

"I like shortcuts. But I *am* a writer."

"So what are you going to write about in this computer diary?"

"Our people."

Tula straightened ominously. "Please tell me that by 'our people' you mean servants, employees, maids, butlers. A sort of *Upstairs, Downstairs* blog?"

"I mean mer-people, and you know it."

Tula rushed from behind the counter, scattering several of her large, slit-eyed, champion Persians. Her shop is large and elegant, filled with twinkling pink-crystal chandeliers and soft Impressionist paintings. The Monet was a gift to her great-grandmother from the artist himself. The Persians sleep on a Louis XIV divan on cashmere throws.

"Writing about us is an invasion of privacy!" she bellowed. "And a sacrilege! And very rude! Wasn't the Trump incident enough trouble for you?"

"Oh, for godssake, I'm not writing about you personally," I lied. "I'm just aiming for a little water-to-land detente, you know, a little understanding between the haves and the have-nots, webbing-wise—"

"It's forbidden! Against the rules! Dangerous!"

I put hand on hip and pouted. "Oh? Because the Council says so? The Council makes recommendations, Tula, not laws."

The Council, you see, is the Mer equivalent of the United Nations, only without diplomatic immunity and free parking passes. It governs merfolk everywhere, slapping hands when need be, sending very unpleasant people to scold the mullet-heads and rakehells of our secretive society, and, in general, making pompous, pain-in-the-ass pronouncements about Mer decorum and relations with Landers. I suppose without it some of our greedier, more maniacal Mers would run amok and take over the world, but aside from preventing a few loony Mers from killing off all the Landers and establishing worldwide domination, I don't see why the Council is so tight-assed. Tight-toed. Whatever.

"I'm just having a little literary fun in the interest of public relations," I said. "Besides, most Landers will assume my blog is fiction. Maybe I'll become the Danielle Steele of Mer lore. Publish books. Have movies made. Be interviewed by Barbara Walters. Her great-great-grandmother was a Mer, you know. There are a few webbed toes hidden in that woman's family closet. I think her tongue's webbed, too. That explains a lot."

Tula groaned and shook her head. "Why don't you do something useful, instead? Like take up water polo."

"I tried. The horse keeps drowning."

"Very funny."

"I want to write about our people. It'll be fun. And harmless. You'll see."

"I predict the Council will send someone to string you up by your webbing until you behave."

"The Council has far more important items on its agenda than little old me and my blog. They're obsessed with UniWorld Oil trying to take over the planet. My little blog is a trifle."

Tula sighed and looked unconvinced. "I don't like the smell of this fish, Juna Lee. You've gotten yourself into trouble, before, but this time —"

"Oh, shut up and sell me something pretty." I smiled, went over to a counter, then cooed in delight. "That little diamond tennis bracelet with the platinum setting will do. Put it on my account."

Tula rolled her azure eyes (and no, it would not be accurate, nor interesting, to call them simply 'blue'). Anyway, rolled her azure eyes and went behind the counter to fetch my bracelet. "You don't even play tennis," she said. "Out of the water, you're as graceful as a beached whale."

"Kiss my blubber," I replied with great drama, then took my bracelet and marched out.

Lilith

೪೪ ೪೪ ೪೪ ೪೪ ೪೪ ೪೪ ೪೪ **3** ೪೪ ೪೪ ೪೪ ೪೪ ೪೪ ೪೪ ೪೪

Of course, it didn't take long for word about my diary to reach Lilith. About two nanoseconds, to be precise. You don't want Lilith mad at you. Picture Katherine Hepburn in her prime, with webbed toes, two yards of wavy auburn hair, and a Southern accent that could melt a martini olive. That's my great-aunt.

As I've said, she's seventy but that doesn't mean a thing in Mer terms. You wouldn't peg her at more than forty — and that's sans any nipping and tucking. She rules the Bonavendier clan and all its subsidiaries, which are spread far and wide. More than a thousand Mers revere Sainte's Point Island as the Mer equivalent of Buckingham Palace, the Statue of Liberty, and Hyannis Port all rolled into one. (Jackie Kennedy had the most discreet Mer family background, by the way. No surprise. Such style. Such intelligence, such class!)

Lilith called me back from a shopping trip in Atlanta on a sultry afternoon decorated with puffy Gulf Stream clouds and warm spring waves. I left my car in Bellemeade and swam across to Sainte's Point. It's an easy swim from Bellemeade, no more than a mile, give or take a small shark or two. The local dolphins chirped at me like disgusted sisters. Dolphins are so full of themselves. "Oh, puh-leeeze, it's only a blog," I chirped back.

After I dried off, wound my red hair up in a hefty braid, and donned a sweet silk sheath with darling little hand-painted Moroccan sandals, I made my way up the stone walkway from the island's docks and boat house. There had been a good deal of hubbub at Sainte's Point lately, what with the elaborate wedding of Ali to Griffin Randolph in the works, but there was a lull in the prenuptial preparations that day. At the sight of me, the household staff — two plump, angelic brothers and a sister — clutched their hearts and staggered about in feigned horror.

Annoying little Tanglewoods. They were only Landers, but generations of their family's spellbound service to the Bonavendiers had given them a Mer-like capacity for appalled attitudes and prissy social judgment. "Just a blog," I flung at them, and hurried by.

In her elegant, sun-filled office, Lilith looked up from an exquisite Russian czarina desk Napoleon shipped home to Josephine during that foolish little trek toward Moscow. Josephine was one of us, by the way. Such a naive child, though understandably caught up in owning lovely jewels and gilded etageres. How foolish to fall in love with a Lander in general and a midget megalomaniac in particular.

My great-aunt frowned at me. I gulped. Lilith looked frighteningly at home behind an empress's desk.

"I hear from Tula," she said, "that you're writing some kind of computerized journal about us, for the whole world to read."

I sank down on an overstuffed French divan with all the drama of a wounded artiste. Me, that is, not the divan. "Go ahead and scold me. Tell me I'll be in trouble with the Council again." I swooned on the divan with the back of one hand against my forehead. "Never mind that I'm a serious writer and scholarly Mer historian, not to mention the daughter of your third cousin once removed —"

"If only you'd channel your melodrama into an acting career, Juna Lee." She smiled, all shrewd eyes and cool mouth, catlike. "You could be the host of one of those reality shows.

I have the perfect name for it. *All Wet.*"

I wound a long necklace of pearls into a faux noose around my throat. "So you'll let me hang in the court of public opinion? You refuse to help me?"

"On the contrary."

I dropped my pearls and lurched upright on the divan. "Really?"

"Yes. I approve of your blog."

"You approve of my blog?"

"Yes. And I'll even allow you to post excerpts from my history of Mers."

I squealed and applauded. "This is wonderful."

"It's not for your benefit. It's for all of us. The world is becoming a very small place, Juna Lee. The oceans are shrinking."

"You mean . . . metaphorically? Because I thought we had that whole *shrinking ocean* thing all taken care of with global warming."

Lilith sighed at my frivolity. "There has always been a delicate balance between us and the immense Lander population. That balance is becoming more fragile as our worlds merge. Humans in a disconnected world, lost to themselves and each other, encased in vast waters or dry cities, while the planet slowly spins out of control toward a frightening future of sterile and regimented loneliness. I'm seeking to draw the faithful together and create a social revolution of sorts, a quiet return to the water in spirit as well as form. Landers share the waters with us, they always have. They are part of us. And we are part of them."

"Only much better dressed."

Lilith arched a brow. I was hopeless, yes. "Go and write your computer journal, your *blog*. Try to spread the good word about us, Juna Lee. See what you stir up and who swims to the surface because of it. You may find a good deal of trouble, but not from the powers that be. I'll speak to the Council on your behalf."

I was stunned. This was much better news than I'd dared hope. I leapt to my feet. "You'll intervene with the Council? Let's celebrate! I'll make a gallon of martinis! And a second gallon for *you!*"

My career as a Mer blogger had been launched.

Crossing Jordan

❧ ❧ ❧ ❧ ❧ ❧ ❧   4   ❧ ❧ ❧ ❧ ❧ ❧ ❧

I hurried to take advantage of my new status as a journalist. My first interview: Jordan Brighton. I headed up the coast in my lovely little yacht, *The Delicious*. Destination: the very rich enclave of Hilton Head Island, South Carolina. Land of fine beaches, multiple golf courses, excellent shopping, exquisite resorts, and Jordan, the most alluring hellion since Rhett Butler (who, by the way, exhibited many of the qualities of your average Mer playboy). I decided I'd wear something expensive, seductive, but very, very strict.

The oversexed dog fish began singing to me even before Hilton Head's beaches, villas, and piney coastline came into view. Singing is a low hum, sometimes wordless but emotional, sometimes filled with images and messages. Who needs a cell phone when you've got a real psychic network?

There's a reason the vast majority of Mer people fall into the Singer caste. We *sing*. We sing to communicate without speaking, we sing to subtly control Landers (who can be maneuvered like remote-controlled toy cars, if one is in the mood). We sing to find loved ones over great distances, and we sing under water (sonar, remember — it's a very useful little tool when you're ping-ping-pinging along some dark, deeply submerged Mediterranean ruin looking for priceless trinkets).

Anyway, singing can be practical. Singing can be soothing. Singing can be a warning. And singing can be a seduction.

Bingo.

The horndog fish was toying with me. Warming me all over with a low-pitched hum. If I gave it a voice, it would be a bass flute, deep and reedy, like a warm breath on my bare stomach. Standing on the deck of my yacht with my head thrown back in the wind, I swayed and clutched the rail.

Stop that you outrageous jerk stop stop or I will hurt you, I screeched into his head. High pitched, lots of vibrato. Designed to pierce the psychic eardrum.

His hum filled with a long, low, deep laugh, but he stopped.

When I reached his villa I found him in his bizarre pool. Its one of those faux rock creations, woodsy and natural with a huge waterfall pouring over boulders, as if someone merely plucked an Olympic-sized pond from high in the Rockies and set it down on the other side of the continent. Jordan Brighton likes contrasts. There he was in the hot, sandy, moss-draped forest world of coastal South Carolina, surrounded by palm trees and hibiscus, and what did he do? He built himself a Rocky Mountain log villa and a mountain pond.

Lander envy, I say to myself. How sad. His lungs would puff up like a blow fish if he tried to live in real mountains.

I heard that, he sings back.

There he was, lounging on the bottom of his silly pool with a high-tech, deep-water, submersible camera weighing him down. One of his experimental toys. I frowned at him. When Mers are underwater they don't get that strangled, hamster-cheeked expression all Landers wear when they're holding their breath. Mers are perfectly comfortable and look at ease. So he looked very handsome underwater.

Planning to tour the Titanic again? I asked with psychic sarcasm.

How boring, he answered. *If you've seen one famous wreck, you've seen them all*. He smiled up at me. Brilliant white teeth enhanced by deep blue chlorine. He was dressed in relatively demure black trunks — naked would have been a rude provocation, and a *Speedo* would just be gilding the lily — so he'd opted for classic and coy.

My heart twisted. I hated him. I loved him. I was terrified of his effect on me. All the usual suspects.

He surfaced with all the sensuous movement of a lazy squid. When his dark-haired head broke the pool's surface he quipped, "You heard me calling, all the way down at Sainte's Point. Couldn't resist. As usual."

"Couldn't resist? It was my choice to come here today. It's been five years since that debacle at Cannes. If I couldn't resist, I'd have strangled you long ago."

Cannes. The famed place, the famed film festival. He and I had gone there together, enjoying what I can fairly admit was the happiest time of my entire Mer life thus far. He'd anchored his yacht off the French coast and we filled it with the most glamorous party people in the world, both Landers and Mer. Mers love the movie star life — I could name names of more than a few superstars who are Mers — so we were there to party hearty with the webbed crowd. And we were there to make love to each other in the warm French waters. Which we did — wildly, wonderfully, and constantly.

Everything was perfect until we had a misunderstanding as to the exact degree of our committed romance. I was. He wasn't. Committed, that is.

"Cannes?" Jordan said now, reading my thoughts. He loved to pretend he was a careless man, but underneath those still waters he was a boiling volcano-Mer. Which is why I couldn't forget him, but also why I kept trying. "Cannes," he repeated darkly, with just the right touch of evil humor. "Ah, yes. Now I remember. When you left me because you were afraid you weren't good enough for me."

I formed a large and exhausted expression, sighing out a tidal wave of boredom. "What a pathetic joke. I gave up more for you than any sane woman would. Cannes. Ah, yes. I remember. Cannes. When you turned two skanky Lander actresses into your personal bedroom pets."

"Cannes," Jordan repeated. "When you assumed the worst and wouldn't listen to reason. When I realized you were looking for excuses to desert me."

"When I found thong underwear on the private sun deck of your suite. And it wasn't *mine*."

"Considering the parties you and I threw, a person could find almost anything on my sun deck. With none of the evidence remotely incriminating me."

"Oh? You *wanted* that underwear there. I *sensed* it."

Jordan began to grow taller, thicker, and madder, at least in personality. A remarkable illusion, really. He towered over me like a Tolkien orc. (Tolkien, by the way? A Mer, on his father's side.)

"Cannes," Jordan said. "When you were terrified I'd want other women enough to be unfaithful to you, and so you used that as an excuse to—"

"Stop. Can the Cannes debate. We're over. Done with. Whether you'll ever admit it or not, you were unfaithful to me, at least in spirit."

He groaned. "You make me wish I could order a lobotomy."

"Mine or yours?"

"Juna Lee—"

"Stop this conversation. I'll put my psychic fingers in my ears at this point and sing *la la la la la*, if you bother to continue."

"If you don't want to talk to me, why did you come here?"

"I came to interview you for my blog. Because you're a perfect example of an arrogant, clueless merman. The pride of faithless dogfish everywhere."

Jordan's expression turned black. I watched in awe as he mutated into the Creature from the Black Lagoon. Psychically speaking, I shrank down to the size of Minnie Mouse but trembled with excitement. A woman craves domination. Oh, not the true kind. Just the take-me-you-beast-but-then-do-what-I-tell-you kind.

Just as I thought he was about to chase me around the pool, a cell phone rang. He snatched it from a pool bench. I sighed with relief and disappointment. Saved by one his business calls. "Yes? Make it quick. All right. The plane's been chartered? Good." He snapped the phone shut and dropped it back on the bench, then stood for a moment, frowning and gazing into thin air.

Jordan was ignoring me. Impossible. Nothing except the most worrisome trouble could distract him from *moi*. I froze. "Wait a . . . you're hiding something. What? Hmmm. Ah hah. I sense it. You're leaving for Scotland tonight." A black tide hit me. "Oh, my God. You're involved in something dangerous in Scotland."

Jordan groaned at my intuitions. "Juna Lee—"

"Don't 'Juna Lee' me. What kind of trouble are you in?"

"I'm not in any trouble."

"I didn't fall off the tuna boat yesterday. I sense something about Scotland and McEvers kin and desperation. Something very peculiar and extraordinary. Murder. Jordan! Have you killed someone?"

"For godsake. Don't be ridiculous."

"Murder. I feel death and violence and misery and your McEvers cousins and . . . murder. Jordan!"

He headed for me with both hands out, a ferocious frown on his face and his dark eyes hard as jewels. He would grab me and distract me, and if I let him do it I'd never get answers.

I spun around and made a perfect arc into his pool. He followed. We engaged in a feverish slap-and-grab in the deep end. Under normal circumstances I'd have wrapped him around my little finger, drained him dry, and left him on the bottom with a silly smile on his face. But the pulse of something dark and sad inside him only grew stronger, and I went still. I shivered. Fear *for him.* Jordan groaned in defeat. We shot to the surface.

"Tell me what's going on," I ordered. "I'll find out anyway if you don't. You *want* to tell me. That's why I came here. I knew you *wanted* to talk to me. I sensed it."

"*I* lured *you* here. I wanted to *warn* you. I want you to go away. You have to leave Sainte's Point."

"Are you insane? Ali and Griffin's wedding is in a few days!"

"After the wedding. Go. Go with the rest of the family on the wedding cruise. Leave the island."

I stared at him. In celebration of Ali and Griffin's wedding, the entire Bonavendier clan from Sainte's Point was scheduled to leave on a leisurely cruise aboard the enormous yacht of Lilith's love, Riyad. Lilith, her sisters, their men, Ali, Griffin, even the servants. Everyone who lived on the island would be gone for at least two months. But I was supposed to stay. "What do you mean, leave the island? Lilith is planning to put me in charge of the place. Tula and I are already scheduling parties that will fill the entire mansion, and —"

"There's been a change of plans."

"No way. Lilith would have told me —"

"She will. Trust me. You can't stay at Sainte's Point. Rhymer McEvers is taking up residence at the island for the next two months."

"Rhymer . . . Rhymer . . . Rhymer McEvers?" I had vague memories of meeting Rhymer once during a McEvers clan shindig at the clan's drafty old castle overlooking a loch. I recalled dark hair, wonderful eyes, a great body, and a Sean Connery voice that could melt a shelelagh, but also I recalled his boring penchant for honor, duty, discipline, shooting people, et cetera. After an early girlfriend of his was killed by European gangsters he'd turned into a vigilante. Now I'm not one to believe rumors, but if one *did* believe rumors, one would believe that Rhymer tracked down and killed a half-dozen Landers he blamed for that girlfriend's death. Dragged them into the ocean and strangled them, one by one.

If one believes rumors.

At any rate, then he'd disappointed his family by join-ing the British navy, thus sinking to the level of a gun-toting Lander and an Englishman. He and Jordan were both far too serious for mermen. Jordan and Rhymer had been friends since they were boys climbing icebergs in the north Atlantic. But what did that have to do with now? "Your cousin Rhymer? The Peacekeeper?"

Jordan arched a brow. "How many other Rhymers do I know? Yes, Rhymer the Peacekeeper."

The Council had its own police force, you could say. *Peacekeepers*, they called them. Hard bodied, hard-assed cops. They were only dispatched in the most extreme cases, when Mers had turned violent or . . .

"What have you done?" I grabbed Jordan's hands. "Is Rhymer coming after you? I'll stand by you. Whatever it is, you're too well-groomed to be a criminal—"

"For the last time, this isn't about *me*, Juna Lee. All I can do is make you leave, for your own safety. That's why I wanted you to come here today. So I could convince you. When I come back from Scotland, I don't want to find you at Sainte's Point."

"If there's some horrible trouble that requires a Peace-keeper, and it includes you, I'm not leaving."

"If I have to shanghai you and send you to the other side

or the world, I will."

I shoved him and stepped back. "Don't even think about it."

"Don't make me."

"What could you possibly—" I searched his mind and shivered. "Rhymer's in trouble. That's it. Oh, I always knew he was too stern and Lander-like. All those solemn allegiances and violent inclinations. He's wrapped tighter than a mummy. He was bound to snap. He killed someone."

"No, no, Rhymer didn't kill anyone. It's not that simple."

"Then what is it?" I shut my eyes. "I feel . . . I feel . . . what? Something I can't even fathom. Something horrible that scares even you. Something that could hurt Rhymer, and hurt you. What is it? What? Either you tell me what's going on, Jordan, or I'll settle at the bottom of your ridiculous mountain pool and refuse to leave. You'll have an easier time scraping pond algae off your rocks."

He sat down on a heavy wooden bench fashioned from thick logs. My sexy, web-footed lumberjack. For awhile he said nothing, frowning at the stone-dark depths of his faux mountain pool. My heart twisted. Jordan was that rarest of creatures — a Mer prince who would have happily given up the tides to live on a simple mountaintop. And yes, his disenchantment with Mer glamour was, in no small part, because of the heartache between him and me.

I sank down in a damp pool of silk at his feet, fixing unyielding eyes on him. He finally looked at me. "Do you believe in Swimmers?"

"Swimmers? Swimmers? Is this a joke?"

"No. Do you believe Swimmers might really exist?"

I gaped at him, realized he was serious, then snorted. "No. And I don't believe in the Loch Ness monster, either."

"Until a few days ago, I'd have agreed with you."

I was speechless. When I recovered, I said, "So . . . you

seriously believe we aren't the only kind of merfolk in the sea. Jordan, I'm sorry, but this is about as logical as debating the existence of fairies, elves, and heterosexual drag queens."

"You don't think there's some kernel of truth to our legends? Why shouldn't there be Mers further up the evolutionary shore than us? We already accept that there are differences between ourselves and Landers. Between ourselves and Mer kin who have no webbing on their feet and no special underwater skills. And we don't dismiss the existence of extraordinary Mers among us — the Healers, for example. So why isn't it possible that Swimmers exist?"

"Because there's no such thing as a shapeshifting merman with retractable claws!"

"A lot of Mers think they've had a brush with a Swimmer, but they can't prove it."

"For the same reason they can't prove Big Foot exists! Because he doesn't! Jordan!"

"I've always heard rumors about Swimmers."

"So have I. But those are fairytales."

"There are plenty of Mers who believe we're descended from semiaquatic mermaids. Lilith does."

"No respect to my great-aunt, but she's a hard-core romantic." When he said nothing but only scowled at me I went on. "And, uh, this has something to do with Rhymer? So Rhymer believes in Swimmers, too?"

"He believes a Swimmer named Orion got his sister killed last week. She was trying to blow up a UniWorld Oil research ship. This Swimmer, this Orion, convinced her to commit the crime. But he didn't show up to help her. The bomb exploded while she was being chased by the oil company's security team. She died in the water off the Scottish coast."

It was literally as if Jordan had told me to look behind the nearest moss-draped oak for the Creature from the Black Lagoon. My skin crawled. "If such a thing as a Swimmer exists . . . if this Orion is real, and he's responsible for the death of Rhymer's sister . . . then why isn't Rhymer asking for help from the Council?"

"If Orion is a Swimmer, he'll evade anyone the Council sends to track him. And he'll kill anyone who tries to arrest him. And he'll seek revenge. We believe he's already planning something. So Rhymer's coming to Sainte's Point."

"Rhymer plans to hide out at Sainte's Point?"

"He's bringing his nieces there. Orion's daughters."

"Whoa, whoa, whoa. His sister had children with a mythological Swimmer?"

"Yes."

"You're kidding me."

"No. She had children. With Orion. And now he wants them. He's never even met them. He may want to hurt them. We don't know what he wants. So Rhymer's bringing them here for protection."

I got to my feet. "I have to talk to Lilith. She knows all about this, doesn't she? She knew when I headed here to see you that you were going to send me away."

He nodded. "She knows."

"I've been ambushed. It isn't fair. I have to talk to Lilith. I'll be back."

"No, you won't. Not unless you want to be shanghaied by me."

"We'll just see what Lilith has to say about that."

I whirled and headed for the pier.

He swept me into his arms from behind, without touching me. He filled my body, filled my mind, nearly absorbed me in a devoted hum of energy. *You still love me,* he whispered inside me. *You'll do what I tell you to do. Because you know you'll always love me and that I'll always love you.*

I moaned but shoved him away mentally. *Someone has to protect you from your own pride and stupid independence.*

And you from yours, he countered.
I ran for my yacht without any dignity at all.

Somewhere off the coast of Scotland, on a state-of-the-art research ship owned by UniWorld Oil

ഇ ഇ ഇ ഇ ഇ ഇ ഇ   **5**   ഇ ഇ ഇ ഇ ഇ ഇ ഇ

The naked body of the stunning brunette lay on the stainless steel gurney, only a small purple area of discoloration marking the side of her face where the underwater concussion had ruptured her brain. Her sea-green eyes stared up blankly into the antiseptic lights overhead. Unlike the emptiness of most dead faces, her expression was tragic, as if her life's mission and the loves she had left behind still lived in the memory of her flesh. A dozen scientists gathered around her, all of them employees of the world's largest oil conglomerate. None of them knew the true nature of the group they worked for, a cabal headed by a man code-named *Leviathan*.

"The corpse is identified as Tara McEvers," a British researcher said into the miniature microphone attached to the collar of his blue scrubs. "A marine biologist alleged to have been involved in numerous vandalisms of UniWorld research vessels in these waters. According to data provided by UniWorld Security, Ms. McEvers was born near or on one of the lochs. Specifics unknown. Only known living relative is a younger brother, Rhymer, age uncertifiable. Former British commando. Whereabouts now unknown. Ms. McEvers also has three daughters, ages six to twelve, whereabouts now unknown. Father of the children — unknown. Ms. McEvers died while attempting to plant an explosive device on the hull of the S.S. Deep Gold, moored off the coast of Arcmoren." The head of the autopsy team turned to his fellow doctors, who were all staring at the McEvers corpse with unprofessional awe and no small degree of grisly attraction. Even dead, she was a charismatic force of nature. "Before we begin dissecting this cadaver, any comments, doctors?"

A female forensics specialist from Nigeria splayed Tara McEver's muscular toes apart. "I want to go on record as saying I've never seen any webbing as remarkable as this before. This is truly a superior specimen." Soft, iridescent folds of skin, as translucent as butterfly wings, unfurled. The webbing extended to the tips of each toe, pliable and yet tough. "This woman was an unusually powerful swimmer," the Nigerian continued. "She easily out-swam Security's dive team for more than thirty minutes in frigid waters at a depth of more than sixty feet."

The British physician said tersely, "That is precisely why Leviathan wants a thorough report on all the autopsy results. All tissue and organs will be sent directly to Research and Development. I intend to dissect and study every centimeter of this specimen. Let us begin."

He turned toward the razor-sharp instruments arranged on a steel cart. As he reached for a scalpel, a chime sounded at the laboratory's windowless steel door. The doctor frowned. "No one is authorized to—" Lights blinked a code on a small console beside the door's latch. The latch opened with the soft hiss of elegant hydraulics. The massive door slid aside.

A slender man in blue scrubs stepped inside. The bright antiseptic lighting did not quite color his eyes; if the men and women standing around Tara McEvers' body had looked closely into those eyes they might have seen the deadly coldness, the flow of bloodlines they had never imagined. "Good morning," the newcomer said pleasantly. "Sorry I'm late."

The heavy security door eased shut.

The team leader stared at the visitor. "Dr. Fortson, I thought you were in London for the week."

The newcomer turned slightly, watching the door's digital panel run through a sequence of numbers that ended with the muted click of the bolts. He was now locked in with the team who planned to cut Tara McEvers to pieces. And they with him. He shifted his gaze to the overhead security cameras. As if disabled by some silent pulse of energy, each made an unnatural whirring sound. Then, silence. Finally he settled his strange, cold gaze on the assembled researchers. They saw the first flicker of change, something impossible to contemplate. Something unbelievable and merciless had joined them.

"Dr. Fortson is in London, indeed," the visitor went on, his voice flowing downward, becoming a soft, fluid growl. "But I am not."

Then he was visible, large and powerful, a shapeshifting fury, an impossible violation of nature as they believed it to exist.

He gave none of them so much as a moment to scream.

A Brother's Duty

❧ ❧ ❧ ❧ ❧ ❧ ❧ **6** ❧ ❧ ❧ ❧ ❧ ❧ ❧

My name is Rhymer McEvers, and I am a Mer Peace-keeper. I have naught against Landers, except that they've overrun the dry world and now believe they can take over the great waters that surround it. They never will, but I bear them no ill will for trying. The waters are seductive. Even Landers realize their allure. I've worked among Landers, protected them, made friends with them, been a lover to more of their women than they'd like to count, and listened patiently as they've told me their version of the ancient history they assume all humankind shares. Which, of course, 'tis woefully ignorant of my kind. So be it.

If Landers will just stay out of my way, I won't be forced to hurt them.

Or any Mers, either.

❧ ❧ ❧

"Stop there, Colonel McEvers."

I got stares. Hard ones. Standing on the steel and concrete dock of the UniWorld compound, with a cold morning wind making everyone but me shiver, I should have sensed trouble. I should never have set a foot inside the electrified gate. But a hearse waited in the parking area; I was ready to tend Tara's corpse. At the moment I had only that mission.

"I've come for my sister's body. I'll take only that much for now, and be back later for answers. She was no terrorist.

The charges against her are a lie. But we'll settle that discussion after I take her home to her daughters."

"You're not giving orders here, Colonel. I am," a snot of a private security chief said, stepping up to me in his heavy camo, one hand on his belted pistol. A half-dozen of his armed lackeys edged into a circle around me.

I contemplated pulling him into the bay and drowning him. Instead I said, "It's not Colonel. The name's just McEvers. Rhymer McEvers. I left the Queen's service two years ago. So drop the formalities. Your bosses have been told to expect me. I've come for my sister's body. *Now.*"

The bloody little tyrant leveled a pistol at me. "Don't move."

"*Now* you've said the wrong thing to me."

"Everyone calm down," a man called. "Colonel, relax." A UniWorld executive strode from the walk of the big ship berthed at the dock. Fine long coat, good tweeds, the look of a smiling bastard about him. "Mr. McEvers. Please come aboard. We'll talk."

A low hum of warning rose in my mind. I had my spies, my people, my kind, in the area. A given. Jordan Brighton suddenly called to me. He was stationed nearby.

Careful, cousin, careful, Rhymer, something's happened. I just got a tip. Don't set foot aboard the ship. He's been there. Orion. He's been there, cousin. And he's killed again. He took Tara's body. The UniWorld people think you have information on the attack. They think you and he are collaborating.

The message froze me in place.

"Mr. McEvers." The smiling executive gestured toward the ship. "Relax. Come aboard. We want to talk with you. That's all. Of course we'll release your sister's body to you. We just want to ask you some questions first."

The broad north Atlantic shifted in gray-green plains before me, empty of all but the massive gray UniWorld research ship and a UniWorld drilling platform in the distance. The emptiness insisted that nothing of humankind lived beyond the rocky shores around us; call us what you will, fact of fancy, but my brand of humankind was out there in the waters. These Landers had no idea. I was in my element.

I shifted my mind and stared at the ship towering above. Mers have a sort of sonar; above water you Landers call it being psychic. A silent song. A vibration. Radar. I searched. She's not here. Tara's body was not inside the ship's steel hulk.

Jordan was right. The bloody bastard, Orion, had taken Tara's body in death just as he'd used it in life. Next he might come looking for her daughters, his daughters, my nieces. They'd never even met him. He had never shown himself to them. Who could say what he intended? To murder them the way a tomcat kills his mate's abandoned litter?

"I have no need to talk," I said to the UniWorld exec. "Let me know when you're ready to release my sister's body. I'll come back. With the Queen's own blessing, if you push me."

"Don't threaten us with rumors of your connections, Mr. McEvers. UniWorld is bigger than the Queen."

"The Queen will be the least of your worries."

I turned to go. The circle of guards stepped closer. Of course I expected that. I was only confirming it. The executive stopped smiling. "We can't let you leave, Mr. McEvers. Now, please, cooperate and come aboard."

"And my choices are?"

The security chief said, "You've got no choices. Shut up and do as you're told."

"Sorry, but I rarely do as I'm told."

I slammed a fist into his face, slapped his pistol aside, dropped two of the guards with more of the same, spun a third hard enough to put him on the ground with a dislocated shoulder, left the outline of my shoe in the groin of the fourth, then snatched a pistol from the hand of another and leveled it at the ones left standing, including the executive. The group gaped as if a sea monster had risen out of khakis and old flannel. "Face down on the dock," I ordered, "or I'll kill you all without so much as blinking."

The men dropped to the gray concrete.

"McEvers," the executive said, muffled by pavement, "your sister's body has been stolen by some . . . some extraordinarily violent and sadistic person, and twelve of my doctors are torn to pieces. I know you're a trained killer, but there's no place you can hide if you had anything to do with their murders."

"I'm a retired navy officer who served Her Majesty, not a trained killer, and I had naught to do with whatever disaster happened aboard your ship. I only came for my sister's body and some answers. I've got neither, and I don't think I'll be staying to hope for better."

"McEvers, you're under suspicion as an accessory. You can't just disappear—"

"Oh? I think I'll be dead, otherwise."

A shot blasted the air, then another, both whizzing by my ears. Bits of concrete sprayed up. UniWorld Security was taking potshots at me from the ship's upper decks. I pivoted and sprinted for the dock's edge, raising the pistol I'd grabbed. I clipped the sideburns of three UniWorld snipers, and they ducked like schoolboys.

It was unbelievable, what he did, they'd tell their mates. *Dropped a cadre of guards with his bare hands, cowed the chief and the division exec, and nearly pierced our ears while running full-out. What kind of man can manage all that?*

No kind like yourselves, you Landers, take my word. And watch this.

I dropped the pistol and went over the dock's edge in a ten-meter dive into the water. By the time I skimmed the bay's rocky bottom they started shooting at me from above.

By the time I was out of the ship's shadow and well into the deep water of the bay I felt the distant vibration of engines. They were after me with small craft, waiting for me to pop my head up as a target.

I thought of Tara — gentle, smart, idealistic Tara, how she must have died being chased by these corporate jackals, down in the black waters beside one of their giant sterile cans of a ship, fumbling with a bit of explosive plastic goo and detonators, trying to blow a symbolic pinprick in a ship's hide, all for the sake of a cause that should not be fought by a woman who had been lured into dangerous acts for the love of an insane and dangerous man who could not even let her body rest in peace. Orion. Goddamn him.

Get your nieces out of Scotland, I told myself. *Before he finds them, too.*

I shucked my clothes and shoes, then knifed through the cold Scottish waters far below the Uzis and speed boats, following the rugged coast northward for over an hour without ever surfacing to draw a new breath. Jordan called to me. *I've sent a boat for you and the girls. Take care. See you at Sainte's Point.*

I'll be there anon, Cousin.

Long after the UniWorld goons declared me shot and drowned I broke the surface of the waves off a rocky beach. Only a pod of whales and a small herd of sheep witnessed me walk ashore in that desolate place. I unfurled the trousers I'd tied around my waist, pulled them on, then jogged, barefoot, to the nearest road. Jogging is not something my kind does well, especially without shoes. Every centimeter of my webbing bled from the trip.

Within an hour I arrived at the isolated cottage where I'd hidden my nieces. By nightfall the four of us boarded a small sloop Jordan had arranged for us, sailing westward, leaving Tara's body somewhere unknown in the care of the man or . . . creature . . . she'd loved so foolishly. Leaving home behind, all the McEvers' wealth and lands, our ancient holdings on the great, deep lochs, the estates on windswept islands; headed like paupers into the great, deep channel between the continents, where no ordinary sailor would be suspected of venturing on such a perilous journey, most likely with a monster in pursuit.

Headed for the sanctuary of our American kin.

The Bonavendiers of Sainte's Point Island, Georgia.

Back At The Island

✎ ✎ ✎ ✎ ✎ ✎ ✎ **7** ✎ ✎ ✎ ✎ ✎ ✎ ✎

"Why, Ms. Poinfax, you look pale," one of the pudgy little Tanglewoods said slyly as I stepped off the *Delicious* at Sainte's Point. "Did Mr. Brighton spank you?"

I stared at the coy hobbit. Tanglewoods were scurrying little toadies of Great-Aunt Lilith's. They knew everything. They spied on me gleefully. They snitched. "Get out of my way or I'll spank *you*, you human hamster."

I stomped onward.

The island's small private harbor was packed with yachts bearing the names of a who's who of international society. The Bonavendier mansion loomed on a knoll above the cove like a fantasy castle. In old paintings it had the look of a straight-faced European country house — no verandas and no turrets yet. Simon Bonavendier built it in the late 1700s, after George Washington awarded the island to him for his service in the Revolutionary War.

But, over the two centuries since then, the Bonavendiers expanded it and dolled it up; fortified it with new walls built of football-sized ballast stones salvaged from the holds of ships that wrecked off the Georgia coast, not to mention fine timbers and antiques that were conveniently lost by those ships. In general, the family had added verandas and turrets, et cetera. So now the mansion is both massive and delicate; solid on its dry knoll but shifting with the beach and tides and the sway of the sprawling maritime oaks around it. Neither land nor sea. Living between the worlds. Just like the Bonavendiers. Just like all Mers.

At the moment, the place crawled with caterers, waiters, decorators, and pre-wedding guests. An enormous white tent covered most of the side lawn, where the wedding would take place. Workers were hanging giant sprays of white roses and exotic orchids from the ceiling. A fantasy wedding. It would be magnificent. How could a murderous boogeyman be tracking Jordan's cousin to this paradise?

I strode up a winding path of broad stone steps and into the house. Lilith's sisters, my beautiful great-aunts Mara and Pearl, were engaged in feverish debate with an Italian decorator who was about to add strings of diamonds to the white roses in the wedding tent.

"These diamonds are perfection," the decorator yelled in a heavy accent. Neapolitan Mers are so theatrical. They think life is a Fellini film.

"Yes, yes, we don't dispute the quality," my sweet Great-Aunt Pearl soothed, "They're magnificent, Sophia, but not quite —"

"I've seen bigger grains of sand," Great-Aunt Mara sneered. "I'm not going to let my half-sister be married under strands of diamonds that look like they came from a pawn shop in a flea market!"

The Italian decorator went berserk. "You insult my diamonds? Last month my diamonds were good enough for the bat mitzvah of the princess of Harynveitch!"

"Well, Sophia old girl, that doesn't mean they're good enough for a Bonavendier!"

Sophia began yelling in Italian and Mara began yelling back in English. Pearl clasped her heart and stepped between them, hesitating only long enough to smile and wave at me. Ordinarily I'd happily dive into a multilingual catfight over carats and royalty, but that day I zoomed past. I found Lilith in her lavish sunroom, dressed in a pale silk sheath and delicate pearls, perusing last-minute changes in menus and music lists. I slammed the sunroom doors. Amidst the clatter of heavy wood and thick glass, Lilith calmly raised her hypnotic eyes to me. "Back from Hilton Head so soon?"

"No disrespect intended, but—" my voice rose "—have you and Jordan gone crazy?"

Lilith rose with willowy grace, glided to the damasked wall across from her desk, and pulled a thick gold rope on a heavy curtain. I knew what was displayed behind that curtain, but under the circumstances the thought of seeing it made me shiver. An enormous oil portrait emerged, towering above us and taking up most of the high wall. An ethereal face looked down at me through eyes the color of the sea. Magnificent bare breasts seemed to glow in the room's filtered sunlight. Green-gold scales glistened like fine jade. A gossamer tail fin — the end of the rainbow was no less amazing — trailed over one end of an eighteenth century divan.

Melasine. She was one of three founding mothers enshrined in Mer legend. The triple play of fantasies. The sacred trinity of fin-dom. The Old Ones.

If I believed Lilith's stories, the portrait had been painted in this very room more than 200 years ago. If I believed Lilith's stories, I and thousands of other Mers around the world were descended from this ancient, half-woman, half-not-woman, being. If I believed Lilith, this chick was still out there in the ocean.

"I believe in the Old Ones," Lilith said, and gave the portrait a nod. "And so, yes, in answer to your unspoken question, I believe there are Mers who are descended more recently from the Old Ones than we, and that those Mers are very different from the majority of us. I believe that Swimmers are rare, but they do exist."

I threw myself into a gilded French chair. "Look, I'm not exactly a fan of logic and science, you know. They're so . . . scientific. I like a cute little fantasy as much as the next girl.

But I'm sorry, Lilith. I can't believe we're descended from a flippered she-fish, and I can't believe in Mer boogeymen."

"Whether you believe it or not, the truth is the truth." Lilith closed the heavy drape. Our mythological ancestress, Melasine the Mermaid, disappeared behind dark velvet. "Melasine and the other two Old Ones do exist. We are the children of that trinity's consortation with Landers over the centuries. We Singers have the best of both worlds. We stand out, but we also fit in. We live among the Landers and they never suspect. But there are other castes — Mers who are more like the Old Ones than like us. Trapped between the ancient world and the modern one. Tragic loners. Only a few of them have ever allowed themselves to be seen by either Landers or Mers. Orion, poor soul, is one of those."

"Poor soul? Jordan says this . . . Orion . . . *seduced* Tara McEvers and *brainwashed* her. He started lurking in the waters off the Scottish coast when she was a kid, and after she was grown she hooked up with him occasionally and, oh, what the hell, it's so bizarre I can only think of it in Victorian terms — he *had his way with her*. She gave birth to three daughters by him but he never even agreed to meet them. Then he lured her into some scheme to blow up one of UniWorld Oil's research ships, but when she got caught red-handed, he deserted her. He let her get killed. And now her brother, Rhymer, is afraid he's going to kidnap her children. Or worse."

"That sums up the known details, yes."

"This Orion sounds like a very bad blind date."

"I doubt we have all the facts about him. He wants it that way. He deals in mystery. He doesn't want to be known. That's a trait of the Old Ones, too. Very reclusive, unless extraordinarily compelled otherwise." She nodded toward the curtained portrait. "Yet Melasine loved Simon Bonavendier enough to share his life. Perhaps Orion truly loved Tara."

"Or maybe — no disrespect now, okay? — maybe he's, hmmm, well, *a murderous psychopath*."

She smiled thinly and inclined her head. "Maybe."

"So if Rhymer's bringing his sister's kids here and Orion is tracking them, and Jordan is intent on helping Rhymer protect those kids, Jordan may be in danger of getting *killed*." I thumped the air with a fist. "My Jordan could get killed by some kind of finned Freddy Kruger! How can you call Orion a 'poor soul?' Are you going to take up a donation for him? Light a candle in the window to welcome him? Try to get him to pose for a tape you can sell to Wackiest Mer-Monster Videos?"

Lilith suddenly loomed over me, her eyes blazing. "Change your tone. Immediately."

She emitted a furious inner song that ricocheted off every bone in my body. I shrank back on the divan. "Sorry. No offense intended."

Lilith stared at me until I was sufficiently shrunken, then relaxed and stepped back. "Apology accepted."

I ventured in a more careful voice, "But . . . but if you really believe Swimmers exist, and you believe this Orion is sympathetic—"

"I didn't say he was deserving of sympathy. But he may be. I know this much: He's powerful. I feel him in the world; I sense him across the deepest waters. He's angry. He's grieving. He's submerged in guilt. Whether that's righteous guilt or criminal guilt, I can't tell. Nor can I tell what he intends for his daughters, or if he can be trusted."

"If he's some kind of freak, why did Tara McEvers —"

"She loved him. It's that simple. I sense her love like a beacon. Her brother doesn't understand. Rhymer's a hardened man; he can't comprehend what drove her to devote herself to such a wayward soul as Orion. But love is never easy to comprehend; it simply exists. I have no doubt that

Orion's power to enthrall is as potent as his power to destroy."

"Jordan ordered me to leave Sainte's Point before Rhymer gets here with Orion's daughters. But I'm not leaving. He can't make me. And neither can you. Please."

She looked down at me kindly. "I don't expect you to desert the man you love."

"I never said I loved Jordan—"

"In fact, I have important work for you to do here."

I gaped at her. "Ah hah," I said slowly. "You gave the go-ahead on my computer diary, but in return I have to grant you a favor. You planned it that way."

She laughed. "Of course."

I sighed. "All right. I'll do whatever you want. Just let me stay."

"I'll speak to Jordan. He'll compromise. You'll be safe enough."

I leapt up. "Thank you, thank you, thank you!"

"Not so fast. I have a job for you to do. You can only stay if you do it well. Do it well, and the Council will clear your record. The Donald Trump incident will be erased."

"Your wish is my command!"

"I've found a Floater I want to contact. She doesn't know she's a Mer yet. She needs to know, to be schooled. She's perfect for Rhymer. Without her, Rhymer won't stand a chance against Orion. He has the courage, and he has the strength, but he doesn't have the faith in humanity. She does. If Orion's innocent, she will keep Rhymer from killing him." Lilith pointed a long, beautiful finger at me. "Her name's Molly Revere. Your job, Juna Lee, is to get her here, keep her here, and bring her and Rhymer together."

I smiled. I was the matchmaking queen of four continents. I'd hooked up more couples than U-Haul. "Is that it? That's all you want? I have to drag some Floater babe here?"

Floaters were Mers without the webbed feet, and most were either ignorant or in denial about their Mer heritage. "I have to clue her about her inner mermaid, then make sure Rhymer heads straight for her inner with his outie? That's *all* I have to do? And in return you'll clear my name with the Council and let me stay here to help Jordan battle Frankenfin?"

Lilith gazed at me patiently. "It won't be as easy as you think."

I laughed. "Oh, yes it will."

Clueless, thy name is Juna Lee.

Molly Revere, Reluctant Mermaid

≈ ≈ ≈ ≈ ≈ ≈ ≈   **8**   ≈ ≈ ≈ ≈ ≈ ≈ ≈

My name is Molly Martha Revere, and on the day destiny came calling I was being stalked by ducks. Not that I hadn't been stalked by ducks — and other adoring small animals — before, but never in the lobby of one of the South's most elegant hotels, where I was about to autograph books for five hundred of my fans. I had just stepped out of the lobby's art deco elevators. The crowd broke into thunderous applause. My publisher's escort team edged closer around me. I peered between the brawny shoulders of my security guards down a red carpet roped off for my procession to a signing table set up in front of the lobby's grand fountain. The aisle was lined by people on the sides — and ducks in the middle.

The last of the dozen mallards hopped off the wide ledge of the lobby's fabulous, mosaic-tiled fountain. Flicking water from their tail feathers, the ducks marched up a red carpet meant for me, their dark eyes enchanted.

Go back, sweeties. Shoo. Go back to the fountain. Agggh.

No duck luck. They quacked louder and kept me in their sights.

"The ducks are caught up in M.M. Revere's magic!" someone yelled. "They're sending out a welcome committee!" The Peabody's chandeliered lobby echoed with laughter. The ducks kept coming. The legendary Peabody Hotel of Memphis, Tennessee, had been, until that day, a glamorous showcase for the disciplined pet mallards.

Now I was responsible for their rebellion. I felt like Mel Gibson in *Braveheart*.

No. Go back. Please, please, my little feathered friends, turn around and go back.

Sometimes when I aimed a thought at my animal fans, they seemed to hear it and obey. Not that I believed I had psychic powers. I was a very analytical thinker, with non-fanciful and pragmatic ideas, except for the fantasy world of my books. It was as if everything fanciful about me lived in the *Water Hyacinth* series, and the rest of me was just a shy little brunette with a bum leg and a penchant for pastel pantsuits. At any rate, the ducks kept heading my way.

"I thought the Peabody mallards were escorted back to their rooftop pen at five p.m. every day," I whispered to a publicist.

"Ordinarily they are, Ms. Revere, but in honor of your booksigning this evening, management left them in the fountain a little longer than normal. They're trained to stay put until their handler comes to get them. I've never seen the whole flock act like this before though. I don't know what's wrong with them."

I knew what was wrong with them: me. The creature magnet. For all of my thirty-five years, pigeons and squirrels had followed me in parks, dogs turned on their leashes, cats purred at me from their window sills, aquarium fish lined up at their glass walls to look at me, and I dared not visit any zoo or wildlife park for fear every winged or hooved or furred or finned resident would rush my way like sailors headed for a strip club. I had no idea why I had such an effect. Frankly, it scared me.

"Ms. Revere! Look this way! Ms. Revere, look over here!" Dozens of cameras flashed. I squinted, put on my public smile, and waved awkwardly at the crowd. Even after three best-selling books and one hit movie — the film of my first *Water*

Hyacinth novel had grossed 300 million dollars, with a second film already in the works — I could barely believe the public acclaim was for me. Didn't they know I was just a Boston librarian who, a few years earlier, had gotten looped on cold medicine during a literary festival and blurted to a book agent, "Just for fun, in my spare time I write stories about children who go to a magical underwater school run by mermaids. I don't suppose you'd want to read something by yet another J.K. Rowling clone, would you?"

The answer was *Yes.* A thousand times yes.

Now I was in the lobby of the Peabody, leaning on my cane, a dozen ducks zeroing in on me like web-footed cruise missiles, while half-a-thousand fans cheered either the rebel ducks or me or both. Camera flashes blinded me. I saw splashes of color punctuated by green mallards. It was like a hallucination starring Daffy Duck.

A cool hand suddenly gripped my arm. "Come with me," a dulcet female voice ordered in my right ear, "before these goofy quackers embarrass us both. And the ducks, too."

The next thing I knew, I was being led into one of the elegant shops that lined the lobby. Blinded, squinting, hobbling along unceremoniously with my cane thumping the marble floor like a drumbeat, I have no idea, even to this day, why I let a stranger lead me off that way, or how my escorts and five hundred fans let her, too. She cast a spell. She was no ordinary stranger.

"My name is Juna Lee Poinfax, and I'm your fairy god-mermaid," she announced the instant she slammed and locked the shop's glass door. Before I could absorb that bizarre statement she shoved me into the shopkeeper's office and shut that door behind us, too. My vision cleared and I stared at her.

I'd been kidnapped by Hairstyle Barbie. You know. The 1960s model with impossibly long hair you could pull from a hole in the top of her head. But this Barbie was real — amazing, auburn tresses spilled from a tight topknot at her crown and spilled in thick waves to her waist. Winged eyebrows flattened in perfect symmetry in a perfect face as she scrutinized me. Green eyes assessed me as if I were up for auction at a slave market. Her cleavage heaved inside a low-cut silk blouse inside a tailored blue silk jacket. She went *Hmmm*, in a beautifully musical way, as she drummed perfectly white-tipped fingernails on one hip of her blue miniskirt. A foot, encased in a lethally pointed high-heeled pump, patted the floor. "This is not good," she finally said. "Lilith didn't tell me you look like a gimpy Allie McBeal."

Splat. The sound of my ego hitting the floor. Hairstyle Barbie was an evil *bee-atch*. An evil, astute *bee-atch*. Yes, I was a gimpy Allie McBeal, but I was no pushover. I leaned on a desk for balance, raised my cane like a sword, and said in a very low, Clint-Eastwoodish tone, "I don't know who you are or what you want. I don't want to know. I'm backing out of this room. Don't try to stop me."

Her hand shot out. Lithe fingers clamped the cane's tip. She jerked, I was startled, and my cane ended up in her possession. She smiled as she slowly twirled it. "What a lovely baton. Hmmm. Mahogany. And hmmm, look at this! I'll have to give you credit for at least a little good taste." She stroked the sterling silver mermaid who formed the cane's handle. "Your great-grandfather, Paul Revere, was such an excellent silversmith."

I held onto the desktop and stared at her. I could walk without my cane, but not fast enough to escape. Surely my security guards would come looking for me at any second. Surely the ducks would rescue me. *Humor her. Stall for time.* "I'm not related to Paul Revere," I said as if having a normal conversation. "My great-grandmother was an actress. She was raised in Boston. She took Revere as her stage name. That cane belonged to her. It's an heirloom. Please, give it back."

"No. If I do, you'll only try to escape." She pointed my own cane at me. "I know more about this cane and your great-grandmother than you do. She wasn't just an 'actress,' she was a writer, a Revolutionary activist, and Paul Revere's mistress. They had a son together. She taught Paul everything he knew about silversmithing. She was the one who inspired him to make that little midnight ride. 'Oh, my, the British are coming. One if by land, two if by sea.' Yada yada yada. And she wrote the poem about it, too. But to be discreet, she let Longfellow claim the credit. Henry Wadsworth Longfellow was a Mer, by the way."

I slid one hand closer to a plastic letter opener on the desk. "Oh? One of the greatest poets of American literature was a merman? And my great-grandmother — not my great, great or great, great, great — my *great*-grandmother was a grown woman in the late 1700s? And she had a son with Paul Revere? And I'm descended from him? Why, you'd think there'd be a historical plaque somewhere. Or a record in *Ripley's Believe It or Not.*"

"Very funny." The stranger sighed, clamped my cane under one arm like a British general, then studied me with obvious resignation. "All right. I know you have to rush back to your little booksigning and your duck fan club, and my personal magic can only hold a lobby full of slack-jawed Landers at bay for so long, so I'll make this quick. Listen up. Whether you believe me or not, your great-grandmother was a mermaid of the Singer class. She died in 1905 at the age of one hundred and seventy. Her son — your grandfather Nicholas Revere — was a halfling, because his father was Paul Revere — a Lander — but Nicholas inherited so many of his mother's traits that he qualified for the Singer category, nonetheless.

"Nicholas married a halfling who was a Floater, producing a son — your father — who was a Singer but who didn't have webbed feet. These classifications aren't rigid, you see. Genetic anomalies, throwbacks, et cetera. It's a very fluid system. Anyway, your father married a Floater — your mother — and that's that." She sighed. "The end result is you — a significantly watered-down Person of Water — no webbed feet, no well-developed psychic or sonar abilities, et cetera. But that doesn't mean you're a Lander. You absolutely love the water and can hold your breath for at least twice as long as the average Lander — a talent you've never dared tell any of your Lander friends about, because you know they'd call you a liar and a freak. You also hide your talent for luring small creatures — a typical charismatic charm of our kind. But you can't hide from the truth. And the truth is that you're a mermaid, okay?" She paused. "Even if you *are* a geek."

I stared at her for a few seconds. *Careful, she's crazy.* Not to mention, long-winded. I edged around the desk's far end, glancing at the plastic letter opener again. If she started to drool and leapt at me, I'd give her a nasty indention. "I'm a mermaid? That's nice. That would explain why I write novels about mermaids. And why I like canned tuna and the Beach Boys. Yes. Of course."

"Oh, please. Drop the pathetic attempt to patronize me. And don't pee on yourself in fear. I'm not a psychopath."

"Of course you're not. Look, I have a lot of avid fans — children and adults — and I'm very, very grateful for them. I understand how easy it is to get caught up in a fantasy world — after all, I do it myself when I'm writing. So I'm not patronizing you, and I don't think you're dangerous—"

"Oh? Then why are you planning to stick me with a plastic letter opener?"

I froze. One hand rested on the desk, inches from the wickedly ridiculous weapon. "What letter opener?"

This brought a sigh from my attacker so profound it

rattled an invoice on a bulletin board. "Okay, time to pull off the kid gloves." She leaned toward me, her eyes becoming slits. "You're dying. And your old cat is, too."

I went very still. "That's not . . . how dare'—"

"Dying. Shriveling. Drying up. You've got leukemia. Or something like it. You've been through two bouts since childhood. Lander physicians freak when they treat you. What amazing resilience. What amazing white cells. They can't quite figure you out. It's a wonder some government research goons haven't spirited you away to a secret lab for testing. No doubt they've got lots of little vials of your blood in storage, all being eyeballed by specialists, trying to figure out what makes you different from the other plain-footed dying leukemia patients in Lander-land."

I leaned toward her, trembling. "I have been in remission for ten years," I whispered between gritted teeth. "And my medical records are private. How could you possibly know—"

"Oh, please. And your old cat — well, he's just *old*. Old and decrepit and sad; your only true friend since your teenage years with a dotty old aunt who took you in after your parents died. Twenty, isn't he, the cat? His kidneys are failing, his heart is weak, and you — you dote on him desperately, because you don't have another living thing that loves you, or that you love."

I stared at her. My hands were not violent of their own accord, not violent or sexy or emotional or reckless, just callused from pecking at computer keys ten hours a day; they were obedient assistants. All my fierce emotions I kept hidden deep inside me, and channeled them into my books, not my fists. So Hyacinth Meridian, the ten-year-old star of the *Water Hyacinth* books, cheerfully thumped sharks on the head. Often.

The redheaded creature from the black lagoon smiled at me. "Hah. *Thump this shark-bitch.* That's what you're thinking. You won't do it. You don't have the guts. To thump me. See? I know what you're thinking. I can hear the furious little song. You could hear me thinking, too, if you'd only listen. You know you can do it. You know you hear the vibrato of our people inside your mind — voices you can't quite make out, messages you can't decipher." She frowned. "If you weren't such as a watered-down specimen of a Floater, you'd have figured it all out by now."

"Why do you keep calling me that?"

"Floater. One degree higher than a Lander. One degree lower than a Singer. Like I said, your father, grandfather, and great-grandmother were Singers. I met your grandfather as a child. Nineteen fifty-three, I think. At a gala in Seoul. He was quite a hunk. Died blowing up Russian submarines for the CIA. What a waste. Only Landers go to war to control land. Why do those pathetic excuses for human beings care about land that much? At any rate, your grandfather died trying to help them."

"Let's see. You were a child in nineteen fifty-three. So you're . . . over fifty years old, now. Hmmm uh. You just happen to look twenty years younger than that. I didn't know a person could get full-body Botox injections."

"Yes, I'm over fifty and guess what? In Mer terms I'm just hitting my prime and you're just a kid, just what — thirty-five? Barely old enough to flirt. Look, Lolita, just because you don't believe what I'm telling you, just because the rules of reality have veered off on a tangent in your boring little assumptions in your boring little Lander world doesn't mean I'm lying. You know, deep down, that you're not a Lander. That you're different. You've always been different."

"My leg was injured in the car accident that killed my parents. I've got leukemia. I've always been frail. I've devoted myself to literature and to writing. Of course I'm different."

"Well, la de dah, you're the Bronte sisters and Emily Dickenson all rolled into one. A delicate flower of martyred bookworm-hood."

What insults! Suddenly I remembered: I was M.M. Revere, the world's bestselling children's novelist next to J.K. Rowling. I was filthy, stinking *rich*. This loony dimwit couldn't talk to me this way. I was M.M. Revere. Ducks adored me.

"*I am leaving this room—*"

"Oh, stop saying that. It bores me. Okay, I grant you: You don't have the feet of a Water Person, but believe me, you've got the intuitions. Despite your tepid personality, with coaching you could develop some respectable abilities. Floaters aren't hopeless, I always say. Just somewhat . . . retarded."

"Your delusions are matched only by your lack of kindness and good manners."

"Delusions? Try this on for size, you dusty little plain-toed ingrate." She shut her eyes. "Lilith? Oh, Lilith? I need some help here. I told you I don't make a good diplomat."

The most amazing sensation filled my head. A beautiful voice sang to me, a voice like the finest alto in the finest choir, yet without melody. It was both sensual and maternal, orgasmic but spiritual.

You know where you belong, you know what you need, to live. Now come along, come along, Molly. Find out who you really are. Don't be afraid. Dive in. Visit us in Georgia.

The voice, the vibration, faded away. I stood there, stunned, hypnotized.

Juna Lee Poinfax sighed dramatically. "I should have known Lilith would sing you into submission with one little pulse from her psychic cell tower. You are so easy."

"What just happened to me?"

"*Destiny*, my little gimpy geek, destiny. That's what Lilith calls it, anyway. You know you'll come. You'll come with me to the coast. If you don't, you will get sick again, and eventually you'll die. You need to be around your own kind — Water People. You need to find someone to love and be loved by before that decrepit Meow of yours goes to Kitty-Puss Heaven."

Decrepit Meow? I snapped back to reality. I *loathed* Juna Lee Poinfax. "If this Lilith wants me to come to the coast and meet my . . . my alleged kind, tell her to write, call, e-mail, or visit me herself with the invitation. I'm certainly not trusting one word you say. You . . . you knot-headed Barbie. May I go now?"

Juna Lee Poinfax gave her last sigh, then handed me my cane. "You'll regret it. Maybe not tomorrow, but soon, and every day for the rest of your life."

"At least issue original threats. Don't spout Humphrey Bogart's lines from *Casablanca.*"

"Bogie was a Floater on his mother's side."

Trembling, I marched out of the shop. The ducks were waiting. The crowd applauded. "Oh, there you are," my publishing rep said, as if I'd wandered off and everyone just noticed. "Ready to sign a few hundred books for your devoted fans?"

I was too shaken to do more than nod. How could I announce that my life had just taken a turn into *The Twilight Zone?*

∞ ∞ ∞

I kidnapped M.M. Revere the next day. Kidnapped her. Me, Juna Lee "Al Capone" Poinfax. So what? Once you've dissed Donald Trump and been banished from polite society, why not go all the way into a life of crime? Landers put up with celebrities who diddle children, with superstar jocks who ought to be neutered, and with politicians who steal the proverbial cookie jar and sell the cookies to China. Compared to that, I'm the Mother Theresa of Fin City. So cut me some slack, okay?

Here's how I did it.

Her literary highness, Molly "Mallard" Revere, was a geek and a gimp, but she was also a Mer, whether she'd admit it or not. Which meant high altitudes made her want to hurl, so she didn't take airplanes. Plus she carted her old kitty around with her when she went on book tours, and she'd decided the old puss needed the comforts of home. So she traveled in a gigantic customized bus, like some kind of gospel choir or country-western singer. Her personal bodyguard and driver was a fat middle-aged Boston-raised Irishman named Scotty. I guess he liked irony. Coaxing him away from the Peabody's parking garage was like shooting Leprechauns in a barrel.

"Scotty, cute, handsome Scotty," I purred, wrapping an arm around him as he stepped from the bus's door. "Molly won't be down from her room for at least twenty minutes. You deserve to treat yourself to a short pint and a smoke at the lobby bar before you steer this lummox back up the eastern seaboard."

"Why thanks, lass, I believe you're right. Uh, who are you? Have we met?"

"Only in your dreams."

He laughed. Then he went inside the hotel, just like that.

Damn, I'm good, I thought. *I'm the Obi-Wan Kenobi of mermaids. May the farce be with me.*

I climbed inside the bus and prowled around. Molly's framed bookcovers, a large poster from the first *Water Hyacinth* movie, and dozens of writing awards decorated the walls. There was lots of sage green upholstery and creamy cabinetry. The bus's broad windows were all tinted a dark blue, for privacy. Shelves overflowed with books and sea-shells. The feeling was submerged and cozy. It was like a lagoon on wheels. Despite myself, I approved.

Thump thump thump. My victim climbed the steps, banging her cane against the narrow well of the entrance as she wrestled a large wicker cat carrier. She was dressed in a floppy sheath dress the tie-dyed color of a bad Easter egg. Her shoulder-length brown hair was stuffed up under a straw hat. She looked like a Holly Hobby. Suddenly she spotted me. And froze.

"How in the world did you get inside my—"

"Nab her," I ordered.

Charley the Tuna leapt onto the bus and grabbed her from behind. My cousin Charley had been hiding on the bus's far side — no small feat for a six-foot-seven, 350-pound merman dressed in jeans and a WWF T-shirt. Charley looked like a Caucasian Buddha. He was hairless from his bald head all the way down to his webbed feet. Most Landers knew him by his pro wrestling nom de smackdown: *The Great White Shark.* But I called him Charley the Tuna. You could say he wasn't a typical merman. Bulky and trusting. Not smart enough to avoid my schemes, I mean.

"Sorry, Ms. Revere," he grunted, then hoisted her and the cat carrier off the floor and elbowed the door lever as he did. The bus's doors accordioned shut before Molly recovered from shock and shrieked. Not a soul heard her except us. Victory.

"What have you done with Scotty?!" she yelled, dangling from Charley's beefy, hairless arms. Inside the wicker cat carrier, a scruffy old tabby hunched down on a sheepskin cushion and hissed at me.

"Oh, please. I didn't hurt your Irish chauffeur. He's in the hotel bar. By the time he wonders why he deserted you for a brew and a smoke, we'll be halfway to Georgia."

"I'm not going anywhere with you!"

"Yes, you are. I'm doing this for your own good. Well, actually, I'm doing this for *my* own good." I stepped aside and waved a hand toward a door that led to a sumptuous bedroom. "Charley, deposit Molly and that ancient, bad-tempered kitty of hers in there. Lock the door. Then let's get this tricked-out Greyhound on the road."

"Are you insane?!" Molly yelled. She kicked and flailed her cane at me"— uselessly, of course. "People will look for me! I'm a celebrity! I'm M.M. Revere!"

I draped myself on a sage-green couch. "Get real. You have no close friends. You have no close family. All your publisher cares about is your next book, and it isn't due for six months. Face it, Molly Mallard Martha: you could jump off a cliff and no one would even notice."

This observation made her shriek again. Hey, the truth hurts. She uttered furious little squeaks and flailed her arms as Charley lugged her and the old cat into the bedroom. "*Ouch,*" he grunted. She'd clubbed him with her cane. He set her down, backed out of the room, locked the door, and lifted a brawny, tanned hand to the welt on his forehead. "She could be a wrestler."

"Sorry, Charley. I'll make it up to you. I promise."

He put a hand to his heart in devotion, then lumbered to the front and climbed into the driver's seat.

Whack whack whack whack whack. Molly pounded her mermaid-handled cane on the bedroom door. "If you let me out of here right now, I won't press charges!"

I rose languidly and went to the door. Leaning close, I said in a pleasant tone, "If you keep whacking that heirloom cane, Paul's mermaid will get dents in her fins. So calm down and shut up."

"You can't just take me prisoner and haul me to the coast!"

"Oh? Watch me." I toyed with her cell phone, which

Charley had pilfered from her purse. "You can't phone home, ET. And if you think you can get help by scribbling *Me And My Geezer Kitty Are Being Kidnapped* on a piece of paper and holding it up to the windows so passing drivers will see, forget it. I'm tuned into you like a baby boomer to an oldies station. I'll know what you're up to. If you try anything I'll come in there and . . . and I'll dunk Geezer Kitty in the commode. *Head first.*"

She gasped loudly enough to hear it through the door. I felt her surge of fury but also her fear for her old pussy cat. She didn't make so much as another gimpy peep. I'd won. I rolled my eyes. Like I was really serious about drowning her elderly feline. Like I'd really stick my hands in a commode.

"I can't wait to get back to the ocean," I said to Charley, settling back with dramatic weariness on the couch as he steered the bus down a Memphis street, heading for the nearest interstate. *I can't wait to get back to Jordan,* I added silently. If Orion the Psycho Swimmer was really out there in the briny deep, and he was looking for his daughters, and he tracked them and their Uncle Rhymer to Sainte's Point, and Jordan tried to help Rhymer fight Orion, and Jordan got hurt, or killed . . .

"Drive faster," I called to Charley.

Charley frowned. "Juna Lee, what exactly are you going to do with Ms. Revere when you get her to the coast? I mean, you can't keep her locked up. And I don't see that your powers of persuasion are working too well. She's a tough little she-crab."

I frowned. He was right. Molly Mallard Martha Revere had given me more trouble than any Mer had a right to. Even Lilith's song hadn't hypnotized her for long. What kind of defenses did she have around that geeky little mind of hers? A shark-proof cage? If she didn't succumb to psychic voodoo easily, how would I ever make good on my deal with

Lilith? How could Molly ever be of any use to Rhymer in fighting off Orion? How could I help Jordan as long as I had Molly hanging around my neck like a pastel albatross? How could I matchmake Molly and Rhymer if I couldn't make Molly even get on her own damned bus voluntarily?

"I'll think of something," I muttered. "Or she'll be sorry."

It never occurred to me that True Love might help me out.

⚫⚫⚫

Uncle Rhymer. Uncle Rhymer? We feel you worrying again. Small voices, singing inside my head. I turned to find three pretty faces peering at me from a porthole in the sailboat's main cabin.

I'm only testing the wind, girls. Stay silent, girls. Just stay silent. Remember. Never sing out.

The oldest, Stella, who was twelve, nodded somberly. The other two, Isis, eight, and Venus, five, whimpered inside my mind, then withdrew from the window. I could not let them keen in vibrant waves of mental song, could not let them heal themselves.

Their father would hear them if they sang. He would track them by the echoes. If he weren't tracking them already.

I had cut across the English Channel in record time, knowing the currents the way only the Water People know them, slipping like a drop of mercury along the curving thermometer of the great summer ocean. I locked the wheel then went to the stern. I watched the receding waters of the other side of the world, my mind open, a net to catch the man, the myth, the thing, the mystery, that had seduced my sister, caused her death, and murdered a dozen people to steal her body before it could be returned to her heartbroken children. I felt his guilt in my soul; I sensed it in the psychic fury humming inside my brain — that poison in him, following me to a new continent. I didn't believe in whimsies and fairytales, either my own kind or Landers', but I did believe in evil, and what I felt seeping after my ship was as unknowable as the darkest evil of an ancient ocean abyss.

Stay back, you bastard. Or come forward and prove you're flesh and blood, and I'll cut the life out of you.

Every sense in my brain searched for him, listened for the low hiss of threat I'd heard from time to time, hummed a sonic minefield, daring him to follow. He was a killer, but so was I. No magic of our kind, no extraordinary psychic powers or other abilities would match the heavy automatic pistol in my belt or the half-moon sword snugged to my left leg. An ancient tradition, that. Bit of a throwback to the old ways, I was. Knight of the watery realm, you might say. A warrior.

A worried man.

He had not killed Tara with his own hands, no, but he'd lured her into his shadow world, convinced her to be a terrorist, and thus she'd died like a thief in the deep, cold waters off our own homeland, where he had not bothered to accompany her. He sent her to her death alone.

Now he wanted his children. Her children. Daughters he'd never even met. My nieces. All that was left of the sister I'd failed to protect. "You'll no' get the girls," I whispered. "Whether you're man or myth, you'll no' get them." My brogue always became heavier when I was worried.

I leaned further over the bow, watching the empty eastern horizon, scanning the vast gray-green surface of the Atlantic. We were along the coast of the States now. We'd make Sainte's Point Island by nightfall, if the wind held.

The wind will hold, an elegant female voice hummed in my ear.

I shut my eyes. *Thank you, Lilith. Please keep steering us to your sanctuary.*

The bow of the large sloop angled leeward as if pushed gently by a hand. The sails bulged, pregnant with the breath of the great waters.

My kinswoman, Lilith Bonavendier, had a way with the winds and the tides. Her island home was the site of old legends, old powers. I could hide my nieces there. I could protect them.

I could wait for their father to find them, if he dared.

And I would fight him to the death, when he did.

Ahoy, Rhymer! The psychic greeting filled my head. *Rhymer McEvers. Come about. Hello. Welcome to America.* A man's voice.

Welcome, Rhymer. Welcome. Let us aboard. A woman's.

I brought the sailboat to a halt and dropped anchor. Surprised, I hung out a ladder then stepped back, watching. A darling brunette climbed aboard, long hair streaming to her hips, sweet breasts and butt outlined nicely in a black maillot. She smiled gently and held out a hand. "I'm Ali Bonavendier. Soon to be Ali Randolph."

"Ah. Cousin Ali. It's nice to meet you. You're a kind of legend. Lilith's long-lost half-sister."

She smiled wider but shook her head. "I'm just one of Lilith's many projects. Rescued from a life of dry futility. Set on the right course by the enchantment of Sainte's Point." She looked up at me solemnly. "It's a safe place. A sacred place."

I laid a hand on the pistol belted to my waist. "I don't need magic. I just need one clear shot."

She frowned, and I felt her concern for my attitude. Before she could counsel me about it, a big lean bruiser hoisted himself up the ladder and bounded onto the deck. He scooped dark hair back with a thick hand. Bit of a rough looker for a Mer, not that I was much prettier. Scars, large and small, pockmarked his bare chest and arms. A wide nylon belt was snugged to the waist of his black trunks; its sheathed knife was long enough to gut a whale. Even his feet were scarred, their webbing gone, snipped out when he was a babe and his mother wanted to hide his Mer heritage. I'd heard plenty about Griffin Randolph on the oceans of the world. The treasure hunter. His father had been a rich, prideful Lander, his mother, a distant cousin to my own. There was a tragic story there — and I sensed the scars inside him. But I also sensed the happiness. It radiated from Ali to him, and back again. My gut twisted. It'd been years since I'd felt any such bond between me and a woman. I was good at sex, bad at the rest.

"Cousin Rhymer," he said, and we clasped hands.

"Cousin Griffin. Should you not be on the island, dressin' yourself up for a wedding to this beautiful woman tomorrow?"

"What can I say?" He nodded at Ali. "On the eve of our wedding she challenged me to a five-mile race from Sainte's Point to your sloop here. It took all my willpower to let her beat me."

Ali clucked her tongue. "You go on believing you let me beat you." To me she said, "Lilith asked us to welcome you and your nieces personally. The island's full of guests, so she couldn't get away herself. It's our honor to be her emissaries. We'll lead you to a quiet cove along the mainland for now. We wish you'd come to the mansion, but Lilith says you'd rather wait until the wedding's over and the island's empty."

I nodded. "The fewer who know about me being here, the better. Orion's listening for hints, keeping his mind open for information. I can't risk him hearing any chatter about me and the girls."

Griffin frowned. "I have a ship off the coast of Costa

Rica. My crew is exploring the ruins of Timaupica, one of the hidden Mer cities. You could take the girls there. And Riyad bin Mahadeen says he can hide you off the coast of Arabia — he never calls it *Saudi* Arabia, because his loyalties are a helluva lot older than the modern regimes."

"Or you can bring the girls and come with us," Ali said gently, "on our wedding cruise around the world."

"Thank you both, but no. We're as safe here as anywhere. And I don't want to endanger more people than I can help. Orion may look on my allies as his enemies."

Griffin laid a hand on the hilt of his knife and scanned the waters, scowling. "I've learned to believe in a lot of things I can't explain. But I'm not sure I believe Orion is a Swimmer. I assume you do? You don't doubt he's . . . different . . . from the rest of us?"

"I don't know *what* he is. My sister guarded his secrets, even from me. All I know is, I intend to kill him."

Both Ali and Griffin looked at me with worry in their eyes. In my mind there was no room for debate about Orion's guilt, innocence, motives or intent; the issue was settled. He'd had years to present himself with honor, years to come to me, Tara's brother, and make a show of fellowship. Now I'd tried and convicted him without his testimony, but it was his own doing. I'm not a brutal bastard, I started to tell Ali and Griffin. I just prize good manners, that's all.

"Hello, sweetie!" Ali said suddenly and knelt down with a hand out.

Venus, the five-year old, peered, wide-eyed, around the corner of the cabin. I groaned inwardly. So much for the girls staying out of sight.

"Are you an angel?" Venus asked Ali, her Scottish brogue lilting like an Inverness butterfly. "Have you talked to me mum, in heaven? Will you tell her we miss her so; tell her to come home?"

Oh, God.

Ali's face convulsed. She put a hand to her heart. I recalled hearing from Lilith that Ali had lost her own mother, a Lander, when Ali was just a babe. A tide of sympathy poured from Ali. Venus gave a little cry and rushed to her. Sobbing, Venus threw her arms around Ali's neck, and Ali held her tight.

Griffin and I, being no more comfortable than Lander men when it came to female tears, harummphed and looked the other way. Suddenly Venus noticed Griffin. She pulled back from Ali's hug and stared up at him, at his scars. One small hand shot out. She laid just her fingertips on a thick scar that crossed the back of his hand.

"Venus, no," I ordered sharply. I scooped her up. "You promised. You promised. You must keep that promise all the time."

She stared at me tearfully. "I couldn't help it, Uncle Rhymer. I couldn't. I'm sorry." She hid her face in her hands and sobbed again. I felt like a monster. I was no good with children. "Uncle Rhymer, I'll take her back in the cabin," Stella said, behind me. "She moves so fast. She got away from me. Sorry."

She and Isis stood there at attention. Isis looked stern as a teacher; Stella looked teary but resolved.

"You'll have to do better," I said. What a beast I was. Not capable of tenderness. But tenderness bred mistakes, and mistakes bred disaster. "You're my lieutenant. I depend on you. Do your job."

"Yes, sir." I handed Venus to her. The three girls hurried back into the cabin.

I turned back to Griffin and Ali. They were staring at his hand.

The scar had disappeared.

When their awed gazes rose to me, I said quietly, "It's

true, what you've heard. The girls are Healers."

Healers. The word hung in the salt air like a bolt of lightning. Most Mers were of the Singer class; only a tiny minority had powers so special they deserved a higher designation. Most Mers had never met a Healer. Some swore the Healers were just entertainers and attention-seekers, concocting elaborate tricks to elevate their social status.

Venus had just knocked that idea to hell and back.

Ali touched Griffin's healed hand. He raised it slowly, then laid the smooth, perfect skin against her cheek. "I've always wanted to touch you without a scar between us," he said gruffly.

She gave a mewl of joy.

I hung my head. Healers. All three of the girls. The instinct ran through every vein of their bodies. They could hardly resist the joy it gave to others. I'd told them they had to control it. When they laid hands on someone, they sang. They sang out like a beacon. And if they did that, Orion would hear them across even the widest sea.

Ali kissed Griffin, cuddled his hand in hers, then looked at me tearfully. "There are miracles in the world. We've just seen one. Rhymer, you have to consider the possibility that there's goodness inside a father who can give the gift of healing to his daughters."

After a long, quiet moment, I said as politely as I could, "He gave them nothing but a dead mother."

And I went, without another word, to set the course toward Sainte's Point again.

Juna Lee's Prisoner

☙ ☙ ☙ ☙ ☙ ☙ ☙ **9** ☙ ☙ ☙ ☙ ☙ ☙ ☙

Trapped. Trapped upstairs, in the dark, in a big, vintage cottage somewhere on the Georgia coast. Imprisoned like a noble heroine in the 1900s dime novels I collected as a hobby. *No, no, she cried, you villain! You'll never keep me here against my will! Tom the Ranger will save me!* I loved the simplicity of good versus bad in those books; the unerring sense of fragile virtue and courageous sacrifice. Oh, all right. I mainly loved the idea of good girls getting tied up, leered at, and rescued. Maybe I had a secret S & M fetish. At any rate, no Tom the Ranger had ever shown up in my life.

"Molly," Juna Lee Poinfax hissed outside the door to my room. "Stop moping around in there. All you have to do is agree to stay in Bellemeade a few weeks and get to know your own kind. Swear you'll stay, and then I'll let you out."

"My own kind?" I said loudly, through solid oak. "My *kind* don't tell elaborate lies about being descended from mermaids. They don't kidnap famous authors, haul them more than one thousand miles in a bus, then lock them in a strange house in the dark."

"Well, turn on a light, you idiot."

I steamed. I'd like to put Juna Lee in a dime novel. I'd play the part of the villain. I'd tie her to the proverbial railroad tracks. And I'd make sure Tom the Ranger got there too late to do more than scrape some of her DNA off a rail for the coroner's office.

She did have one good point: My noble virtue wouldn't

be compromised if I turned on a lamp. I made my way to a table, fumbled with a cord beneath a glass shade, and pulled it. Soft light lifted the shadows. I looked around, stunned.

My prison was lovely.

The room made me think of a romantic cabin on an eighteenth century pirate ship. Heavy, curving beams formed the ribs of the ceiling. All the furniture was ornate, handsome, and antique. In an alcove, a pretty four-postered bedstead was plumped up with lacy white pillows and a marshmallow-like comforter. Beneath my sandaled feet, fishtailed mermaids, mermen, and other mythological beings cavorted in the design of a beautiful rug. I turned slowly, pirouetting around my cane, studying that woven world.

The lamp I'd turned on? Tiffany. And I'd bet it wasn't a reproduction. Jasmine and vanilla scented the air, along with the aroma of maritime oak, fine brocades, and silk.

An unhappy meow came from the carrier by the door. Big, apologetic Charley had deposited my cat and my luggage inside the room right after he deposited me there.

"Heathcliff," I moaned. "I didn't mean to ignore you. I know you've been traumatized." I rushed to the carrier, opened the door, and gently lifted Heathcliff into my arms. The old tabby purred. His fur felt even drier and more scruffy than usual. "I'll give you your medicine in just a minute," I whispered, stroking his head. "And then I'll unpack your tuna and we'll have dinner. I hope you don't mind sharing."

I set Heathcliff on the plush bed. He lay down gratefully, easing his bony bottom into the luxurious comforter. I reached for another Tiffany lamp on a bedside table. I listened to a low purr of sound outside. The tide. The ocean.

I hurried to a huge bay window. I loved being near the ocean, any ocean. My skin tingled. I'd grown up on Cape Cod, right on the beach. How many times my father had scooped me up in his arms and plunged into the tide with me, laughing as I laughed, burrowing into the ocean as if tunneling into a beloved nest.

I felt the magnetic pull. I believed I could see underwater; maybe I had a compass in my head, like the fish and the whales. As I grew older, alone, after my parents died in a land-bound car crash, I started to worry that I was deranged, that losing them, particularly losing my father, who lived in the water as if he preferred it to land, had damaged some rational part of me. So I submerged all those wild ideas about the water, and let them surface only in my books.

I remembered giant bluefin tuna, slipping up almost to the shallows like huge pets when my father whistled; seabirds gliding overhead not in raucous greed but to cluck lightly, sweetly at friends; the iridescent sheen where the surf licks the outreaches of wet sand. The world, my father said, is a beautiful woman. The ocean is her necklace. There, on that edge between water and earth, I could see it shine.

My father. My father was descended from Paul Revere and a mermaid. A *mermaid*. That meant I was descended from Paul Revere and a mermaid. Holy Nonsense, Batman. *If* I believed a word Juna Lee Poinfax said. I didn't.

"Agggh," I said aloud. But I looked out the window and gasped.

I saw the island. Out there in the moonlight, a golden island shielded the bay of this Georgia hideaway. *Sainte's Point.* Juna Lee had prattled on about it endlessly during the drive from Memphis. Home of the Bonavendier Mer clan since the 1700s. A beacon for Mers in this part of the world ever since. Not that I took any of her delusions seriously.

Despite myself, I trembled. Sainte's Point was majestic. Magical. Ethereal. Lights winked among the moon-tinged outline of the forest. The island was like some great ship anchored to the heart of the ocean floor, beckoning me with the glitter of its lanterns.

Your metaphors are as overwrought as your books, Juna Lee snarked.

I swung around, stared at the door, and raised my cane like a sword.

No, she hadn't slipped into the room. I was still alone. She'd spoken to me inside my mind.

I reeled. Just my imagination. Just like that strange moment in Memphis, when the mysterious Lilith had "spoken" to me psychically. I was overwrought, yes. The dime-novel heroine needed a *Zanax*, that was all.

Juna Lee rapped on the door. "You're a Mer. Tranquilizers don't work for you. Drink a cola. Eat some fish and a bowl of high-fat chowder. Now, that's comfort food."

She was reading my mind. Just like in Memphis. "You should work as a lounge act in Las Vegas. Do card tricks and tell fortunes."

"And *you* should drink a couple of stiff colas out of the miniature fridge in your room. It's in the armoire in the corner. A couple of colas will loosen up those sissy nerves of yours."

"I'm allergic to cola drinks. I get dizzy and disoriented."

"No, you get *drunk*. Admit it: you like the way they make you feel. They make you tipsy. You know that sounds impossible — it's another one of your secrets, like being a duck magnet. But you're not nuts, you're a Mer. You can swig booze all day without getting a buzz, but anything carbonated throws off your blood gases and makes you giddy."

"That's ridiculous pseudo-science. It's not physiologically—"

"Admit it. You love to climb into bed at night with Geezer Kitty, a stack of books, and a fizzy cola. You guzzle the stuff, get looped and fall asleep in a stupor, with romance novels and self-help books scattered all over you."

"Stop doing this . . . this cable-TV mind-reading act!"

"Chill out. Look, I'm going to a wedding on the island tonight. Charley's downstairs, so don't get any loopy ideas about escaping. Gulp some cola, get drunk, and read the books I put on the nightstand for you. There's a history of Mers that Lilith wrote, and a book about Sainte's Point. You *read those books. Read them*! You like books! It should be easy! Read! There'll be a quiz when I get back!"

"You're going to the island and just leave me here?"

"To a wedding on the island. If you'd be a nice little Floater, you could go, too."

"I rarely enjoy weddings I attend as a *hostage*."

"All righty, then. Be stupid. Stay here. Practice your psychic e-mail. If you need something, just think about it. Charley will hear you."

"Pardon me, but that's insane."

"Have it your way, idiot."

I heard her footsteps on the landing, then receding down a heavily carved staircase. I moved closer to the bay window and craned my head, trying to see her leave. A few seconds later she strode out of the cottage along a sandy path lined with pink oleander shrubs and palmetto. A flirty little silk robe twitched around her in the warm night breeze. I watched as she passed an elaborate stone boat house, then out to the end of a long pier.

When she reached the end, she shucked the robe and stood naked in the moonlight.

My jaw dropped. She pulled a fastener off her hair, and the auburn mane fell down her back. She dived into the dark bay with a smooth arc. I gripped the windowsill and strained to see her swimming. Finally, a good hundred yards beyond the shore, she surfaced in a pool of moonlight. She turned my way and said inside my head, "Read those books!"

Stick 'em up your tailfin, I blurted mentally.

The low hoot of her disdain popped my eardrums. *I*

don't have a tailfin. I clasped my head. She'd spoken. And I'd answered. And she'd heard me.

She dolphined beneath the water. I didn't see her surface again. I stumbled back from the window. I was trapped in her fantasy. I needed a big swig of something fizzy.

But then . . .

If I *was* trapped in *The Twilight Zone*, shouldn't I might as well play by the rules? If I really could talk to other . . . other mer-people, psychically, then maybe one of them might hear me calling for help. Maybe all Mers weren't snarky loons like Juna Lee.

There's no such thing as mer-people. No such thing. Don't let her brainwash you. This is how well-meaning human beings are lured into cults and gangs and American Idol auditions. Brainwashed. It's the Stockholm Syndrome, where kidnap victims start to trust their kidnappers. Find a phone. Call 911, not the psychic hotline.

But I couldn't resist.

Help me, I whispered inside my mind. Could one whisper inside one's mind? I thought louder. *Help.* I threw back my inner head and yelled. *Help!*

Nothing. No one answered. Heat zoomed up my cheeks.

I fed Heathcliff some tuna, drank some cola, turned off the lamps and sat by the bay window in the dark, drunk and upset. All right, instead I'd pretend to be a lighthouse sending an S.O.S. Only the light was a song, and I was singing it. Or something.

Help please help help I'm losing my mind help I'm a harmless, hypnotized lunatic, I thought. Sang. Hummed.

Not really believing that anyone would hear me.

The loneliest sound in the world is the silence when no one answers.

Help me. Help. Please.

The voice was soft and female and desperate. In other words, I could no' resist listening. Whoever she was, she hummed inside me as if I was exactly who she needed to find. Some women's voices are an instant warning. Some are an instant hard-on.

Hers was both.

Uncle Rhymer, what's wrong? Stella whispered. She stood beside me in the dark of the deck. We were moored in a hidden river inlet on the mainland near Sainte's Point. With barely enough room to maneuver, I could spit and hit the pine forest just beyond the gray muck of the banks.

Ssssh. I'm listening to someone who doesn't quite know how to sing. I touched a fingertip to my lips. Stella stared up at me, her eyes so wide I could glimpse the white rims in the moonlight.

A terrible thought loomed inside me. Was the call for help a deception? The bastard, himself, Orion, mimicking a woman? Did he have that kind of power? Not that I knew of, but then, who knew exactly what a Swimmer could do?

"What's the problem?" Jordan called in a low voice. He made his way along the sidedeck from the bow, one hand on the Uzi hanging from his shoulder. He was dressed all in good linen, as if for a round of golf at St. Andrews. The man took facials and got his nails buffed. Having him aboard as a bodyguard was a bit of a strange combination, like Cary Grant playing a commando. But Jordan and I'd always been like brothers and in fact were some degree of distant kin; Mers are a close-knit bunch, for obvious reasons, with a labyrinth of family ties not even the Queen can best. Jordan was one of the few men, Mer or Lander, I trusted completely. Even if he did buff his nails.

We traded a look, channeling a thought over Stella's head. Mers can control who hears what they think; I didn't want the lass worrying more than she already did.

Do you hear her? Hear the woman calling for help?

Jordan frowned in the moonlight. *No. Nothing. Is it Orion? Is it a ruse?*

I don't know. I intend to find out. I nodded to the east. *What's over there, on the coast?*

Randolph Cottage. Belongs to Griffin's family. It was his parents' lovenest. Haunted, in my opinion. But Griffin and Ali love it.

"Stay here with the girls. I'll go and have a look."

I was already dressed in a black wetsuit — not for warmth or protection, since Mers need little of either in the water— — but for fading into the night. I belted a pistol to my waist in a waterproof case; my short sword was already lashed to my thigh. "I'll be back soon."

And over the rail I went, into the black water.

❧ ❧ ❧

I was so proud of myself. *Juna Lee Poinfax, Successful Kidnapper.* Not a soul, not even Lilith, suspected that I had Molly Revere caged up at Randolph Cottage. The cottage belonged to Ali and Griffin, but they let me use it as a guest house.

Hah! Did I have a VIP guest or what? Lilith thought I'd had to give up on Molly in Memphis. She thought I was defeated, that next I would be forced to traipse all the way to Molly World in Massachusetts and beg Gimpy The Wonder Writer to listen again. Hah! As if Juna Lee Poinfax ever accepted secondhand couture, secondhand men, or secondhand kidnap victims.

So there I was at Ali and Griffin's post-wedding gala, basking in my secret victory, dressed in a slinky Versace gown, wearing some of my best diamonds, partying beneath elaborate Japanese lanterns on the leeward beach at Sainte's Point with several hundred other fabulous Mers. On a stage among the dunes, Gloria Estevan sang Latin pop with a full orchestra. She's a Mer, you know, on her mother's side. I was dancing a barefoot rumba with Billy Dee Williams, the actor, who is just a Floater (no webbed toes inside those imported loafers of his) but who perfectly represents the stylish, cavalier charm of mature Mer playboys everywhere. By the way, yes, Mers come in all colors, religions, and places of national origin.

"I hear you and Jordan are back together," Billy said, as we rumba-ed back and forth. The man moved like chocolate ice cream, cool and sweet.

"Hah. In his dreams."

"Where is he tonight?"

"Oh, I don't know. Probably twiddling jellyfish somewhere out in the shallows."

Billy laughed. I frowned.

Truth was, I'd expected to see Jordan by now, and I was worried. I planned to seduce him into telling me when Rhymer and the girls would arrive. I assumed they were still somewhere in the English Channel, trying to hitch a ride on the Gulf Stream. I figured I had at least a day to browbeat Molly into submission so I could turn my full seductive powers of concentration on the whole psycho-murder-mystery Swimmer thing.

"Maybe I should go find Jordan—"

"Yo, yo, yo, Juna girl!"

A sturdy little Lucy Liu look-alike in see-through silk and tattoos sauntered through the dance crowd. She had the Chinese symbol for luck tattooed on one perky little breast and the Chinese symbol for water tattooed on the webbing between the big toe and first toe of her bare feet. Ouch. She was Anna Chin, Miss Masochistic Mer from San Francisco. A bad-girl rapper with two platinum CDs to her name. A Bonav-endier cousin. Jordan was a partner in the Mer-owned label that produced her music. I slapped her hand. "Homegirl!"

"Word. I heard you and Jordan are doing the nasty again. Where's he at?"

"Why would I know? He's not hangin' at *my* crib. And, no, we're not getting our freak on, or whatever. Hey, check out my bling bling." I pointed to a new diamond choker. Yes, there's nothing goofier than a white mermaid trying to talk like a Mer from the hood, but then, I was saying this to a rap geisha Mer who went by the silly stage name Lady Tyg R S. Which *Entertainment Tonight* pronounced Tigeress, though it always seemed to me that it should be pronounced Tiggeress, which would be, one assumed, a rapper from the Pooh hood.

"Nice ice," Anna opined. "Check this." She held up a diamonded hand. "Tula made it for me. I'm wearing it to the Grammys."

"Six carats. Excellent. Subtle, but not."

She hooted. I faked a laugh while wondering, again, just what my personal Loch Ness Monster was up to. Didn't Jordan understand that I couldn't let some creepy Mer mobster rip his heart out? That ripping his heart out was *my* hobby? For the first time in my life, I caught myself looking out at our beloved ocean with fear.

∞ ∞ ∞

The big, bodybuilding Mer recognized me as a Peace-keeper the second I slipped out of the tide and laid the tip of my blade at his throat. He was lounging on a teak deck chair in the dark with headphones on his tanned ears, connected to a portable CD player tucked into one beefy hand. Plus he was a little drunk on Alka Seltzer and Sprite. When I prodded him with the sword, he rolled off the lounge and nearly pissed on himself.

"I heard the lady in the cottage over there calling for help," I said calmly, as he scrambled to his feet with his earphones dangling from one ear. "I'm a Peacekeeper."

He groaned. "Oh, man, I should have known the Council would send a Peacekeeper over this. I'm Antoine de Breneaux. But you can call me Charley the Tuna. I shouldn't have let Juna Lee talk me into kidnapping somebody. But we grew up next door to each other in Charleston. She's my cousin."

"Sorry, but I know Juna Lee's rep, my friend. Do no' try to defend her."

Charley sighed. "Okay, so once, when I was about ten, she talked me into building a bamboo raft and playing explorer. 'You be Thor Heyerdahl,' she said. 'I'll be Jacques Cousteau.' We ended up somewhere around Costa Rica. But she apologized. Sort of. Well, okay, she lied to everybody and said it was all my idea. My parents were so mad they sent me to boarding school in Iceland, and her parents sent her to school in Europe. I got glaciers. She got *Paris*."

"Sorry about the glaciers, Charley. Into the boathouse with you. I'm sure the Council will take your cooperation as a plus. Not to mention that you've been under the influence of a notorious woman."

"I should have known Juna Lee would get me in trouble again."

He trudged toward the boathouse.

∞ ∞ ∞

Speak your name and convince me not to kill you.

Those were the first words my potential rescuer — or murderer— spoke inside me.

I jumped up from my spot by the cottage window, grabbed my cane, and limped to the far side of the bed in the moonlit darkness. I cradled Heathcliff in one arm. My old kitty and I, barricaded behind a four-poster with lacy linens, would hold this psychic fort. Shaking, I offered a feeble rebuke: *I was only signaling for help. No need to be rude. Exactly who are you?*

Speak your name, the voice ordered again. It soaked my brain with a masculine timbre. I felt like a rum cake, drenched in rich liquor. Though the voice was a kind of vibration, not an actual sound, I deduced that it was . . . Irish, English, Scottish? Scottish, yes.

Speak your name.

This time the voice was louder, meaner, closer. It hummed inside my skull, vibrated off the bones of my face. I stared toward the window. Was he outside by the water? How close was he? Who was he? Did the prison doctor know he'd stopped taking his medication?

Speak your name, he ordered again. *If you're innocent, I mean you no harm.*

Well, that's good to hear. How do I know you're innocent?

Speak your name.

I shivered. Did I have a choice? I was holding a psychic conversation with a Sean Connery sound alike. Did trauma produce hallucinations based on vintage James Bond films?

I'm Molly (No! Sound stronger, fiercer, unconquerable!) *I'm Molly Martha Revere, of Boston, Massachusetts. I was kidnapped in Memphis, Tennessee, yesterday, by Juna Lee Poinfax. She says I'm descended from a mermaid and that I have to acknowledge my Mer heritage. All I know is I spent all day locked in my own bus and now I'm locked in a bedroom somewhere on the coast near Sainte's Point Island, and nothing like this has ever happened to me before. Who are you, please, and do you hear other voices inside your head besides mine? Don't listen to them! Merge your personalities! Merge!*

Silence. My ridiculous tirade was being assessed. I could feel him probing for lies. My breasts and thighs tingled. Probing for more than lies. *Yes*, I sputtered mentally. *I'm not just pretending to be a woman. I do have a vagina.*

He was convinced. *Come to the window*, he said. Amused, surprised, and almost gentle. Usually, men were bored with me until they found out I had money. *Show your face. Don't be afraid.*

Don't be afraid? You threatened to kill me.

Sorry. But now that I've confirmed you have a vagina, you're safe. Show yourself.

I set Heathcliff down on the bed, then slowly edged over to the bay window. Its window seat was cushioned with sumptuous silk pillows. I eased down on them, craned my head, and peeked down at the beach.

My breath caught in my throat. He stood, a dark, masculine silhouette with moonlight carving his face, at the edge of the tide. The foaming water curled around his feet like cream being whisked. From the tilt of his head I knew he was looking up at me. That we had found each other. *Found each other.* What a thought. I was too used to loneliness to believe I'd found or been found by a man.

Well, Molly Revere, it's good to see that you look none the worse for being kidnapped by Juna Lee.

How can you know anything about me? I'm just a dark shape in the window.

Some shapes are better than others.

Oh. Plus, I have a vagina.

Do no' be pretending you don't appreciate the fact that I have the opposite.

Ah hah. *The opposite.* He was a gentleman. A gentleman didn't say *penis* until the lady said it first. Shy. No. Not shy. *Gallant.*

But I was in no mood for gallantry. *You have a big, wagging, testosterone-overloaded penis, you mean.*

He gave a psychic cough. *That would be the technical term. I prefer to call it my Moby Dick.*

I burst out laughing, then stopped, horrified. I clasped a hand to my mouth, as if my mouth was working without me. Not only had I lost my mind, I was casually discussing penises with a stranger. Me, a Presbyterian librarian from Boston. While I was still being held prisoner in Casa de Juna.

About my circumstances, Mr. Dick . . .

I'll have you out in a minute.

My nameless visitor stepped out of the surf and strode across the sandy yard toward the cottage. I watched, breathless and intrigued, as his tall, muscular form disappeared beneath my window.

Be careful! You'll have to get past a huge wrestler named Charley the Tuna.

I already have. He's locked in the boat house.

I sank back on the pillows, speechless.

I was being rescued.

☙☙☙

The peal of a ship's bell in the mansion's turret at Sainte's Point interrupted mine and Anna Chin's meeting of the Diamond Appreciation Society. We followed the crowd to the lawn below the mansion's broad verandas. Oil lamps and lanterns flickered everywhere, casting lovely fingers of light up into the moss-draped oaks. Deer, raccoons, wild turkeys, and other wildlife stood respectfully in the shadows, munching a wedding feast of fine grains and corn, while spectating on our sport. Behind us, the Atlantic kissed the shore, drew back coyly, then kissed and withdrew again. A number of guests wore soaking wet gowns and tuxedoes, having succumbed to the usual Mer fondness for a tipsy tickle-and-grab in the ocean. Waiters and waitresses handed out tall crystal flutes filled with lots of vodka and a little tonic (a Bonavendier tradition at celebrations).

Amidst a glow of lights and applause, Lilith and her two full sisters, Mara and Pearl, appeared on the veranda. The three of them made an awesome sight: stately Lilith, sarcastic, beautiful Mara (my favorite), and sweet, flaky Pearl. Imagine an eagle, a hawk, and a parakeet. Talk about birds of a finned feather. Their men — Riyad, C.A. and Barrett — stood behind them, as men should.

"When we found our half-sister, Alice, in the mountains of northern Georgia," Lilith said, looking like a dream in a strapless Oolterang, with her silvery auburn hair up in a pearl-wrapped chignon, "we prayed that she'd become a happy part of our family and our heritage. That dream has come true. And now it's our immense pleasure to present her and her husband, who is also a dear part of our family. My friends, my kin, let us toast Ali Bonavendier Randolph and Griffin Randolph!"

Cheers erupted. Crystal flutes were raised. In the cove that served as the island's marina, dozens of dolphins raised their heads from the water and chittered their congratulations.

Ali and Griffin came out of the mansion, hand in hand, him big and rough-edged (his father? A rich, brutal Lander!) but handsome, dressed in a tuxedo yet shirtless and barefoot; Ali glowing in an antique wedding dress that had belonged to some Victorian Bonavendier, her long brunette hair streaming over the fine silk and tulle in gleaming rivers. Saltwater dripped from the couple; Ali plucked a bit of seaweed off Griffin's lapel.

Everyone laughed and applauded. In true Mer style, the newly married duo had christened their union in the bay, making love under the water, surrounded by guardian dolphins.

My heart twisted with envy. Oh, what a sucker I was for weddings. What an absolute, sentimental idiot. As Ali and Griffin waved to their guests, and everyone toasted them, I blinked back tears.

I dodged out of the crowd, into the darkness along the beach. *Stupid, stupid, stupid,* I chanted silently. *You wouldn't marry Jordan, even if he asked you. Not that he's ever asked.*

Help, a voice grunted in my head. I halted, listening. *Uh, help,* it said, plodding and masculine, a little embarrassed.

Charley? What's going on?

Uh, well, nothing. Sort of.

Charley.

I'm locked in the boathouse at Randolph Cottage.

I groaned. And?

I'm never letting you talk me into building a bamboo raft again.

Molly And Rhymer

∽ ∽ ∽ ∽ ∽ ∽ ∽ **10** ∽ ∽ ∽ ∽ ∽ ∽ ∽

My rescuer — whatever his real name, I refused to call him Mr. Dick again — my rescuer jerked open the cottage's massive front door downstairs, sounding as if he'd nearly ripped it from its hinges. Upstairs, I hurriedly guided Heathcliff into his wicker carrier, then grabbed my cane and waited.

Soft thuds on the staircase. The rescuer was barefooted. I heard the sensation of his naked feet, I felt his thoughts — or, at least, some of them. Briefly I had dated a *New York Times* book reviewer who claimed to be psychic. "*I knew you were going to say that,*" he often claimed. He dropped me for a woman who wrote true-crime novels.

"You can predict her reviews before she gets them," I told him. "And help her solve who-dunnits."

But this, this involvement with the amazing stranger who'd come out of the bay at my call, was nothing so silly as that. I could feel his strong and steady heartbeat in my mind. His heart was coming up the stairs with him. I put a hand over my own heart.

"Stand back, Moll," he said through the door.

Moll. I was a racy Scottish Moll now?

"Moll is standing far, far away," I confirmed.

He kicked the door open. The lock ripped from its berth. Heavy wood splintered and sprayed. The ghostly fingertip of an oak tree stroked my cheek.

My stranger stepped inside the dark room. Suddenly, he had a scent — a good scent, of salt and water and moonlight and sand — and a presence, a brisk warmth, an impression of broad shoulders, long legs, shadowed eyes. He towered over me.

"Where do you want to go?" he asked.

Wherever you are. Thank goodness, that thought didn't escape my own head. He would have commented, surely. "Anywhere. I have a bus."

"Not anymore. It's nowhere to be seen."

Juna Lee had hidden my bus? That woman. I sighed. "I noticed a beautiful little bayside village on the way here. Maybe it's close enough to walk?"

"Hmmm. Bellemeade. I'll take you to the inn there. Good enough?"

"Oh, more than . . . thank you." Silence. I stepped into the moonlight, squinting as it bathed my face. I wanted a good look at him, but he stayed in the shadows. His face was beautiful, harsh but gentle, with big, sea-gray eyes and dark hair. I could feel him studying me, making my heart race. In my new mode as a psychic soothsayer, I could swear his heartbeat matched my own. Except yours truly was not the type who gave men palpitations.

Tired and suddenly sad, I said crisply, "To whom do I owe the honor of rescuing me?"

"Well, it's not *Tom the Ranger*."

Exposed like a bug under a flower pot.

"I have no idea what you mean by that."

"Right. But call me Tom, if that suits you. Come along, Moll." He reached for the cat carrier. "You and your worried puss, too."

"My puss and I," I said drily, clutching the carrier's handle, "can make our own way downstairs, thank you."

"Ar." Some Scottish invective. Burp a haggis. That sound.

I had a small problem. I was lying about being able to lug the carrier down a steep flight of stairs. Nonetheless, I picked it up and balanced heavily on my cane. Like most handicapped people confronted by able-bodied arrogance, I had a fierce need to appear completely and totally independent. "Excuse me."

He stepped aside.

I lumbered past. *Thump, step, thump, step.* The dance of my daily life. I hated my scarred right leg. Hated the memory of the car accident on Cape Cod that had taken my parents and left me crippled when I was only fifteen. Hated the rare blood disease — leukemia, or whatever it was — that haunted me. Hated being an easy target for cheap pity and petty humiliation. Hated feeling Tom the Ranger's dark eyes on me.

"Moll, I'm in a bit of a hurry — sorry," he said suddenly. He scooped me up into his arms, cat, wicker carrier, and all. "I'll no' drop you. Or your puss. You have my word."

I hugged the carrier and peered around it, staring at him, open-mouthed.

"You better not drop my puss, at least."

Five minutes later we were standing on the sandy front walkway outside the cottage. At least, *he* was standing. I was still being carried. He shoved the pathway's curlicued white gate open with his bare foot. I still had no idea who he was, where he'd come from, or why he happened to be barefoot and wearing a black wet suit, not to mention armed with what appeared to be a waterproof gun holster and a small, ceremonial sword belted to his waist.

"I can walk now, Tom."

"Too slow for my purposes, Moll."

"Smile when you say that, stranger."

"I'm not making fun of you, and I'm not pitying you. You've had a hard day or two, Moll. Relax and enjoy the ride. Just do me a favor, will you? Latch your inside arm around my neck. I don't fancy a mile walk to Bellemeade with your nicely pronged elbow in my ribs, hmmm?"

"At least you didn't call it a *bony* elbow."

"There's nothing bony about you. Just . . . precise. The arm. Around my neck, Moll."

I slowly curled one arm over his shoulder, curved it behind his neck, and just as slowly unfurled a hand on the hard surface of his opposite shoulder. I felt his muscles shift under the thin wet suit. I forced my fingers not to stroke the movement. They curled and uncurled, despite me. "Your ribs are safe now."

"But as for the rest of me?"

A heat lamp scoured my face. No doubt, I turned rose-red. "Perfectly safe, I assure you."

"Then you're a grand challenge, Moll."

Inside the cat carrier, Heathcliff began to purr loudly. Tom the Stranger had that effect on a puss. As we stepped through the gate, fireworks burst from the island. Enormous chrysanthemums of gold and white bloomed over the bay, then streamers of magenta and multicolored whirls. The beautiful kaleidoscope sprinkled us with ethereal light. I was being showered by magic in the arms of a gallant, mysterious stranger.

"Ah. The wedding," he said. "It's officially celebrated now. 'Tis a good thing, the honoring of bonds between a man and a woman."

I gazed at the beautiful night sky over Sainte's Point with awe. This coast was full of magic. The lure was powerful. I wasn't sure what to think, what to believe, or whom to trust. Except the man who held me in his arms. I'd finally been rescued.

Don't let him hear you thinking.

Too late. He turned, frowning and tired, his head near mine, his lips near my ear. As the boom of the fireworks continued before us, he spoke intimately, brushing my skin with his breath. "The name's Rhymer McEvers. And yes, if you and I had naught else to worry about, I'd love to dance with you under those lights."

With that — my heart and puss clutched firmly in his possession — he carried me to town.

∞ ∞ ∞

I've known women, lots of them — wink and a nod — but I'd not met one like this one, before. This Molly Martha Revere, as quaint as an old-fashioned pudding, as unpredictable as a minnow in the shallows, perched in the window above me, in the dark. I knew nothing but that Juna Lee had caught her up in some scheme. Kidnapping a fellow Mer — which this Molly was, even if a bit unsure about it all — kidnapping a fellow Mer was against the rules I was sworn to enforce, as a Peacekeeper for the Council. Beyond that, I shouldn't have cared about Juna Lee's victims one way or the other. I helped this little Molly minnow out of her puddle, admired her with a tug at my heart and my Moby, then disappeared back into the bay.

But I could no' forget her.

∞ ∞ ∞

"Give her back, Tula."

"I will not. Unlike you, Juna Lee, she's a *real* writer. And a fan of serious fiction. I like her. We may start a book club."

Tula was pissed at me. After the wedding she'd returned from Sainte's Point and dropped by WaterLilies Inn (which she co-owns with our Great-Aunt Pearl) for a nightcap, only to find a message from Rhymer McEvers about my perky little escaped prisoner, who he'd left at the sushi bar. Tula found her calmly nibbling steamed soy beans and *ahi*.

"I can assume you're my cousin's kidnap victim?" Tula asked drolly.

"Yes," Her Mollyness replied. "You don't seem surprised. She's a sociopath, you know."

"I know. I'm so sorry. Truly."

"May I borrow your cell phone? I'd like to hire a hit man to break her kneecaps."

"Oh, please," I said to Tula now, "like I haven't been threatened by worse." I jerked my head toward the broad windows of Tula's Victorian marsh cottage. Bellemeade Bay shimmered in the moonlight beyond the gently swaying marsh grass. "Look, I don't have time to argue. I didn't know Rhymer had already reached Georgia. That means Jordan is out there in a cove somewhere, playing bodyguard to Rhymer's nieces while Rhymer's been rescuing Little Miss Molly Muffet from my evil tuffet, and he needs my help. So don't piddle around. Give me my gimpy author back. She's the ticket to my redemption with the Council. She's the reason Lilith cleared me to stay here. All she is to Rhymer is an *appetizer*."

Tula waved both arms. The silk sleeves of her antique kimono fluttered. She looked like a big butterfly with red hair. "Juna Lee, haven't you done *enough* damage? Leave Molly alone. She's in my guest suite upstairs. Happily stoned on vodka tonics. I went up to offer her a midnight snack and she was out on the balcony, crying and looking toward Sainte's Point. When I asked her what was wrong — besides the obvious, you know, like being *kidnapped, transported across state lines, and held prisoner at Randolph Cottage* — she hiccupped and smiled and said, 'Who am I? Where am I? *What* am I? I've never found the real world particularly romantic before. But this world is a *very* romantic place.'"

"So? She's babbling. She's one lipstick shy of a makeup kit. I'm telling you. It's like trying to hold a conversation with Anna Nicole Smith."

"Juna Lee! Don't you get it? Despite everything you did to her, she's *happy* to be here. Rhymer rescued her and carried her all the way to the inn. Something happened between them. Something sentimental. Something good."

I gaped at my cousin. Finally, I smiled. "Ah hah! My matchmaking plan is already working!"

"You call this a *plan?*"

"Whatever. It's working."

"Hello, Juna Lee, you bee-atch," Molly said, drunk but dignified, above us. We turned and looked up. She wobbled then leaned rakishly on the white rail of the upstairs landing, which overlooked Tula's luxurious, sea-colored wicker den. Her fine, short brown hair fluffed around her face, electrified by some alchemy of salt air and Rhymer lust and cola-induced inebriation. One of Tula's slinky silk robes draped her like a Greek toga. She glared down at me. She looked like an enraged Tweetie Bird.

I batted my eyelashes. "So you and Rhymer hit it off?"

"He's a gentleman. I appreciate a gentleman. That's all I'm going to say."

"Too bad. So nothing fun happened?"

"I want to know more about him. Tell me. Does he live near here? Is he some kind of law enforcement officer in the States? FBI? CIA? Navy Seal?"

I snorted. "Maybe a selkie. Not a seal."

"*Tell me more.*"

"So Molly The Magnificent admits she needs my help, hmmm?"

"It's research on mermen. For a future book."

"Oh, sure, you drunken little geek. Research. All right, I'll tell you all about Rhymer. But *only* if you do something for me in return." I smiled up at her. "You have to spend the summer at Randolph Cottage. And you have to promise to keep quiet about our little road trip from Memphis. Don't use the k-word, again. Kidnapping. You won't file charges. *Capice?*"

She stared down at me, her fine-boned face working up a delicate pucker of disgust. I wouldn't have been surprised if she hawked a loogy at me. I subtly moved out of range. Her eyes narrowed. "Don't worry. I never spit in public."

Damn. She was hearing my thoughts. Her Mer talents were developing quickly. I put a hand on one hip. "Don't get uppity, you stubby-toed Floater."

"*Juna Lee*," Tula scolded. "How tacky. Picking on a fellow Mer's toe status."

But my former captive wasn't chastened. The smug little shark smiled, showing pearly teeth. "You need me. I need you. Fine. Tomorrow, I'll move into Randolph Cottage. And I'll pretend to forget that you k-worded me." She turned away, then hesitated and looked back. "I want my bus here by eight a.m. With your lipstick stains washed off the glassware and your crayon marks scrubbed off the dining table. Good night."

She limped back to the guest suite while I went *ah-ah-ah* with my speechless mouth, then noticed that Tula was biting her fist to keep from laughing at me.

∞∞∞

Hello, hello? Calling Rhymer McEvers. It's Molly Revere. The psychic pen pal you rescued earlier tonight. Testing. One. Two. Three. Testing. Oh, this is ridiculous. I can't believe I believe this is possible. It's not. I'm hallucinating. Suffering from PJSS. Post Juna Lee Stress Syndrome. Rhymer McEvers is out on the ocean somewhere, and I'm here at Tula Bonavendier's home, and if I want to talk to him in the middle of the night I'd better pick up my cell phone — which would be way too bold for a Boston librarian turned world-famous author to do. I'm going to sleep, now. Sleep. Sleep. Concentrate on sleeping. I'm drunk on cola with a chaser of rum and I'm growing sleepy—

'Tis no hallucination, Moll. You sing out, I hear you. But

any woman who calls out to me at this time of night had better be naked.

One if by land. Two if by sea.

Is that a yes as to nakedness?

One if by — sorry, it's a slight obsessive compulsive twitch of mine. When I'm upset, I think of the famous Longfellow poem. Like a chant. It blocks out anxiety. Hello!

A famous poem?

I forget. You're Scottish. The poem's about a hero of the American Revolution. Paul Revere. Juna Lee says I'm actually related to him; I thought the surname was just something my father's notoriously flamboyant grandmother adopted as a stage name, but apparently I was wrong. The poem is The Midnight Ride of Paul Revere. *The most famous line is 'One if by land, two if by sea.' It refers to a lantern signal warning the American colonists that the British troops are coming. Did I wake you up?*

No. I don't sleep much. I'm sitting on the bow of my boat, watching the ocean. My nieces are in the cabin. Jordan Brighton is bunked on the stern. Tomorrow we'll move to Sainte's Point. But tonight we're on the boat, hidden in a cove. So, this poem about your famous ancestor helps you avoid thinking naughty thoughts?

Naughty? *Am I that Victorian?*

I ask if you sleep without clothes, and you start reciting poetry.

Okay, I'm a little unhinged by recent events.

Aye, that's understandable. I have nothing against unhinged women. Be that as it may — I take it you want to talk to me?

I . . . yes. Yes. All right. Yes, I want to talk. I was just . . . testing the system. The Mer psychic call-in line. I'm sorry. I disturbed you. I didn't really think this would work.

Where you're concerned, I'm awake and at attention. And only disturbed by your effect on me.

One if by land, two if —

Easy, Moll. I apologize. Bit of a lout, that's me. Sorry.

*You're not a lout. A man who rescues me and carries me —
plus my cat — all the way to Bellemeade is no lout.*

*You throw me off guard with such flattery. I'm fair to mid-
dling blunt with people. Not good at the niceties. I can't recite
poetry to you in return, Moll. But I don't mean to embarrass you.*

*Embarrass? No. Startle. Yes. Naked in bed. Me? Hah. I'm
not a naked kind of woman.*

It was a serious question, Moll.

*One if by land — naked. Naked. I sleep naked. All right?
Yes. I admit it.*

*I hear you breathing too hard. Relax. This conversation is
just inside our heads. Remember that. Phone sex without the
phone.*

I'm psychically hyperventilating. And you?

I take it you're in no trouble, not asking for assistance.

No, no. No trouble. Phone sex without the phone?

Tula Bonavendier is a fine hostess, and you like her?

Yes. She's very pleasant and rational. Not like Juna Lee.

*Juna Lee has a bit of a bad rep. Do no' take her to heart. At
least she got you here. You're safe and sound, none the worse for
wear. And you're learning who you are. That's good. The unhap-
piest Mers are the ones who don't know what to believe of themselves.*

Do you? You know what to believe of yourself?

*A glorified guard dog, that's what I am. I don't mind. Suits
my temperament. My ancestors died at Culloden. Always fighting for the losing side, we McEvers.*

No. Not a guard dog. A . . . lion. A noble lion.

A sea lion, maybe.

*But what does it feel like to be a Mer? To be a member of a .
. . a sub-species of humankind that couldn't possibly be real?*

*Not real? We are real, Moll. You and I and the others. Very
real. And we're not a sub-anything. We're the dominant species.*

Homo Swimmians, *if you like puns. Small in numbers but vast in influence.*

You do realize that the existence of mer-people defies every known law of genetics and evolution? Not to mention the entire canon of human history?

Lander *history, Moll. Not human history. You and me — we're just as human as any Lander. Only different.*

How can an entire minority society of, well, unusual human beings, exist for thousands of years without the majority discovering them?

Landers see what they've been taught to see. We just help the situation along with a few illusions. The poem you quoted — —one if by land or two if by sea? *Landers look for the light on land, Moll. They never think to look for the light by sea.*

You're a philosopher. A poet in your own way.

I've never rhymed two words in my life. Despite my name.

But you love books. You love to read. I can . . . feel it. What a strange thing. There's this wonderful hum inside me, and it's you, and I know things about you because of it. Am I prying?

No more than I'm prying into your mind. I feel you inside me, too. Like a flow of electricity.

This is how the 'singing' ability works? This tingle?

Aye.

There's no medical or physiological explanation for this ability. None.

Do no' be telling the great sea mammals that. They'll laugh at you. When a dolphin laughs, it feels like bubbles in your brain. It tickles.

Well, of course, whales and dolphins and other marine animals have sonic abilities; to find fish, to use as a compass when they migrate, to communicate. That's proven.

See? They communicate. Just like us. So hard to believe?

Then why can't ordinary people communicate this way?

Because they're ordinary.

Ah hah. Well, there's the scientific explanation I was hoping for. Do you let just anyone blow bubbles inside you?

No.

I'm honored.

Now that you've got your foot inside my door, you're welcome to a tour.

Bubbles. I feel bubbles. You're teasing me.

I'm no' teasing you, Moll. I'm sitting here in the dark on the boat. It's so quiet all I can hear is the surf and the wind. There's a million stars above me and a whole world of water before me. From here to forever. Hills and valleys and canyons deeper than the Grand Canyon and plateaus broader than the prairies. All under the oceans. Most of the world. Hidden from Landers.

It's the edge of forever. Oh, I'm sorry. That sounds like an old soap opera. 'Tune in tomorrow, as we continue The Edge of Forever.'''

Do no' be sorry. I like how you see things. How you see me. Kindly.

I see the truth.

Kindly.

I'm not kind. I'm vain and selfish and greedy. I love being a rich author. I love having people treat me like a celebrity. I had sterling silver faucets installed in my RV. But then I felt such shame I donated a huge amount to charity.

You give money to charity all the time. You're generous beyond all expectations. I feel it.

But I give lots more money when I install silver faucets. Oh! Bubbles!

It's been a long time since I smiled. Thank you.

About that tour. May I visit any part of you I wish to imagine?

Do no' go playin' with fire . . . ah.

You feel me thinking about you? Thinking about—

That's the part, you bet.

I'm thinking about your chest. How strong it felt against my side when you carried me.

Close enough.

Now I'm thinking about, yes, all right, oh, my—

Me too.

What are you —

Just thinking about you and your parts, Moll.

Oh. Oh! Oh!

Jordan Takes Charge

෴ ෴ ෴ ෴ ෴ ෴ ෴ **11** ෴ ෴ ෴ ෴ ෴ ෴ ෴

The round-the-world-in-eighty-days cruise, celebrating Ali and Griffin's royal Mer wedding, sailed the next day. Dozens of elegant yachts, large and small, made a raucous flotilla off the Atlantic beaches of Sainte's Point. Leading the way was their flagship, The Lady Lilith, Riyad's floating villa, staffed by a crew of handsome Saudi Mers whose allegiance was not first to Allah or country, but to their own Water People. No religion or race or national alliance turned a Mer away from his or her truest obligations; our kind maneuvered beneath the Lander world like a slow, deep current of primordial lava, slowly carving new waterways into the face of the planet.

". . . carving new waterways into the face of the planet," I finished typing into my laptop. I hit *Send*. A wireless widget flashed my new post to my on-line diary. I smiled fiendishly. "Done. Another fabulous entry."

"Juna Lee, I hate it when you're premenstrual and philosophical," Tula sighed. We lounged on blankets, naked except for thongs, on an isolated beach at the island. We were backed by huge sand dunes, the dark oak forest, and the prying eyes of wild ponies who lived like fat little hobbits under Lilith's care. I watched the wedding armada leisurely sail for the deep, summertime waters off the continental shelf.

"There they go. Leaving me to supervise the island and help Jordan fend off a murderous, mythological Mer. While at the same time trying to matchmake between the Clint Eastwood of Scotland and an obnoxious, wimpy writer who hangs around my neck like an albatross. I swear, I don't know how I multi-task so brilliantly."

Tula rolled her eyes. "Has Jordan actually asked for your help? Hasn't he emphatically ordered you to stay away from this island after today?"

I looked at her over my retro Ray Bans. "Do I look like I take orders from men?"

"Juna Lee, this is one time you shouldn't be capricious—"

"Eeeeee." Which is approximately the sound I made, accompanied by various obscenities, as a nylon lasso snared my bare left foot.

Jordan rose from the surf. He wore baggy silk swim trunks but might as well have been naked, considering how the silk was plastered to his erection. But even aroused, he looked serious. "Here, Juna, Juna," he called dryly, as if I were a cat. Then he dragged me into the water.

I barely finished squealing, kicking, and yelling, before the tide rushed over my head. I continued my protest in sonic trills that sent all the neighboring dolphins skimming away with their flippers covering their ears. I swallowed a gallon of saltwater, regurgitated it with a fierce spit (it's nearly impossible to drown a Mer) then finally managed to grab the tow line. I was in twenty feet of water by then, with jellyfish and crabs slithering by, giggling at me, and Jordan was towing me at a speed just short of a warp-speed skier.

Don't even try it, he growled inside my head, as I latched one hand around the rope at my ankle. He curled around me, rolling me inside the rope and three feet of my own auburn hair. Fly, meet Spider. I tried to pop his eardrums with my sonic shriek, but it didn't do a damn bit of good. He wrapped me like a seafood burrito, arms pinned to sides, thigh clamped to thigh. Only my boobs were free — or, at least, bulging out between two rounds of rope.

Maybe they'd signal for help.

Jordan, I'll never forgive you, you scum of the ocean, you amoeba-balled sneak, you—

I warned you I'd have you shanghaied if you didn't leave the island.

I popped to the surface alongside him, bobbing like a cork. "Lilith told me I could stay—"

"I didn't get that message." He stuck a finger in one ear. "La la la la la," he deadpanned. "I can't hear a thing."

"Liar! Cheater!"

"So sue me."

He levered himself up the ladder of a small sailboat, grabbed me by my rope corset, and lugged me aboard. I might as well have been a netted tuna. I lay there on the deck, fuming. This mermaid was steamed.

Jordan knelt beside me. My heart caught. Damned heart. His eyes were hard but also dark and sweet. Sure, he had regrets. Sort of. "If only you were always this easy to control," he grunted. He pushed my streaming hair away from my face, gently plucked a wet wad of it from my mouth, then gallantly arranged thick strands over my breasts. His knuckles brushed my skin, rousing a nipple or two.

Damn nipples, as well as hearts.

"I'll drop you off near Cuba," he said. "The Araizas will meet us there. They'll take you to one of their hotels. Maybe in Cozumel, maybe Cancun, maybe the Caribbean. At any rate, they'll make sure you stay put."

The Araizas. A Mer clan who owned resorts, cruise ships, and casinos. They ran their empire with an old-world mafia attitude. Picture the Godfather with webbed feet. "You're letting the Corleones of the Caribbean hold me hostage?"

"Hmmm. Holding you hostage? How melodramatic. What goes around comes around, right? Now you know how Molly Revere feels."

"Jordan, please. Don't make me leave. I know I look like a fluffy angel fish, but I'm a piranha when it comes to you."

"You've chewed my ass off a few times, that's for sure."

"Please."

His face softened. He leaned down, feathering my lips with his. "I love how you love me."

I never said I love —

He planted a long, slow, wet kiss on me, and I let him. Damn heart, nipples, and lips.

Traitors.

ᗧ ᗧ ᗧ

My name, I typed, *is Moll Revere. No longer Molly. Not Molly Martha. Moll. Moll the Mer.*

Maniac.

I deleted all of that then dutifully typed on my laptop, *Water Hyacinth, Book 5, Hyacinth and the Cave of the Argonauts. Chapter Seven.*

I sat at a wicker table at the end of the dock at Randolph Cottage, beneath a pastel beach umbrella. Enya sang her ethereal Celtic love songs on a CD player. My laptop was neatly arranged on the table, along with a notepad, a crystal pitcher of water, and a cell phone. Heathcliff lay beneath the table on a sun-shaded pillow of silk and lamb's wool. He calmly watched the ocean through cataract-clouded green eyes. I was dressed in an ivory cotton jumper over an ivory cotton tank top, with ivory cotton mules on my feet and a white-washed straw sunhat on my head. Yes, I looked prim, like a vanilla ice cream cone, as the loathsome Juna Lee would have noted, but I felt very wild and provocative in that tank top. If you pulled the bib of my jumper out and stared straight down at the tank, you'd have seen that I'd impulsively cast off my bra. Gasp. You'd see the bumps of my nipples.

Secretly rebellious bumps. If that isn't wicked, I don't know what is.

I stared at the blank computer screen, and I sighed. Moll, the Mer, muses. And mopes. Mostly over a man.

"Molly?"

A polite female voice made me jump. I looked around wildly. A wet, gorgeous woman poked her head over the edge of the dock. She held onto the wooden ladder and gazed up at me as if she were selling Mary Kay and just happened to swim by with my order.

Tula Bonavendier. I liked Tula. She was an oasis of friendship in the delusion that had swallowed me.

"Tula, hello!"

She climbed out, naked except for a thong. I looked away, peeked, looked away, drank some water, peeked. She calmly pulled a silk shirt from a waterproof fanny pack, languidly covered herself, then sat down cross-legged on the dock. "Juna Lee has left for the Caribbean on a . . . business trip. She asked me to check on you."

I stared at the transparent silk shirt over her breasts. I sighed. Just when I thought I'd liberated my own repressed bumps, she showed me how carefree bumps could be. *Note to self*, I thought. *Get one of those see-through shirts.*

"Are you writing another *Water Hyacinth* book?" Tula asked, watching me pleasantly. "I'm such a fan."

"Oh. Yes." I nodded. "I always carry my laptop in the bus. I write every day, even when I'm on a booksigning tour. Stories have to be told."

"This is the perfect setting. You'll be inspired. Your best book, yet. I bet."

"You're such a gracious person. Why do you put up with Juna Lee? Does she blackmail you with secrets? Were you and she separated surgically, at birth?"

Tula laughed. "No, but we're like sisters. I've known her for. oh, forty years. Since we were teenagers in Charleston. The South Carolina Mers are very tight. A society thing. Very Charleston. I grew up near Juna Lee in a pre-Civil War mansion with a view of the water and Fort Sumter. We were debutantes in, oh, the 1950s."

I stared at this youthful creature. "You're—"

"Older than you think."

"Oh. Tell me, how do Mer people get away with looking so young? Don't people notice you've been around for a long time? Don't they check your Social Security card?"

She laughed. "Not if we tell them not to notice. People believe what they want to believe, Molly. That's why Mers with webbed feet can go barefoot among Landers. The Landers don't see what we don't want them to see." She slid a bare foot forward. "What do you see?"

I leaned forward and peered at the sinewy, beautiful sculpted foot. "Not webbing, but, something glimmery between your toes, something—"

"Now look. Because I let you." She pushed her foot a little closer. Suddenly, as if my vision had cleared, I saw a human foot that was not quite human, extra wide across the toes, and the toes were longer than normal, and between those toes — between them, was the most beautiful, iridescent webbing.

I put a hand to my heart. "Butterfly toes."

She laughed.

I kicked off a white mule and looked down at my ordinary right foot, on the damaged leg, somberly. "I wish—"

"You're a Mer, regardless. Having webbed toes is just the icing on the fish cake."

I sighed. *Change the subject.* I always changed the subject when the scarred leg was involved. Under my concealing jumper, the leg was an ugly landscape of surgical scars, divets, and puckered skin. When I undressed at night I never looked at it. I pretended I couldn't see it. Maybe, like a true Mer, I would teach myself to see an illusion instead, some day. Maybe some day Rhymer McEvers would look at me, naked, and only see what I wanted him to see. My heart sank. Daydreams. "So. Juna Lee has gone to the Caribbean. Perfect. The jerk chicken of the sea."

Tula laughed again. "You're a match for her."

"She was supposed to tell me about Rhymer McEvers. We had a deal."

"I know. I'm here to honor it."

"Tell me. Is he . . . what? Sixty? A hundred? Sean Connery's long-lost younger brother?"

Tula sighed. "He's a lost soul."

I settled back in my chair. *So am I,* I thought. "And?"

"Many years ago, he was in love with a member of the British royal family. The house of Windsor has a strain of Mer, you see. Why do you think they send the young princes off to join the navy, not the army? Mer instincts."

"Of . . . course."

"Anyway, Rhymer was in love with a sweet girl, some cousin of a cousin of the future Queen's, but she was killed. Murdered. They say it was a revenge killing over some elaborate international business deal of her father's during World War II."

I took a deep swig of water and wished it was nerve-soothing cola. "Rhymer was a young man in the nineteen forties?"

"No, he was just a child, then. But this complex business relationship of the girl's father stemmed from the 1940s. And had something to do with Nazis."

"Please don't tell me there were Nazi mer-people."

Tula arched a brow. "Of course not. Only Landers kill each other over land, politics, and religion. Mers have no interest in any of those things—" her voice became sardonic "—as long as we control everything else."

"I see."

"To continue, Rhymer was in love with this girl, but her father, a Lander, owed some secret debt to Hitler's top cabal, and the high-ranking Nazis who escaped to South America needed money to fund their exile, and the father refused to pay, so they sent assassins." She paused, her face sad. "And they dragged Rhymer's girlfriend from her country home along the English coast, and they killed her."

"Oh, Tula, how sad." *Good. She's definitely dead.* I gasped inside. *What a horrible thing to think.*

"Rhymer tracked them down. All of them. And he, well . . . I'm only relaying gossip—"

"Tell me."

"He killed all the assassins. Then he went to South America and killed the old Nazis who'd ordered her murder."

I sank back in my chair, speechless.

Tula looked up at me somberly. "I don't know Rhymer very well. No one does. He spent years as some kind of commando for the British. Now he's a Peacekeeper for our Council. But I knew his sister, Tara." Tula paused. "Now, I'll tell you what happened to her."

I continued to sit in hypnotized silence as Tula related the story of Tara McEvers and her . . . her Mer lover/monster. A sensation like cold lizards crept up my arms and spine. Tiny lights sparkled in front of my eyes. Occasionally, my migraine headaches started this way. Only without the sensation of pure horror and incredulous terror.

Tula halted, watching me. "Take it easy, breathe, breathe, don't pass out."

I gulped some air. "A few days ago I was just an ordinary person, living an ordinary life. All right, an ordinary person with odd little traits and unexplainable impulses. But certainly not less mainstream than, say, your average Goth computer gamer or audience members at Jerry Springer tapings. Then I was jerked out of my psychologically insulated world by Miss Barracuda, aka Juna Lee, and told that I'm descended from a mermaid, and that all my quirks are actually Mer traits, and now I'm conducting psychic cell-phone chats with various merfolk, and trying very hard not to bolt for the nearest police station and beg them to lock me up until appropriate psychiatric help can be summoned . . . and now you expect me to believe that *my new family tree includes shapeshifting mutants.*"

"Now, now, I never said Orion is a 'mutant.'"

"If no one's ever seen one of these rare and incredibly secretive Swimmers, how do you know they exist?"

"Well, obviously, Tara McEvers believed Orion was one. Tara wasn't fanciful. She wasn't foolish. And there have always been reports, rumors, sightings — just never any proof."

"So . . . this Orion might look like something subhuman, or he might look like Barney Fife."

"Personally, I think he's somewhere in between."

"Well, that's comforting." I sat there, chewing my lip, absorbing and sorting information. "He wants to kill his own daughters?"

"We don't know what he wants to do with them. He's never visited them. Tara would meet him at the ocean. He never even contacted his daughters psychically. Tara insisted he didn't want to frighten them. But now, suddenly, he's looking for them. He's looking for them, and he's violent. He murdered all those UniWorld scientists and took Tara's body." She paused. "Not that the scientists didn't deserve being murdered, for treating a Mer like a research object."

I gaped at her, trying to focus on this bloodthirsty facet of her personality. Jewelry designer, elegant middle-aged youngster, lover of good books, the antidote to the awful Juna Lee, and gleeful pro-murder advocate? "I take it we, hmmm, don't like UniWorld?"

She arched a reddish brow. "To say the least. Most Mers have a slight problem with greedy Landers prowling around the coasts ruining the view with oil derricks, not to mention the occasional disastrous oil spill from a leaky tanker. Especially when UniWorld also owns dozens of other coastal industries, including marine labs doing unethical research, plus a couple of volatile nuclear power plants *and* private weapons labs selling the latest killing machines to the highest bidders."

"But I thought Mers controlled the waters. Aren't Mers powerful enough to stop this conglomerate?"

She gave me a grim look. "We don't like to admit what I'm about to tell you. I won't go into the details now. Really, Lilith will have to tell you the whole story sometime." She paused, almost stricken with humiliation. "UniWorld is owned by Mers."

This jaw-dropper set me back in my wicker chair, speechless. Before I could find my tongue again, Tula blinked and looked away as if listening. "Lilith says hello."

Lilith. The ethereal voice that had filled my head in Memphis. I reached out tentatively. *Lilith? Hello? Can we . . . talk face to face? Mind to mind, that is?*

My dear Molly, of course we can talk.

Lilith, I'm floundering. I'm in information overload. I might sink.

No, you won't. Just keep treading water, and you'll find your way to shore.

Lilith —

Trust your heart, Molly. The human body is 98 percent water. Listen to your own tides.

Tell me what else I should know about Rhymer McEvers. Is

there any way I can help him?

I can tell you this much — he needs you. And you need him.

Am I losing my mind?

No, dear. Only your unnecessary illusions. Au revoir, Molly Martha Revere. I'll see you when I return to the island in two months.

Two months? But I don't know if —

I'll see you, my dear. By then you'll be an old hand at Mer life. You'll glory in your liquid substance. You'll dive into the depths and breathe the elixir of joyful truth.

And then she was gone.

Dive into the depths, and breathe. I looked at Tula. "Can I breathe underwater?"

She nodded. "All it takes is practice. And faith."

Whammo. All these years, I'd thought I was just good at holding my breath.

∞ ∞ ∞

"Onto the shore, girls. This is Sainte's Point."

"It is a magical place, Uncle Rhymer," Stella said.

"Aye, it 'tis." Let them have their fancies. I was certain only that the island was far from Orion's grasp. I hoped.

Stella, Isis, and Venus stepped off the dock and, holding hands, gazed up at the pretty ballast-stone walls and delicate turrets and general oddities of the Bonavendier mansion. The bleached shells of sea turtles decorated a wall beneath the massive beams of the veranda, like warrior shields. Anchors and ships' cannons perched grandly on stone pads about the yard. Ships' bells swayed gently from tall posts. From Spanish galleons to Yankee submarines, the Bonavendiers had collected quite a commission from the shallows off their island.

"Look, sisters, a lovely fountain," Stella said, directing a slender finger at a statue of a sexy mermaid holding a large shell, from which water trickled into a basin. "Such a pretty Mer. A Greek *Nereid.*"

"Oh, Mother would have loved it here," little Venus sighed. "It's wrapped in a lovely shade of happiness."

"Looks as though they like war a bit much, if you ask me," Isis grumped. She prodded an 18th century cannon with her sandaled foot. "Perhaps, if our father shows up, we can shoot him with one of these things."

Venus began to cry. "I don't want to shoot him. I don't even know him. Why does he want to kill me and eat me?"

Stella gasped. "Where did you get such an idea?"

"I felt Uncle Rhymer thinking it."

I groaned. Shaking my head, I dropped to my heels before the threesome — stately Stella, jaunty Isis, sweetheart Venus. "You did no' hear me thinking such a thing. Tis your imagination, Venus."

"Mother always said he loves us dearly, in his own way, but that he wasn't meant to be with us. But if he loves us, wouldn't he at least talk inside our heads? But he never has."

"That's right," Isis grunted. "He doesn't call, he doesn't write. Not so much as a holiday card."

Stella hissed at her. "Whatever the truth, we're here with Uncle Rhymer, so let's make the best of it. Let's go inside. Miss Lilith left us all manner of good things to eat. Shrimp and chowder and chocolate and deviled crab with butter sauce. She spoke to me just this morning, and she said if we walk to the far side of this island we can see the village of Bellemeade and, farther up the coast, a lovely little cottage where a Mer storyteller lives."

"A Mer storyteller?" Venus whispered, wide-eyed.

All three girls caught my surge of thought. They pivoted toward me as neatly as a platoon on drill. "Who's Molly, Uncle?" Stella asked.

"Someone you like immensely, we take it," Isis echoed.

"And what's this about her puss?" Venus chimed. "She has a lovely kitty, you say?"

I groaned inwardly and squelched my thoughts. "She's a nice lady who's taken up residence across the water, just as we have here." I pointed a lecturing finger at the girls and put on my sternest face. "But we'll have no visiting, you hear? It's no' safe to leave the island."

Stella stared at me, picking up on details even I couldn't hide. Healers are even more sensitive to intuitions than most Mers. Her eyes went wide.

"Molly is . . . she's M.M. Revere. Molly is M.M. Revere. Uncle!"

"I don't care if she's the queen of Persia. There'll be no visiting."

"M.M. Revere?" Isis squealed. "M.M. Revere lives nearby?"

"Aye. Now you have the truth. But still, there'll be no visiting—"

"We have all her books! We have the DVD of *Hyacinth and the Mermaid's Torch*! We've watched that movie a thousand times!"

"Hyacinth?" little Venus shouted. "The Hyacinth lady lives near here? Oh, Uncle, I want to visit the Hyacinth lady!"

"No visiting."

They moaned. Stella beseeched me. "But you said she's one of us. She's a Mer, and her books are so special—"

"She's in seclusion, as we are. Do no' be trying to see her. Enough. *No visiting.* That's the last time I'll say it."

I was reduced to waving my hands and making a deadly face. In the service, I'd grunt a one-word command and armed men would jump to follow the order. But three little girls made me flap like a deranged seagull.

They looked absolutely crestfallen. I felt as if my own

crest had taken a tumble, too. 'Twas no fun to be a father figure. "Into the house with you three," I ordered. "And not another peep. Not so much as a hum."

They dutifully trudged up the knoll to the house, their delicately webbed feet beating a soft rhythm in sandals, thin summer smocks floating around them like upside-down buttercups, their heads bowed.

I stood for a moment, looking up at the grand, empty house, then scanning the grand maritime forest behind it, before turning to look at the quiet harbor where my boat was now anchored. Sainte's Point. A safe sanctuary, I prayed.

I thought of Moll. Another kind of sanctuary, quirky and sweet.

But I could not risk visiting her, anymore than the girls could.

⬳ ⬳ ⬳

Moll, I could still hear Rhymer saying. Speaking my name in that deep, Scotch whiskey voice of his. Almost as if he'd just said it again. He made my knees weak. Not a good thing when one knee was already tricky.

Leaning on my cane, I stopped suddenly in the sandy yard outside the shingled walls of Randolph Cottage, my adopted summer home. Heathcliff snoozed heavily in his carrier, an old kitty-man who spent all but an hour a day in deep, tired rest. I set the wicker carrier down gently, then, trembling, hunched over my cane and peered at a sandy spot between two pink oleanders.

Rhymer's footprints, from the other night. Big, strong, barefoot, manly imprints.

With the outline of webbing between the toes.

I maneuvered myself into a kneeling position on the sand, then slowly touched a fingertip to the prints. As I traced the outline just above the sand, not wanting to destroy them —*to hell with the Zen of the moment,* I thought grimly, *I like things that last* — a sexual warmth came over me, highlighting specific regions, and no respecter of dignity. I shut my eyes.

Dance, Moll, Rhymer whispered. *You can do it.*

Then he was gone.

I opened my eyes, sat down on the sand, and looked out over the bay at the low green mountain of Sainte's Point. The island rode the blue-gray crest of the horizon, the rim of the world, the curving waters. I drew a shaky breath. This was all real. I was not immersed in some hallucination, some waking dream, some malfunction of fragile brain tissue. Rhymer McEvers was real. mer-people were real. I was real. A real Mer. Floater class, no webbed tootsies, but still.

You, too, I whispered back to him. *Dance. And stay safe.*

Trapped in the Land of Rum Cocktails

❧ ❧ ❧ ❧ ❧ ❧ ❧ **12** ❧ ❧ ❧ ❧ ❧ ❧ ❧

Dear Diary:

I hate steel drums and blackened flounder. In my opinion, the entire Caribbean, along with every fruity rum drink, jerk chicken dinner, 'Hallo, Mon,' accent, and Rastafarian dreadlock should be swallowed by a massive tidal wave.

But then, maybe I'm just in a bad mood because I'm locked in the Jamaican equivalent of a Vegas high-roller's suite.

"Juna Lee?" my guard called through the teak double doors in her coy Hispanic drawl. She was six feet tall, two feet wide, and built like a brick lighthouse. An Amazon. A freakin' Amazon Mer was guarding my door, night and day. The Queen Latifah of Mer Mamas, guarding me. "Juna Lee, you prissy little *puta*, you better answer me."

I stood and yelled, "Listen, you Araiza-employed knuckle-dragger, obviously I'm not going to throw myself off a fifth floor balcony when you're not looking. I'm not a flying fish."

"Jordan Brighton sent you a gift. Behave and I'll open the doors and hand it to you. *Si?*"

I was off to the doors in a flash. My warden unlocked the door, opened it a few inches, then thrust a beautifully wrapped little box at me. I grabbed the box and made a poofing sound at her. "Scared of me? It's not as if I'm going to arm-wrestle you and bolt."

Snow white teeth gleamed in the polished chocolate

stone of her face. A whiff of Chanel wafted off her pale silk suit. A plus-sized designer Amazon. Her eyes narrowed. "Oh, *senorita*, I *wish* you'd try to escape." She pulled the doors to, and locked them again.

Muttering under my breath, I hurried to my bed — a lonely fantasy island, draped in white netting and plump with sea-peach silk finery — where I curled up and ripped the wrapping off Jordan's apology.

I forgive you for being a pain in the fin, his note said.

"You forgive *me*?" I popped open the jeweler's box and glowered at a tennis bracelet engorged with diamonds and pearls. "You know I don't play tennis! You know I don't *ever* sweat deliberately!" I stuffed Jordan's note into the box, ran to the balcony, scoured the palm trees, beaches, pools, and cabanas below for a likely target, then drew back my arm ferociously.

I sent the jeweler's box so far it probably hit a pirate in his *Yo-ho-ho*.

Then I latched the bracelet around one wrist and went back to my computer.

Never throw diamonds away. It's bad luck.

Molly Embraces Her Inner Shopping Mer

∞ ∞ ∞ ∞ ∞ ∞ ∞ **13** ∞ ∞ ∞ ∞ ∞ ∞ ∞

I stood on the sidewalk before a boutique in Bellemeade, clasping a small shopping bag containing a clingy, diaphanous silk dress the clerk had talked me into buying. I wasn't sure I'd be wild enough to wear something so un-Molly-like, even in the privacy of my own home, but I loved the idea of putting it on a hanger and looking at it.

"Ms. Revere, your Jaguar is waiting," a voice said.

I turned. "I beg your pardon?"

"Tula Bonavendier said you needed a car to drive during your visit to the coast."

I looked from the well-dressed young man to the gleaming silver Jag he'd parked on the bayfront street. "A Jaguar? I told Tula I was thinking of renting a nice little sedan with a pine-scented air freshener. Something fragrant and inconspicuous."

"No need to worry about your privacy here, Ms. Revere. Bellemeade belongs to *our* people. *Our* Landers are well-trained and polite. They won't harass a celebrity."

Ah hah. He was a Mer. I should have known. Second, he was a Mob Mer, or talked like one. Our people. Our Landers. It was almost medieval. The beautiful little village was awash in nice people — Landers, there, I said it! I made the distinction! — who hurried to help me, welcome me, and compliment me on my books. I buzzed with guilty pleasure. I was a princess here. I had peasants.

"The car, ma'am?" The well-dressed Jag-delivery Merman was looking at me.

"Sorry. Lost in thought. I . . . can't drive a stick-shift, I can't manage the clutch."

"Oh, I know. So I brought you an automatic."

I stared at the magnificent sports car. From the silver cat on the hood to the cat-eye tail-lights, it was one racy feline. I had millions in the bank, but up in Boston I drove an ancient Volvo with a *Save The Oceans, Love A Whale* bumper sticker. "You don't have any Volvos to lease, do you? With bumper stickers?"

"Are you all right, Ms. Revere?"

"Yes, yes. I'm sorry." *I'm just not used to life as a mythological sea princess yet.* "The car's fine. Thank you."

"Please. I'll take your package."

He whisked my shopping bag over to the car and put it in the back seat. Then the man strode back to me, bowed slightly, and placed the remote, and its attached key, in my hand.

"Thank you," I said uncertainly.

"You're most welcome. Would you mind autographing a set of your books for my son? His name's Noah. He's seven, and he's a huge fan."

"Of course I wouldn't mind."

He shifted a handsome leather tote off one shoulder, dug into it, and produced all four of my *Water Hyacinth* books, well-thumbed. *Hyacinth and the Mermaid's Torch, Hyacinth and the Temple of Neptune, Hyacinth and the Curse of Poseidon,* and lastly, *Hyacinth and the Surreal New Life.* I mean, *Hyacinth and the Siren's Ghost.* The surreal new life was mine.

He held each book open to the title page, and I signed *To Noah, from Hyacinth, aka M.M. Revere. Dear Noah, never look a gift whale in the mouth.*

"Oh, he'll love that. Thank you, Ms. Revere."

"You're welcome. Thank you for the automotive boost to my pedestrian image."

He laughed, then headed off down the sunny, oak-shaded street, which fronted a beautiful little marina where shrimp boats mingled with small yachts. I hung the Jag keychain on the tail of my mermaid cane handle, then made my way down the sidewalk. Moll Revere, Mer-babe, driving a Jaguar. The Minnie Mouse of children's literature, driving a supermodel's car.

Sunlight glistened on the bay. In the distance, Sainte's Point was crowned with a blue mist of late-morning fog. I gazed hypnotically at the island, trying not to worry about a murderous mutant named Orion, who might show up on Rhymer's doorstep one day soon. A dilemma. I'd finally met the man of my dreams, one worth fighting for. But no one had ever mentioned defending him against a web-footed monster. At least, that's how I pictured Orion.

"Molly!"

Tula waved at me from the entrance to her jewelry shop. On either side, tall, moss-speckled flower pots of a vaguely Grecian nature brimmed with ivy and perfect burgundy roses. She'd invited me to come by, and then we'd do lunch.

"Sorry, I'm a little late," I called, and limped up the cobblestoned sidewalk as fast as I could.

"No problem. I have a customer to take care of first."

"I love your faux-Grecian urns. They look like something out of an archaeological exhibit."

"Thank you." She smiled. "They are."

"Are what?"

"Real. Coast of Crete. Around the time of the Minotaur, give or take a century."

A thank-you for the Jaguar stuck to my tongue. I chewed it — my tongue, that is — as I studied Tula's unvarnished smile. She wasn't kidding about the vases. Apparently, Mers scattered priceless antiquities around them the way seagulls scatter shrimp shells. She laughed as she caught my thought.

"We Mers know where all the good stuff is hidden." I made my way through the door she held open for me. Speaking of *hidden*. I looked around furtively. I hadn't seen Juna Lee since that night at Tula's cottage. I hoped she'd been eaten by a shark.

"Where's Juna Lee these days? Still out of town? Having her fangs sharpened?"

"I'll tell you over lunch. It's a story that deserves martinis."

I gaped at the array of intricate, unique jewelry spread among glittering glass display counters. "What a beautiful shop! Your jewelry! And, oh, your cats!" The Persians rose from their luxurious beds, stretched languidly, and came to me, rubbing my legs and purring. I bent to pet them. "What pretty meows. I wish my old kitty could still get around as well as you do. I miss having him do a figure-eight around my ankles. Not that I didn't take a few falls that way."

"All right," a gorgeous man said, striding from a doorway to a back room. "This one, Tula. I'll send this one to her next. Maybe she'll stop throwing the gift boxes off the balcony. She hit a cabana boy the other day." He held a fantastic emerald choker in one hand and a jeweler's eyeglass in the other. I stared at him. He was no Rhymer, but he'd put your average Hollywood hunk to shame. He saw me and halted. Offering a perfectly mannered but stunning smile, he gave me a graceful up and down then said, "Rhymer's finally gotten lucky."

What was that supposed to mean? What I hoped? I went all hot and fluffy, mumbling, "Tula? Hmmm?" until she rescued me with an arm through mine. "Molly, I'd like to introduce you to Juna Lee's better half — some would say, far better — Jordan Brighton."

I was speechless for a moment, which didn't stop me from broadcasting my newly acquired Mer radio frequency.

Jordan arched a brow sardonically. "Yes, I know. How could she possibly deserve me?"

"I . . . well, I . . . where *is* Juna Lee?"

Tula and Jordan traded a look. He nodded. Tula turned to me. "She's been exiled."

I looked from Tula to Jordan. "Did she leave willingly, or was an exorcism required?"

Jordan laughed, then held up the magnificent necklace. "Let's just say this: It was my doing, and my apologies are expensive."

A man of courage and good taste, at least in jewelry. What could such a man see in Juna Lee? Tula linked an arm through mine. "I'll tell you what: Loyalty, passion, and the challenge of surviving the Mer equivalent of a pet tigress."

"Who says I'll survive?" Jordan said with an edge to his voice.

I decided to change the subject. "Speaking of large cats, Tula, thank you for leasing a Jaguar for me. I signed some books for the Mer, hmmm, Mer-man, who delivered it. He was very nice." There. I had acknowledged Mer-dom openly. I had voluntarily entered the Mer Matrix.

Tula's smile vanished. So did Jordan Brighton's.

"What Jaguar?" Tula said.

"*What man?*" Jordan asked darkly.

꜃ ꜃ ꜃

That night I caught the bloody liar outside his posh digs up at Sea Island, off the coast of St. Simon's. Kings, queens, presidents and movie stars bunk there. A favorite Mer stopover.

"Fight me, and your throat will be wearing a smile," I said. I slung him and his Armani suit face-first against a wall hidden by oleander shrubs and kept my sword pointed at his

Adam's apple. "My name's Rhymer McEvers. What's yours?"

"I see you're a Peacekeeper," he managed, recognizing the vibes, speaking into the wall. "But I've done nothing—"

"Don't make me give you that smile."

"I'll report you to the Council! This is not how Peacekeepers are supposed to treat—" His voice ended in a gasp as I pressed the sword's tip deeper into his skin.

"Do no' be tellin' me you weren't lying to M. M. Revere today. I feel the lie like it's a train vibrating on the rails. Speak, or I'll let it run over you. Who are you, and what do you want with her?"

"All right, all right. I'm Alamande Oltovelli. From New York. I deal in books. I wanted her to sign some first editions. Her autograph on first editions is worth a small fortune."

I bored into his thoughts as best I could — Mers are good at hiding guilty thoughts from other Mers — and after a few seconds I had to admit I sensed no other deception. He wasn't Orion in disguise. He was a rare book dealer, just scoring Moll's autograph by means of an elaborate ruse to deliver a car. I lowered the sword. He looked up at me with the terror of a blowfish cornered by an orca. "I meant no harm," he said. "I just heard through gossip that M.M. Revere had come out as a Mer, and was summering in Bellemeade, and I wanted to—"

"Trick her and take advantage of her."

"Do you know what her autographed books will sell for among our people, now that she's out of the closet? Mer children haven't been this excited about a Mer author since Hans Christian Anderson."

"She'd have signed the books without your lie, if you'd asked."

"Don't be so sure. She's notoriously shy. Some authors don't do many public signings, so autographed first editions are rare. In her case, I can see why she stays away from her fans. The bad leg. And she's skinny. She's not exactly an attractive — agggh."

I stuck the sword's tip in his side. With a quick, upwards slice I opened a good length of suit, shirt, and skin. Just a scratch. He reeled back, clasping his nicked ribs, too scared to utter a yelp, but staring at me as if I might turn cannibal on himonly next. The bastard didn't dare say again, 'I'm reporting you to the Council.' Not if he wanted to see his tailor in the morning, instead of a surgeon.

"Be gone with you," I ordered. "Stay away from her."

He nodded wildly, clasped his sliced Armani jacket to his bloody side, and dashed down a path that led to one of the resort's doors.

I let the sword sag to my side. Around me, frogs sang to one another, and the damp, sexual heat of a coastal night rose inside my senses along with the aroma of fine flowers and nearby ocean and decadent luxury. A night for lovers. Wishes and regrets were all the courtship I could manage for Moll. I had a bad feeling I wasn't going to live long enough to earn her love.

∞ ∞ ∞

Moll stood on the shingled front porch at Randolph Cottage, wearing a silk robe that clung to every slender curve and would have been see-through, dammit, if only the dawn light would hurry up. But the sky was just the palest pink over Sainte's Point by the time I returned from Sea Island, and I couldn't stay for the sunrise. I stood in the yard, keeping my distance, catching traces of her fine, soft scent, thinking immoral thonly oughts. She latched one hand at the robe's bosom and one hand down at her thighs, over the other portal of embarrassment. Shy, no. Not shy. Dignified. And worried. About my exploits and my safety. I pretended it was something else.

"No need to worry, Moll. He was just after your auto-graph."

"I smell . . . I sense . . . blood. Not yours. His. He paid a high price for my signature."

"I just scratched him. He'll be fine. I've gotten worse diving among prickly fish."

You threatened that man on my behalf, I heard her think. *You drew blood, for me.* She gave off a silent song of pleasure.

God, I adore this honest woman.

She heard me think that.

"Okay," she said quietly. "I admit it. I'm medieval and bloodthirsty." *Now, come here and ravish me as your reward. Ohmigod, he didn't hear that last part, did he?*

Oh, yes, I did, and, when she realized it, a chorus of *Omigods* skittered from her psyche like a rapper's chant. *Omi, omi, omi, omigod god god.* She wasn't used to being undisciplined about sex, much less sharing her brainwaves on the subject. She'd spent years ignoring all that bottled up heat, subconsciously waiting for a man of her own kind — a real man, yes, I'm no' too humble to put it that way — to deserve her. Now she was aching to give as good as she got. And I wanted to take her up on it.

Moll, if it makes you feel any better, I'd like to rip that robe off you and carry you into the bay and have my way with you.

Quaintly put, but the style suited her.

She fumbled for the arm of the wicker chair behind her and sat down weakly on its seashell cushions. "Okay," she said out loud, very prim. "You have my permission."

I laughed like a pirate, trying to be jaunty. "Save your booty for later. I've got to get back to the island."

"I know." She almost moaned the words. "Can't you call the . . . the Mer police, or some such thing, for back-up?"

"Afraid not." I touched the small, curving, jeweled sword strapped by a leather band across my chest. *Change the sub-*

ject. "Do no' worry so much, Moll. I'm a tough piece of work, and this blade, in my hands, will be more than a match for Orion, should it come to that."

Her worried eyes went to the sword. "It's beautiful. And deadly looking."

"'Tis a holdover from older times. The blade was forged of metal by a famed Mer swordssmith in Scotland. If you believe fanciful legend, it's the only kind of sword that can harm a Swimmer."

"Can't I help you some way? At least let me meet your nieces. I've very good with children. Couldn't I visit the island and keep them company?"

"No." The word rang out harder than I liked.

"Please. I'm not afraid of Orion."

"You're terrified. I don't blame you."

She got up from the chair proudly, wavering a little without her cane, but straight as a sloop's mast. What a looker she was, slight as a wisp of cloud, teak-wood hair moving in soft flutters around a smart, big-eyed face — it was like meeting an elf in modern times. And the rest of her, delicate but not so fragile as she thought — the rest of her was more than fine. I felt the warmth in her, and the tart sweetness, and that steely pride.

"I may not look like much of a fighter, but I am. Not in the physical sense, but I am very good at emotional support. I've taken care of myself since I was fifteen-years-old. When it comes to solid stick-to-it-tiveness, I'm the Rock of Gibraltor."

"No doubt, Moll, but if you're a rock, then I'm a hard place." I pointed to myself. "I'm harder around you than you know."

You could say I made a Freudian slip. She tried to blush but it was more of a glow in the pink darkness. I kicked myself on behalf of my lusty rocks of Gibraltar. "That is to say," I went on grimly, "that is to say . . . No. Simply that. *No*. I won't let you get involved. Stay here. Stay away."

I nodded my parting to her, then turned and strode manfully out of the yard as if I weren't a wreck. I did the manful walk to the end of the cottage's pier, then dived off into the cold, dark brine. I felt her silent keen all the way to the island. And my own.

Wrestling Aphrodite

∞ ∞ ∞ ∞ ∞ ∞ ∞ **14** ∞ ∞ ∞ ∞ ∞ ∞ ∞

Dear Diary:

Shit. Sorry, but that's the best word. Shit. I climbed five stories down the pink-flowered lattice of a mandevilla vine outside my balcony at Chez Prison de Araiza, while everyone was distracted by some gaudy Caribbean festival involving lots of steel drums, fireworks, and rum hurricanes. Just as I stepped off onto terra firma, my Amazon warden grabbed me by one arm, threw me down on my back, then straddled me and sat down on me. "Juna Lee, did that vine *look* like the guest floor elevator to you?" she asked drily.

Gasping, I stared up at two hundred pounds of cocoa princess poured into a strapless white mini-dress. Her long black hair was wound up with pearls, and a huge cluster of pearls and diamonds hung from a heavy silver chain around her neck. The brooch nestled between breasts bigger than my head. "Don't let your boobs fall out of that Versace. I could get a concussion."

She leaned over me, smiling wickedly, threatening to let the mammary twins do a bungee jump on my forehead. "The Council would give me a medal."

"Do you have a name, other than *Shamu?*"

"The name is *Aphrodite.* I've told you more than once, but you never pay attention."

"I don't listen to the hired help."

"*Hired help?*" She slid to one side but kept me pinned with one long, gleaming brown leg. She pointed to the coral-tipped toes peeking from a high-heeled white sandal. Dusky pink webbing glimmered in the light of a nearby lamppost. "I keep telling you I'm a Mer. An Araiza Mer."

"Oh, please. I've never met a Mer with the body mass index of a Sumo wrestler. And I've never met an Araiza who—"

"Watch it, white girl."

"— who had such a . . . dark tan."

"Araizas are Latin. Latins come in vanilla, chocolate, and everything in between. My mother came from Cuba. My father was Hernandez Araiza. They met in pre-Castro Havana, the 1940s. He owned a casino. She was a star performer there. A novelty singer and comedienne. She wore headdresses of fruit and painted her lips such a bright red she could signal Miami with her smile."

"Oh, great. You're a cross between a black Carmen Miranda and Ricky Ricardo."

"You obnoxious little *puta*."

"Fine. You hate me. I hate *you*. We're even. Just sling your enormous thigh toward the nearest Weight Watchers meeting and let me escape."

"Oh, I wish I could. I wish I could escort you to the ocean and throw you in. Headfirst. *On a shallow sandbar*."

"Wait a minute. I'm feeling something, sensing something—" I put one hand to my head, ala Karnak the Magnificent on the old *Johnny Carson Show*.

Aphrodite drew back at little. Her black eyes flashed. "Keep your claws out of my psyche, Senorita Sinister."

"I'm sensing — ah hah!" I jabbed a finger at her triumphantly. "You're doing community service, just like me! The Council has sentenced you to house arrest here on the islands! House arrest *and* community service! Hah! Compared to you, I'm an angel! What'd you do — smother some old sugar daddy during rough sex?"

She wrapped a hand around my throat. I coughed and struggled, which only made her tighten her grip. She looked down at me with disgust, then spoke a long stream of obscene but well-educated Spanish. She switched to English at the end of her little speech with "and the Council said I'd already been warned twice to stay away from UniWorld's London office. So I'm being punished. I have to spend a year doing chores for the Council, so here I am, performing warden duty for a prissy little Southern belle Poinfax."

"Don't tell me you're one of those paranoid Mers who's convinced UniWorld has some dastardly plans *beyond* world domination. You couldn't possibly be a violent sociopath *and* a crackpot conspiracy nut all rolled into one."

Her long, coral fingernails dug in. "I wonder if I could squeeze just right and make your larynx pop out."

I squirmed. "Tara McEvers got herself killed pulling pranks on UniWorld. Wasn't that a good lesson to the rest of you boringly obsessed activists?"

"Pranks? Tara was a hero."

"Right. She hooked up with a boogeyman Swimmer and let him talk her into a goofy plot to blow up a research ship, then he betrayed her, so now she's dead, and her daughters have no mother, and their boogeyman daddy may be out to kill them for some insane, possessive reason, and *Jordan Brighton is in danger because of it all.*"

She released my throat with a disgusted little shove. "Think whatever you want. UniWorld is scheming against Mers as well as Landers. Some of us are trying to prove it."

I sucked down some air. "And then you'll move on to other ludicrous theories, such as 'Elvis — alive and hiding his webbed toes?' and 'Madonna — Mer, or just a pretentious twit?'"

"I'm wasting my time talking to you." She dragged me to my feet. A pair of hunky boy toys appeared from nowhere and took me by the arms before I could make a break for the ocean. I moaned. The shore wasn't more than a hundred yards from the hotel. If I could just get to that surf, get out into the deep, I'd swim the whole way back to Sainte's Point if I had to. I had to get back to Jordan.

I felt Aphrodite, queen of the Amazon boobs, probing my thoughts and studying me. "Why, I do declare," she said in a Spanish-accented southern drawl. "Scarlett has a heart."

"Stuff it, *Mammy*."

She laughed fiendishly.

And then I was hauled back inside.

๛ ๛ ๛

I should have known my nieces were up to no good.

"We're going back to the mansion for a nap, Uncle Rhymer," Stella announced, as a pretty afternoon sun blazed over the island beaches. The four of us sat on soft silk blankets under the shade of an oak, looking out at the beach and the ocean. The girls were nearly frantic to dive into the Atlantic, where young dolphins kept poking their blue-gray heads from the water and chattering, *Come and play. Come and play.*

Out at the island's western point, Jordan, armed with his buffed fingernails and Uzi, had given me some rest time. He stood guard beside the remains of an old lighthouse, aided by a pod of dolphin elders who patrolled the island's waters like guard dogs as a favor to us.

I turned a suspicious eye to Les Sleepy Femme du Threesome. "A nap, is it? I can't recall a single time when you three have napped during full daylight."

Isis pouted. "We might as well sleep. We can't go swimming. We're shriveling up."

Venus added with a sad face and the slightest lisp, "The

130

baby dolphins think we're naught but sissies."

"Dolphins are a bit cheeky that way. Pay no heed. All right, off to the house with you. But stay on the path and go straight inside. I'll be there in a bit."

Stella smiled, grabbed the younger ones by their hands, and they trotted up the sandy path through the deep arbor of giant oaks and draping moss. Squirrels, raccoons, birds, two lizards and several deer, who had all been nibbling bread from the girls' palms, looked disappointed. Frowning, I watched until the girls disappeared

The mansion is naught but a stone's throw from here. They'll sing out if anything or anyone startles them.

I got up and paced, windblown and barefoot in old khakis and a thin cotton shirt, stomping web-toed prints in the sand. I pulled a slender, intricately carved pipe from my shirt pocket. I filled it from a leather pouch, lit the bowl with a good, god-fearing sulphur match, and took a deep draw. Merkind can no' touch tobacco — it's as deadly as a poison to our oxygen-rich lungs — but we do love our herbs. No, I'm not meaning your obvious cannibis, but rich, guarded mixtures of exotics from all over the world, blended by hand, given as gifts by proud Mer growers, guaranteed to mellow the most worried soul.

I puffed and inhaled, blew out and puffed again. I saw Moll's worldly innocence in the smoke; I saw my sister's smile. I saw the memory of the girl I'd loved and killed for decades before. But I saw nothing of the unknowable, unpredictable Orion. I emptied my pipe, brushed sand over the wisps of its leavings, then returned the pipe to a back pocket. There would be no mellowing of my mood anytime soon.

When I got back to the Bonavendier mansion I scaled the grand staircase two steps at a time and padded silently down a Picasso-adorned corridor to the girls' suite for a quick check. I sensed them sleeping, sprawled like pale angels on a big bed they shared. Yes, the girls could broadcast illusions, could fool even the toughest Mer heart — that I knew because they were Healers, and Healers are so charismatic, when it suits them. But they and I had a military respect, an understanding, an agreement. I expected to find them snoozing innocently.

They were gone.

☙ ☙ ☙

Hyacinth swam swiftly through the sky-blue water, I typed, *past the sign that read,* Do Not Venture Beyond These Boundaries, By Order Of Finster's Academy Of Mer-misses and Mersirs, *past the dozing tentacles of Octivant, the academy's guard-dog octopus, and past the Reef of Giggly Silliness, which made a pretty coral crescent along the outer edge of Finster Academy's magical underwater world. She knew only one thing: She had to get to the deep, dark, abyss that led to the Cave of the Argonauts, if she was ever to solve the mystery of Orion.*

Orion. I groaned, then deleted the name from my laptop's screen, and instead correctly typed *the mystery of the dolphin queen.* I nervously scruffed my bare foot over Heathcliff, who lay on his pillow beneath my table on the pier at Randolph Cottage. He dozed in the table's shade, cooled by the bay breeze despite a hot afternoon sun. He'd been sleeping even more than usual. Winding down. I was worried about him.

Must concentrate. Must . . . write. Must stay focused.

The dolphin queen. The . . . dolphin . . . queen. But nothing popped into my head as a follow-up. I took a break and spent several minutes rearranging the folds of my floppy white sundress. When the words won't flow, writing is like sitting in heavy traffic listening to static on the car's radio. "Oh, who am I kidding?" I said aloud. "I'm only *feigning* normalcy. Working on the next book and pretending to be calm, just as if I haven't been set down in Oz. Heathcliff, maybe I'll just give up and carry you inside and try to perk you up with some tuna, and then get drunk on an entire six-pack of the first diet cola I can lay my hands on."

Heathcliff snored on in tired disregard.

I forced my fingers back on the keyboard. *Stop worrying about Heathcliff. Stop worrying about Rhymer and his nieces. Stop thinking about Orion. Stop thinking, period. Write. Go on, fingers. Type something.*

Nothing happened. My fingers wouldn't strike. They were *on* strike.

I sank back in my wicker chair, pulled my sunhat low over my face, and recited the last few paragraphs in a loud, muse-commanding tone. "Hyacinth had to get to the deep, dark, Abyss of Forever that led to the Cave of The Argonauts if she was ever to solve the mystery of the dolphin queen." I took a deep breath and continued. "As . . . Hyacinth flicked her lovely pink tail fin and gathered herself for a burst of speed into the fearsome darkness, a hand grabbed her arm. Rapid-fire fingertips tapped on her skin, spelling out words in the secret underwater language that had been used by Finster students for generations. *Hyacinth Meridian, don't you dare go out there alone.*

"*Agggh. Barney,* she thought. *I should have known you'd follow me.* Barnacle T. Tradvorius, Barney to his friends, scowled at her when she tried to pull away. Hyacinth slapped a hand on his bare shoulder and tapped out a fierce rebuke. *Barnacle, you let go of my arm or I will . . .*"

I halted, struggling. "I will . . . uh . . . I will . . ." I sighed. "I don't know what she'll do to him."

"Pound him into crab snot!" a little voice supplied.

"Pound him into . . ."

I leapt up, grabbed my cane, and looked around wildly. I saw only some seagulls and, out in the bay, the dorsal fins of a few dolphins who dropped by to chatter at me occasionally, like native hosts politely trying to teach their language to an immigrant.

"Who spoke?" I called. Silence. Chills ran down my spine. The voice had been small, childlike. Would Orion imitate a child? Was he about to rise from the water and attack me? Had he already attacked Rhymer and the girls, and now I was to be his next victim?

Not without a fight.

I knotted a fist to my chest and limped to the end of the pier, ferociously thumping my cane on the wide boards. Small monkeys pound sticks on the ground to make themselves seem more fierce; so did I.

"Who's there!" I demanded, reaching the end railing and grabbing its weathered wood for support. "I'm not afraid of—"

I looked down.

Three small, beautiful faces looked up at me.

The smallest one gave an anxious mew. "Please don't pound us into crab snot, Miss Revere."

Scottish. The little voice had a Scottish lilt.

Rhymer's nieces. "What in the world . . . don't worry. I'm sorry, I didn't mean to yell at you. Come out. Climb up. There's a ladder right over—" A terrible thought struck me. "Is everything all right? Where's your uncle?"

The largest of the girls looked up at me solemnly. "He thinks we're napping. I'm sure he'll come after us soon. May we visit until then?"

"Of course you may visit! Climb up!"

I gazed in wonder as they swam to the pier's ladder. They moved like glimmers of sunlight flashing on the water, graceful and effortless, arms and legs barely flicking, their bodies undulating. I'd never seen any human being swim the way they did. The smallest one climbed up first, a perfect little doll in a yellow swimsuit, her skin creamy pale, her eyes bright green and extraordinarily large. Wavy, black hair streamed all the way to her knees. When she stepped off the ladder her delicate feet hardly made a sound. I stared at elongated toes linked by gossamer webbing the color of peaches.

And at beautiful little hands with peach-hued webbing between the fingers.

Toto, we're not in Kansas anymore.

The older girls were just as ethereal, with manes of black hair and huge green eyes and webbed feet and webbed hands. The tallest one wore a black swimsuit, the middle one, jade green. The one in black said quietly, "I'm Stella. This is my sister, Isis, and our little sister, Venus. We do hope we're not intruding, Miss Revere. We love your books."

"I'm honored. Please, please, call me Molly."

That brought smiles. Their eyes gleamed.

Venus, the smallest one, spotted Heathcliff beneath the table. "Oh, dear, oh, dear, old kitty, old, sick kitty," she moaned. "I'll just pet the old, sick kitty a bit—"

"No," Stella ordered, and Isis grabbed her by the hand. Clearly, something about my cat was forbidden. Perhaps little Venus had an allergy to animals. But then all three girls leaned down and studied Heathcliff with expressions I can only describe as wistful and tormented. They swiveled those gazes to me, then to my cane. They trembled.

Stella exhaled. "If you don't mind us asking . . . how were you hurt?"

I explained briefly, and delicately, that a truck had hit my parents' car when I was not much older than they. That my leg had been badly injured, and my parents killed.

"And you've been sick at times," Stella said. "In other ways."

"I have a small problem with my blood. But I'm fine."

"No, you're not," Isis said bluntly. "Some people have blood diseases from being part-Lander. They don't understand why they're so sickly, but it's because they're Mers and don't know it."

Venus looked up at her sisters. Her expression was agonized. "Couldn't we —"

"No," Stella said firmly but gently. "Not right now."

Venus whimpered.

I didn't know what they were trying to tell me, or each other. I didn't like discussing my blood so I changed the subject to a seahorse of a different color. "So, you're fans of my books?"

They nodded eagerly. "We want to know what happens to Hyacinth in the next novel," Stella said.

"Did you know you were a Mer when you wrote the first Hyacinth book?" Isis asked.

"No, but I suppose I suspected it, deep down. I just didn't know what to call myself."

"But you knew you were *special*."

I smiled sadly. "I knew I was different."

Their eyes widened. Different, yes. *That* connected. "You were so sad and lost when your parents died," Stella put in. "You even wanted to die."

I froze. "I beg your pardon?"

"We can feel the story inside you," Isis said flatly. "The time you tried to drown yourself in the ocean — but someone special saved you."

"Now, girls, I never tried to —"

"The year after the accident," Stella supplied. "You could barely walk. You couldn't even swim anymore. You were so lonely. Friends of your parents took you to stay with them. You wanted to die. You went into the water. You lived in a small part of your mind then, shut off from everything else. But you didn't drown — you couldn't drown, not like a Lander

— and you remember an extraordinary moment when arms gathered you, and long hair floated around you, and a very old, very beautiful voice said inside your mind, *The water is your friend. The water can never hurt you.* And you lived from then on. But you weren't sure why, or what for."

"How do you know that about me?"

"I can feel it. We all can." The three girls nodded in unison. Venus added solemnly, "It was Melasine The Old One who rescued you. She knew you were special."

I sank down in my chair and said nothing, a knot in my throat. They crowded around me. "About Hyacinth," Stella said. Apparently, being rescued by the founding mother of mythological mermaids was just chitchat.

I recovered enough to say, "What would you like to know about her?"

Stella looked at me sadly. "I'd like to know what she finds beyond the Abyss of Forever. I want to know if there's anything on the other side."

Isis peered at me, frowning. "I'd like to see her escape from school and have her pet stingray electrocute anyone who tries to stop her. I like revenge."

Venus clasped a hand to her heart. "I want to know if she'll ever discover what became of her parents. Won't her parents please, please come back from the Disappearing Sea?"

Their wistful requests left me speechless again. They didn't have to sing inside my mind. I knew how it felt to be an orphaned child. "I promise you this much," I said gently. "Hyacinth will have a family again. She'll be happy again, some day."

We heard the distant rumble of an engine. Across the bay, a sleek speedboat zoomed toward us. Rhymer.

"Oh, crap," Isis said. "Uncle Rhymer is boiling mad. He'll never let us out of his sight again."

"He's very strict," Venus whispered to me. "We adore

him, but he is awfully frightful."

"Better him being frightful than our own father trying to kill us," Isis intoned.

Stella hissed at her and cut her eyes at their little sister, who looked horrified. Isis sulked at the rebuke. Venus teared up.

I stood. *The chicken of the sea* morphed into a protective Mer mother hen. "Move aside, girls," I said crisply, "I'll talk to your uncle." I planted myself in front of them. My heart pounded. I could already see the grim set of Rhymer's jaw. I cleared my psychic throat and sang out silently, *These children are desperate for your approval and affection. Don't you dare lecture them for visiting me.*

Rhymer thundered inside my head, *Approval and affection will do them no good if they're dead. You're a lure they can't afford.*

Lure? A lure? I didn't lure them here.

Nor did you chase them away, I see.

What harm has been done? Please, let us visit.

Did they sing to you? Did they touch you? Did they lay hands on Heathcliff?

No. Why would they? What are you talking about —

If they sing, Moll, he'll hear them. And he'll come.

They didn't sing, but I don't understand —

"Come aboard," Rhymer said loudly, as he swung the speedboat into place beside the pier. "*Girls.* Into the boat with you. Not a word. Into the boat."

The girls looked up at me with quiet regret. I nodded, defeated. "It was very nice to meet you all. When things are better, I'll tell you everything you want to know about Hyacinth."

Stella sighed. Isis pouted. Venus moaned and reached toward me. That small, beautiful hand, laced in see-through webbing that folded like invisible silk when the fingers were closed, opened like a diaphanous wing. It took all my will power not to place my open hand against the magic of hers. "Your mother," I said hoarsely, "is with mine. They live in the most beautiful lagoon of the Disappearing Sea. They want us to smile and be happy."

Venus's eyes widened, then filled with joyful tears. She leaned forward. "Melasine sings to us sometimes," she whispered. "I'm sure she's very fond of you and glad she rescued you." Venus and the others climbed down the ladder and into the boat. Rhymer gazed up at me, frowning, his eyes dark and hooded. *Stay here and stay safe, Moll. Don't call to them. It's for your sake as well as theirs. And mine. Stay safe, Moll. I don't want to lose any other people I love.*

I couldn't even form an answer. As he gunned the boat and headed back toward Sainte's Point I stood there on the pier with my hand still held out to Venus, to Stella and Isis, and to him, pledging a troth to mysteries and magic and love I had only imagined, before.

Had I been saved by the ancient and wonderful Melasine years ago? I'd always thought it was a delusion. A mermaid off Cape Cod? And yet, I knew it was true. *The water is your friend. The water can never hurt you,* she'd said. I'd survived on those words from then on, though I wasn't sure why, or what for.

Until now.

Meanwhile, Back in the Caribbean

❧ ❧ ❧ ❧ ❧ ❧ **15** ❧ ❧ ❧ ❧ ❧ ❧ ❧

Araizas are like a box of chocolates. I wanted to bite them and spit out their nuts.

"Oh, come now, Juna Lee," a silver-haired *patrone* said in a Ricardo Montalban accent. He laughed. "Look at this wonderful party we're throwing for you, just to keep you entertained."

My suite was full of people, all Mers — all of them gorgeous, exotic Araizas decked out in the best resort wear and world-class jewelry, not to mention a lazy aura of privilege with a side dressing of dangerous charm. When I called them the Corleones of the Caribbean I was exaggerating a little, but they *do* have several centuries of, shall we say, *creative buccaneering* to their credit. Even by Mer standards they've collected a few too many ships' cargoes the old-fashioned way, without even bothering to leave a tip on the nightstand. I'd always heard juicy rumors about their Soprano-like penchant for sending Landers to sleep with the fishes.

"Yep," I mused, "It's always fun to party with kidnappers."

"You aren't going to write about us in that blog of yours, are you?" Aphrodite asked, her white smile a wicked sliver. "You like having *both* your ear lobes, don't you?"

That was just an idle threat, because no matter what Mers do to Landers, they generally don't touch their fellow Mers. No, even Araizas would complain to the Council instead. Then a Peacekeeper like Rhymer would show up on my doorstep, and I'd find myself exiled somewhere on a rock.

Those old seafaring stories about sirens singing on rocks? They were doing time.

"Of *course* I'm not going to write about you," I lied.

Around dawn, when the party broke up and the bartenders carted the last of the rum fizzes away, I eyed my two new gorgeous boyfriends. Aphrodite's boy toys. *Guards.* They lounged, looking like pouty male supermodels in their open shirts and oh-so-clingy trousers on the deck chairs of my balcony, ensuring that I'd never climb down the mandevilla vines again. So they thought.

"Boys, I'll slip into something comfortable," I called, "and then we'll smoke some herbal stogies and order breakfast." *And after that I'll turn you into sexually hypnotized guppies, and then you'll get the hell out of my way so I can escape.* They smiled at me and flexed their bare webbed feet. A subtle Mer flirtation.

I went into a bath boudoir about the size of a Manhattan apartment, rummaged through several enormous closets full of fab clothes (Araizas knew my weaknesses all too well), and selected a vintage silk nightgown from a 1930s Claudette Colbert movie. Claudette was a Mer on her grandmother's side, by the way.

The gown was more see-through than silk. I fluffed my hair down my back, spritzed myself with extra Chanel, a fave fragrance of Mers (oh, yes, Coco had webbed toes), then sauntered onto the balcony with everything set on High Jiggle. "Good morning, boys," I drawled. "How do you like the view?"

They looked up at me without batting a single pouty eyelash. "We're gay," they said in unison.

I stared at them a second.

"Shit," I said. "Get your own breakfast."

And I went back inside.

Venus Shines

☙ ☙ ☙ ☙ ☙ ☙ ☙ **16** ☙ ☙ ☙ ☙ ☙ ☙ ☙

A dogfish trying to keep order in a catfish aquarium. That's what you are, McEvers.

I was no good at daddying my nieces, and not much of a catch when it came to romancing Moll. The incident at the pier made that clear. I'd hurt her feelings. Female-wise, I'd always gotten by on good military manners and a big, thrusting attitude. But with Moll I was swimming in uncharted territory. As for the girls, they needed a daddy, not a sergeant.

Not that I intended to change my bullish ways, you understand. I wanted the girls and Moll to stay alive. I wanted Orion dead. Nothing else mattered.

Uncle Rhymer. Help!

The shriek of dual voices inside my mind. Stella and Isis. I left my station on the mansion's veranda and bolted upstairs.

The two girls met me at the landing. "Venus has disappeared," Stella said.

☙ ☙ ☙

Heathcliff was just a kitten when my parents died in the car accident. My mother gave him to me on my fifteenth birthday, only a few weeks before she and Dad were killed. At the hospital, family friends sneaked Heathcliff into my room several times. I was barely conscious, fading in and out between physical pain and grief. Heathcliff would sit delicately on my pillow and nuzzle my face with his head, sometimes licking the tip of my nose and purring. He was my one link to happy sensations, the last remnant of comfort in the world.

In the twenty years since then, he and I had rarely spent a day apart. Now I watched him everyday, my heart breaking, wondering which day would be our last together.

"You didn't eat well this morning," I said to him. I cuddled him in my lap as I sat down in a heavy wicker chair on the veranda of Randolph Cottage. He sighed. I stroked his head and pretended to gaze out over the bay, toward Sainte's Point, while I fought back tears. With all the miracles I'd discovered recently, there was no miracle for him. He had been my dearest friend, my only family, for two decades.

I feared he was beginning to die.

"I'm going inside and get a small can of your favorite fancy tuna," I announced. "And we're going to sit out here in this wonderful ocean breeze and nibble on tuna. If you just get some breakfast in your tummy, you'll feel better."

I gently set him on the chair's thick cushion. He sighed again, and curled up with his eyes closed.

I can't let you go without a fight, I thought, then scrubbed a hand over my eyes and hurried inside.

I was reaching for a small bowl in a glass-fronted cabinet of the cottage's cozy antique kitchen when I heard a thump on the veranda's wooden floor. *Oh, Heathcliff, no*, I whispered, rushing back through the cottage. I pictured him falling off the chair. "Heathcliff." I slung open the screen door.

I halted, staring.

Venus stood there, her back to me. She was soaking wet; her pale sundress dripped saltwater. A bit of seaweed clung to the hem. She swayed and hummed and hugged Heathcliff. I could just see the tips of his ears above her shoulder.

"Venus, honey, you shouldn't be here. What are you—"

She turned around. Her eyes glowed with tears, and her mouth trembled. "Please don't be angry," she said in her soft Scottish burr. "I couldn't let the wee old cat keep hurting. And I could hear you crying about him." She set Heathcliff down. The breath stalled in my lungs. He looked up at me, bright-eyed. His fur was soft and smooth again, each black tabby stripe standing out like the vivid bars of a military chevron against the silver-gray background. He meowed with robust delight, then launched himself at me. I caught him in my arms. He nuzzled his head against my cheek, then licked the tip of my nose.

"Now he's young and happy again," Venus said. "And he can be your friend for a long, long time yet. Your heart doesn't have to break."

I sank down in the chair, hugging Heathcliff, making small, incoherent sounds of awe and crying. Life always comes with a price. Venus had restored a piece of my heart but may have doomed herself, her sisters, and Rhymer in the process.

Venus, aware only that life can be saved, smiled.

❧ ❧ ❧

I could no' yell at little Venus. I couldn't do it, though she'd gone against every word I'd said on the subject of healing. Nor was anything Moll's fault. She hadn't called for help with the dying old cat. Now a teary-eyed Moll stood in front of Venus like a female tiger shark, holding Heathcliff in her arms, staring at me sadly but firmly.

Don't you yell at Venus, she ordered in my head. Venus peeked up at me. "Uncle Rhymer, I did no' sing out very loud when I healed Heathcliff. I promise. Just a little hum. I could no' help myself. With scary things all about, and sadness, and worry, Moll needed her kitty fixed. So I fixed him. It was quick, quick and quiet! I promise!"

"All right. I'm not mad, I swear it. Go get in the boat and wait for me."

"And you're not mad at Moll?"

"No, I'm not mad at Moll. Now scoot along."

"I won't heal anything or anyone else! Except for a wee butterfly with a torn wing here and there. I promise."

"Aye, we'll have a talk about your promises later. Now go."

She scampered off the veranda and through the oleanders, then turned and waved. "Bye Moll, bye, Heathcliff! Oh, but he looks so fat and fine!"

Moll waved and blew her a kiss. The old cat, not old anymore, purred.

When Venus stood safely in the well of my speedboat, I looked at Moll grimly. "You understand what's happened?"

She gave a pained nod. "Isn't it possible she only sang out 'a little,' and Orion didn't hear her?"

"Her by herself — maybe not. If it had been all three girls singing together, he'd hear for sure. But even just her alone is too much. This isn't good, Moll."

"I know. Rhymer, if I did anything, thought anything, wished anything that drew her here, I'm so sorry. I didn't mean to."

"She's had her eye on old Heathcliff all along. It's near impossible for Healers to resist healing. Especially when it comforts them to do it."

She hugged the new Heathcliff to her chest. "I'm so glad to have him *restored* — but not at the risk of the girls' safety." She looked tortured. "And yours."

"I want you to move out of this place. Go stay with Tula."

"Move out? Why?" She froze, reading fears I couldn't hide quick enough. "You think he might come *here*? Looking for *me*?"

"I don't know how he might track what he heard. Just to be on the safe side, move in with Tula. Go get your things. I'm not leaving this yard until you're packed and settled in your car."

"But—"

"And whatever you do, don't sing out to me anymore. Not for any reason. Keep your mind quiet." I paused. "I'll miss you."

Her face paled. She understood. We looked at each other sadly. We'd never been together, except in our minds, but that was the most powerful bed of all. And now even that would be empty.

◌◌◌

"Molly, I'm taking you someplace fun and decadent to get your mind off what happened," Tula announced. "You're going to see hot, wild, mermen in action."

Since I had spent the two days since the Heathcliff incident in deep brooding at Tula's cottage, I looked at her blearily over an empty soda bottle and said, "In case you're wondering, I'm not a naive, thirty-five-year-old virgin who goes dewy over male hotness. I have managed to lure a couple of fully accredited men into my lair over the years. But frankly, they didn't fulfill my fantasies the way Rhymer does. So I'm not interested in hooking up with some merman." I paused. "Or maybe the operative term is 'hooking' a merman."

She smiled. "I'm not taking you to a Mer brothel, for goodness sake. Just a nightclub."

"Under the circumstances, I have no intention of partying. Because of me and Heathcliff, Orion may be on his way to Sainte's Point. I can't just—"

"Rhymer asked me to take you out."

I stared at her. "He *asked* you to find me a man?"

146

"No, he asked me to keep you distracted. He says there's no point in you sitting and worrying. It won't help. Think positively and cheer up."

"Think positively and cheer up?" I stood furiously, pounding a fist on my bad leg. Heathcliff leapt from my lap to the back of Tula's overstuffed white couch. He loved racing around her cottage, amazed at his own new youth. "Do you know what would cheer me up? If I could make my gimpy leg work well enough to swim long distances! If I could find Orion and lead him off the track of Rhymer and the girls! I want to help Rhymer defend Stella, Isis, and Venus!" I searched for a mantra. "I want to be a Singer, not a Floater, with real webbed feet!"

"Well, in the meantime, let's dress your inner Mer in something sassy and go see some naked men. I brought you an outfit."

She held up black leather pants low enough to show my inner Mer's hipbones and a white leather bustier barely long enough to lace under my inner Mer's outer boobs. Even Britney Spears didn't show that much stomach.

I took a last, long swallow of soda. On the melodrama meter, my mood clicked from depressed to reckless. "Give me those clothes," I told Tula.

∞∞∞

It was the Mer equivalent of a Chippendales show. A girls' night out at the most elegant nightclub imaginable on the decadently elegant riverfront of one of the south's most decadently elegant old cities, Savannah. I stared as a sleek, gorgeous, web-toed man wearing nothing but a flesh-colored thong undulated to the ethereal beat of some New Age Celtic rhythm, flexing with provocative masculine grace as a coordinated lightshow of shadows cascaded over and under him.

His powerful body and barely concealed erection weren't more than a quick tickle away from me. I could have stroked him, except for four inches of brilliant glass between us. He floated inside a giant tank as large as a room. He smiled at me from inside a glorified goldfish bowl.

A penis on the half shell.

"Blow him a kiss," Tula whispered. "You're the famous Mer author, M.M. Revere. Everyone's watching you. It's only polite for a celebrity to flirt with the performer." Thank goodness for the darkness, which was lit only by the flickering light of our table lamp. Tula's breasts were barely visible inside a diaphanous blouse. Her long legs were sparsely topped by a black leather mini skirt. She should flirt with Mr. Penis, not me.

When I continued to sit there like a red-faced monkey, she elbowed me gently.

"Tula," I finally managed, "if I lift my arm to blow him a kiss, one breast will fall out the bottom of this bustier."

"So? Be brave. Risk flashing a nipple."

Slowly I put my fingertips to my lips. I kissed them, then reached out to tap my fingertips on the glass in the general vicinity of the swimmer's smiling lips. But at the last second he swirled upward and, grinning, pressed his pelvis to the glass.

My fingertips planted a symbolic smooch on his erection.

Everyone laughed and applauded.

I slumped back in the shadows, mortified. Tula put an arm around me. "Now see, you're becoming a wild libertine, just like the rest of us. Mers aren't shy. We're the beautiful people. That was fun, wasn't it?"

"I just wish he'd kept his waterlogged woody away from my fingers."

Tula laughed until her eyes watered. I hunkered miserably over my tumbler of vodka, then pushed it aside and downed a chaser of fizzing tonic water. The hard stuff. Cool, sea-scented air curled around my bare midriff like a seductive breath. *Leave me alone*, I told it. *I'm a librarian-slash-author from staid old Boston. I'm not here to be seduced. I'm worried about Rhymer and the girls.*

The haunting Celtic music faded away, and the handsome male performer disappeared through a nearly invisible tunnel at the bottom of the enormous tank. Seconds later the music changed to a throbbing dance beat. A magnificent young couple plunged from perches high in the nightclub's elaborately carved rafters. They speared the water of the giant bowl, then curled toward one another in perfect symmetry. He wore nothing but a bulging thong of gleaming fabric; she wore little more than a shimmering band of ribbon between her legs. As the lighting system strobed them, they entwined, touching, kissing, undulating in a yin/yang dance of pure, fluid sexuality.

I lost myself in their thrall. *This is what I want. To be made in the water, by Rhymer. To be made of water, with Rhymer.*

Beside me Tula gave a soft, unhappy sigh. Loneliness suddenly radiated from her like a bleak aura. Someone had hurt her, or she'd hurt him, and the memories returned. I wasn't drunk enough to ask for details, and her thoughts were closed. She proceeded to polish off nearly a dozen glasses of bubbly water over the next two hours. I designated myself the chaperone and switched to straight vodka.

By the time we left the club, Tula was wobbling and I had to take her by one arm to keep her on course. I thumped my cane's silver tip on a rustic, cobblestoned path that led to a patio overlooking the river. "Follow the sound of the tapping cane," I quipped. "What kind of stones are these? It's like an obstacle course." The stones were rounded. Even sober, it was like walking on stone eggs.

Tula lurched and nearly pulled us both down in a heap. "Ballast stones. Thousands of 'em. Tossed from the hulls of big ships coming up the river to harbor since the sixteen hundreds. They're everywhere in the old part of Savannah. Streets, walls, you name it. The weight of old trade, under our feet. That's what life is all about, isn't it? The weight of our trades? Our compromises? Trying to walk when we just want to fall down?" She stumbled again. "I'm so sorry," she moaned. "Juna Lee always says I shouldn't watch the couples' acts. She says I get morbid and start babbling clichés from old soap operas. She's right."

"Let's sit on the patio edge over there." I guided her like a tugboat pushing a tanker. We made our way to a heavy wooden railing, which gave us something to hold onto. A lamp post cast a soft cone of light around us. We sat down and dangled our legs over the side. A dozen feet below us, the Savannah River made a slow, deep highway to the Atlantic. Across the river, the lights of the city's historic cotton exchanges winked in the hot night air. Now the grand old buildings were full of shops, restaurants, and bars. I heard the faint sound of music. On a summer night the riverfront surged with young people, rowdy and carefree. I had never been rowdy or carefree, at least not outside my imagination. An enormous freighter slid by, heading downriver to the ocean, blanking out the scene, a peaceful monolith in the moonlight.

I clasped Tula's hand. "Feeling better?"

"A little." She slumped a little, staring into the blackness. "I owe you an explanation."

"Being a newly liberated Mer who air-kissed a stranger's penis tonight, I'm now frank enough to say, 'You betcha.' So explain. Is this mood of yours about a man?"

She nodded wearily. "He was a Lander. But not just any Lander. Most Lander men are easy for a Mer to control; they're as docile as pet puppies. They can't resist us. They're fun to play with and easy to forget. We use them; we break their hearts. For that reason, conscientious Mers don't indulge in Lander romances. But there are the rare ones — the special ones — the ones who catch a Mer off guard." She exhaled wearily. "And in those cases, the outcome is almost never good."

"But there are *some* happy cases?"

"Yes. Lilith's younger sister, Mara, tormented a Lander for years, and he tormented her. But now they're together, and happy. He's Griffin Randolph's uncle. Griffin is only a Mer on his mother's side, you see. Randolph men are notoriously strong-minded when it comes to Mer women. But the story of Griffin's *parents* — now, that's a different story. A typical Mer/Lander tragedy. His mother was a beautiful McEvers, from Scotland."

"Related to Rhymer?"

"Yes. An older cousin of his and Tara's. Undiline McEvers. She came here to visit the Bonavendiers, then fell in love with a Randolph shipping heir. Porter Randolph. Pure Lander, through and through. She hid her Mer heritage from him." Tula raised a foot, clad in a shimmering, high-heeled sandal. She spread her toes slightly, showing off the beautiful webbing. "She even mutilated herself for him. She cut the webbing from her feet."

I raised one of my low-heeled, sandaled feet, staring at my plain toes wistfully. "How could she bear to do that?"

"She adored him. He adored *her*. She feared he couldn't accept the truth. So she hid her Mer status from him and married him. They were deliriously happy when Griffin was born. She had a doctor secretly remove his webbing, too. So Griffin was raised not knowing he and his mother were Mers."

"Oh, Tula."

"But eventually Porter discovered the truth. She'd been

right to worry about his reaction: He couldn't take it. Couldn't comprehend that Landers aren't the only kind of human beings in the world. Couldn't accept that the essence of reality, as he knew it, wasn't real. As I said, Randolphs are strongminded. Meaning hard to control. Otherwise she'd have saved him'— soothed him, planted sublime understanding in his mind. That's how we coexist in the Lander world. By putting forth our illusions."

"What happened to her? And Porter?"

Tula looked at me sadly. "He killed her. And then he killed himself. They're buried on a bluff at Sainte's Point. Their graves face your cottage. They built it. They were happy there."

I stared at her, speechless. Another giant freighter inched past us, blocking out the view. Eventually it slid by, a manmade eclipse, and the bright necklace of Savannah's riverfront appeared in the distance again. Tula frowned. "Landers and Mers shouldn't mix. Juna Lee always says so. She's right."

"My mother was a Lander. She and my dad were very happy. I have only good memories."

"She wasn't a Lander."

"*What?*"

Tula gave me a gentle smile. "There are a lot of people in the world who love the water beyond reason, who have special talents, who know they're not quite like everyone else. Almost always they're Floaters, like you. They have Mers in their recent bloodlines. They just don't know it. Your mother was a descendent of a Mer clan in northern California. Lilith told me so, before she left Sainte's Point. Your mother was a Miakawa."

"A Miakawa? But . . . that's a Japanese surname, and my mother wasn't Asian-American. She was a brownish blonde with light eyes. She and Dad ran a bookstore on Cape Cod. She grew up on the coast of Maine, helping her father catch lobsters."

"But her great-grandmother was a Miakawa who migrated from Japan. A full-fledged Singer. So you're a Mer on both sides of your family tree. That is, your family river, as we Mers say." Tula smiled. "Did she ever mention whether she and her father caught lobsters in a trap — the Lander way — or *by hand?*"

After a long moment, I said numbly, "She did mention something about the fun of outwitting the average crustacean."

"There you go. A true Mer. She loved a hands-on hunt for shellfish. For Mers, chasing lobsters is the equivalent of fox-hunting. Royal sport."

I held my head with both hands. "Let's get back to the present. About your own romance — wasn't there *any* hope?"

She hugged herself and shut her eyes. "No. When I let him know about me — about being a Mer — when I dropped the illusions and let him see the real me, he was . . . repulsed."

"No. Surely—"

"Repulsed, yes. Horrified. Afraid of me. Is it so hard to imagine? Look at you. If you weren't a Floater, with an inborn instinct to accept what Juna Lee told you about yourself when she kidnapped you, wouldn't you be in shock? Traumatized? Afraid? Wouldn't you question your own sanity?"

"I suppose. Yes. Yes, all right. I've questioned it anyway. But I've accepted my new reality easier than I expected."

"Because you're a Mer."

"Just a Floater."

She squeezed my hand. "You're one of us. That's all that matters."

"The man you loved. What happened to him?"

"I made him forget me."

"Made him? But I thought you couldn't control—"

"There are ways. Drastic ways. Lilith helped me find a Healer."

"Like Rhymer's nieces?"

She nodded. "They're rare. But effective."

"This Healer—"

"Had the power to heal the mind as well as the body. She healed him."

"You mean she made the man you loved forget he ever loved you?"

"Yes. It's as if I never existed to him."

"Where is he?"

"He travels a lot. He lives in London, New York, Los Angeles. Other places. He has plenty of women to keep him company. Lander women. But he's never married. I think, somewhere deep in his soul, he remembers me."

"Couldn't the Healer have made you forget *him*, as well?"

She looked at me with tears in her eyes. "Yes. But I didn't *want* to forget him. No matter how much it hurt."

"Oh, Tula."

We hugged. She drew back, crying a little, wiping her eyes. "Enough. *Enough.* I was supposed to take you out for a good time, but here I am, stoned on tonic fizzes, depressing you with tales of my morbid romantic history."

"At least you didn't air-kiss a penis tonight."

She laughed hoarsely. "I'm going inside and wash my face. I'll be right back. Then I'll take you to a club out on Tybee Island. We'll eat raw oysters and watch an Elvis impersonator."

"As long as he's fully clothed."

Laughing harder, she got up and headed back inside the club.

I sat there on the shadowy river's edge, growing somber and sad. Given the chance, would I ever want to forget

Rhymer — the most compelling man I barely knew?

No. Never.

"It's never easy to forget what we can never have," a female voice said.

I turned, startled. A beautiful woman stood on the patio behind me. Black hair cascaded over her simple black minidress. Her eyes were dark and large. No, not just dark. Deep. As deep and mysterious as the river water moving slowly beneath my feet.

A little rattled, I said, "I'm new at Mer social rules, but isn't it rude to listen in on someone's thoughts?"

She smiled. "Perhaps." The dark eyes never left me. She glided up to the rail and lounged gracefully, gazing down at me with that unblinking stare. And yet I didn't feel afraid of her. She was only studying me, curious. "Quite a show in there," she said, nodding toward the club. "Distractions are welcome in long, bored lives."

"It seemed to go on forever."

"You were embarrassed?"

"Not embarrassed, precisely. But I've spent so much time alone in my life that I treasure intimate privacies. Public displays of powerful emotions — erotic or otherwise — make me feel naked. So much about our lives is exposed. Why add the most personal desires to that list?"

"Nicely put. But you were a good sport."

"I had no choice."

"You want to do the nice thing. Not offend. Not judge."

"I try to be equitable." I shifted under her stare.

"I'm making you uncomfortable."

I smiled. "I'm always uncomfortable."

"No. You have a remarkable ability to bring out the best in people. They sense your innate fairness."

"You've never seen me around my distant cousin. One Juna Lee Poinfax."

"Children adore you. You have an endless capacity for understanding and forgiveness. They know it."

I stared up at her. "Have we met before?"

She ignored my question. Her dark eyes seemed bottomless. The Abyss of Forever lay behind them. I felt a chill up my spine. "Are the local children coming to see you?" she asked, leaning toward me. "I'm sure they must want to. Tell me. You're a magnet for the lonely children of the world. Tell me about the children you've met during your stay here on the coast."

One if by land, two if by sea.

I didn't speak that verse from the famous Longfellow poem about my ancestor, Paul Revere, but I thought it — loudly — like a protective charm. Paul Revere had seen trouble coming and risked his life to warn his compatriots. I sought to warn *myself*.

The dark-eyed stranger tilted her head slightly, studying me harder. "One if by land, two if by sea," she repeated, mulling the words. "When you were young and alone, you chanted that to yourself, for courage. *One if by land. Two if by sea.* To make yourself believe that you weren't alone. On land, yes. In the sea, no. You knew, even then, that you would find the other half of your heart in the ocean. One if by land. Two if by sea. To shut out the pain, to shut out the fear. To shut out all other thoughts, and keep your peculiarities only to yourself. Very effective. I can't hear a thing you're thinking when you're in that mindset. I'm impressed."

"Who are you, and what do you want from me?"

She leaned closer. The head tilting. The eyes like black tunnels. She . . . flickered. Like an old television screen. As if revealing some subliminal image. Just hinting. I thought I glimpsed . . . something, someone. But then I blinked, drew back, and she was a dark-eyed stranger again, frowning slightly, as if puzzled at her own reaction. "I'm not quite sure what I want from you," she said. "I'm still deciding."

I didn't like the sound of that. I opened my mouth to say so.

"Hey! Baaay-bees! Show us some tit and ass!"

The loud, drunken male voice was underscored by the raucous laughter of other males and the quick putt-putt of a skiff engine. I craned my head and stared past my unnerving companion at some *new* unnerving visitors. An overloaded rowboat wobbled down the river, angling our way. A half-dozen blitzed college students leaned over the sides, waving their arms. The little boat looked like some kind of large water beetle floating on its back, its legs fanning the air.

"Give it up!" they bellowed. "Let's see some booty! Shake it and spread it!"

I unleashed a righteous librarian glare on them. "You must be very entertaining at fraternity parties. Take your drunken obscenities elsewhere."

They hooted. A couple grabbed their crotches. "Entertain this, bitch!"

I grabbed a lower railing and hoisted myself to my feet. More hoots and catcalls accompanied my actions. Nothing to do but make a dignified retreat, if possible. I refused to look over at the dark-eyed woman. She, no doubt, was about to desert me quicker than a heron deserts an empty beach. I cringed at the thought of the catcalls I'd get as I limped slowly up the sidewalk in my lowriders and skimpy top, a scrawny Britney Spears imitator with a bum leg.

I heard guttural sounds. When I looked at the rowboat crew, they had stopped flapping, stopping laughing, stopped breathing. They looked terrified. Their eyes were riveted on some sight other than me. Had someone walked up behind me and the dark-eyed woman? Someone much taller than me and her, judging by the angle of their stare? Someone much scarier?

"Let's get the hell out of here," one of the boys finally said, his voice choked. "Please."

The navigator fumbled frantically with the outboard motor. Everyone else began scooping their hands into the water, trying to help by paddling. The boat's little engine strained and sputtered. The skiff disappeared in the darkness.

I whirled around to speak to the dark-eyed woman. "Did you see someone behind—"

I was alone.

She'd vanished. Or shapeshifted.

My legs turned to rubber. I swayed and held onto the railing.

Orion.

ॐ ॐ ॐ

I didn't tell Tula what had happened. I put up a great pretense of being so tired I suddenly wanted to skip the Tybee Island club and go home. She was subdued from her own emotional turmoil and agreed readily. Inside, panic ruled. I was afraid to even *think* about Orion, afraid to call out to Rhymer in warning — afraid Orion would tune in to my distress call, that he'd follow me.

Maybe he's trying to find Rhymer and the girls through me. But why can't he locate them himself if he's this close? Something is keeping him at bay. Or he's waiting. Watching. Deciding whether to kill us all? Deciding whether to risk the wrath of the entire Bonavendier clan and all its many familial tributaries?

After Tula went to bed I slipped into my rental car and drove to Randolph Cottage I hurried to the end of the pier and stared helplessly at Sainte's Point. There was no moonlight that night; the island was just a barely discernible shape on a black horizon, haloed by stars.

My heart raced. I looked at a mile of dark water.

One if by land. Two if by sea.

I came from the blood of patriots and mermaids. I had to get to the island and warn Rhymer without Orion hearing.

I undressed down to my bra and panties, carefully laid my cane atop the discarded clothes, then limped to the open gate where the pier's ladder disappeared down into the water.

Taking a deep breath, I dived in.

Learning To Breathe

👁 👁 👁 👁 👁 👁 👁 **17** 👁 👁 👁 👁 👁 👁 👁

The dolphins were screaming.

I woke to the sound and leapt from a deep teak chair on the veranda at Sainte's Point. The dolphins massed in the cove just off the docks, a dozen or more of them, calling me in a high-pitched trill that vibrated inside my skull. The air was pink with dawn; the brisk rumble on the seaward beaches said the tide was near its peak. Jordan came running outside, looking more than a bit half-asleep and rumpled. It had been his turn to grace a couch in the front parlor, while I sat guard duty outdoors. "What are they calling for, Rhymer?" he yelled.

"Someone's needing help, they say. Stay here. I'll go see. You go upstairs and station yourself outside the girls' suite."

He ran back inside. I slung a gun over one shoulder and ran down the knoll to the marina. The dolphins chattered and squealed. We do no' share so much a language with them as an *understanding*. Akin, you might say, to Lassie rushing home to bark: *Timmy's down the well!*

Your she, your she, your she, they were telling me. *Hurt, hurt, hurt*.

My *she*. Dolphins were none too concerned with niceties. They decided things by blunt observation; they were practical matchmakers. *My she. Moll. Hurt*.

Tell me where, I signaled. They did. I ran back up the knoll and plunged down a forest path, headed for the island's bayside.

Deborah Smith

I found Moll unconscious in the sand of a gray little shore facing the mainland. The currents built grand beaches on the island's seaward edge but little more than narrow strips of muck and sand on the bayside. Moll was streaked with mud the color of pewter. She lay on her back, barely clear of the water, dressed in naught but her lingerie.

"Moll," I groaned. I scooped her up and carried her onto dry sand, then knelt with her draped across my arms. She was cold as ice, but then, our kind are cold-skinned in the water, conserving our warmth deep inside, the way the other sea mammals do. I bent my head close to hers and sighed with relief when I felt the faint puff of her breath on my cheek.

She was not near-drowned — for a Mer, even a Floater such as she, drowning is a rare concern. But she *was* exhausted to the point of forgetting to breathe. I rimmed her lips with a fingertip, gently forcing them open. Then I sank my open mouth onto hers, and exhaled into her lungs.

Her heartbeat quickened; I felt the rhythm in my blood. But it wasn't enough. When a Lander performs mouth-to-mouth resuscitation on another ailing Lander it's a mechanical action, inflating the lungs, coaxing the muscles to flex, the nerves to fire. But the procedure for us Mers has a different intent. It's an infusion of oxygen, a gift of living breath. I had to remind Moll's lungs to search out the deep stores of oxygen that can let a Mer stay underwater for an hour or more at a time.

I needed the water's help.

Trust me, Moll. I carried her into the bay, covered her mouth with mine again, then sank beneath the surface. The water was black and murky. Dolphins surrounded us, fighting off everything from curious minnows to aggravating jellyfish. I breathed into Moll; I held her tongue aside with my tongue. Moll and I shared an essence of ancient water memories; the unseen vapor of our kind. We were bodies of water and, for us, the water breathed.

Moll came to with a languid start. Her tongue curled around mine sweetly. She knew it was me. Her body arched in my arms; I held her tighter and continued to breathe into her. Slowly, she lifted her hands and stroked the sides of my face. Then her arms slid around me.

I'm no fool. No monk or saint. I was instantly hard, instantly needing her. *You're here,* she whispered in my mind. *You're inside me already. More. I want more. I want the rest of you.*

You own all of me, Moll. With a quick fumble of my trousers and her panties, I slipped inside her.

She curved her good leg around my back. I eased the other one close to my hip, and stroked the scarred thigh.

Together, we came back to life.

⚭ ⚭ ⚭

They knew. Stella, Isis, and Venus knew I'd made love to their uncle.

"Good afternoon, *Aunt Molly,* " they said in unison, smiling, when I woke with them sitting in chairs beside my bed. I blinked. The world came into focus. I was submerged in the deepest feather mattress at Sainte's Point, in a golden guest room of antiques and fine brocades. The early afternoon sun streamed across my silk comforter. I pulled it higher on my chest and did a quick mental checklist of my hidden parts. Muddy, sodden bra? Gone. Muddy, sodden, ripped panties? Likewise. Rhymer had tucked me into this gorgeous bed, naked, kissed me, and held me until I fell asleep.

Now, I was wide awake.

Aunt Molly was wide awake.

"Good . . . afternoon."

Little Venus looked at me sweetly. "You've very brave for swimming the bay with an unwilling leg, Uncle Rhymer says." Black hair streamed over her soft white jumper. Isis wore faded jeans and a white T-shirt.

"Very brave," Isis echoed.

Stella, stately young preteen Stella, was dignified in a pale silk blouse and baggy silk harem pants. She steepled webbed fingers beneath her pale-moon face and looked at me worriedly. "Did you really meet our father last night?"

I sat up slowly, hugging the sumptuous bed coverings to my chest. "I think I may have, yes."

"What did he look like?"

"I don't know. I'm sure he was in disguise."

"Was he awful? Terrifying? Were you afraid?"

I thought for a moment. Then, honestly, "I don't know."

"Did he threaten you?" Stella persisted.

"No. In fact, when some unpleasant men came along, he frightened them away." The three girls straightened, traded astonished looks, then gazed at me, wide-eyed. Hope flowed from them in rivers. I knotted my fists in the covers. "I don't know that you should trust him. I can only tell you that — if it was, indeed, him that I met — he didn't seem to want to hurt me."

Heavy footsteps sounded in the hall. Rhymer appeared in the doorway, frowning. He carried a delicate silver tray with a silver tea service on it. Steam wafted from the pot. Slabs of yellow butter melted atop scoops of scrambled eggs and caviar. A large flute of champagne, lightly colored with orange juice, completed the meal. Did I mention that Mers are the original Atkins diet afficionados? Fat, protein, and alcohol is their creed.

"Let Moll recover from her swim a bit longer and have some brunch," he ordered. "Out with you. And no more questions."

The girls stood. Stella faced her uncle stoically. "We believe it's possible our father is not intent on harming us."

"That's something I don't know yet. In the meantime, I don't want any of the three of you outside this house. Stay inside. And stay together. And if you sense the least odd thing, sing out only to me and Jordan." He paused. "Or to Moll. Let there be no doubt that you can count on Moll."

They smiled at me. I nearly burst into tears of gratitude and smiled back.

After they left the room he made a pretense of setting the tray down just so on the side of the bed, being quite formal about it, not looking at me as he pulled a chair to the bedside and sat down. "Glad to see you're awake," he said brusquely, pouring me some tea. "Let's get some food into you—"

"Now I know I really can breathe underwater," I whispered. "Because of you. You changed who I am. What I am. How I exist."

Slowly he met my tearful, smiling gaze. His eyes were intense, trying to be businesslike. But he failed. "You're a wonder," he said softly. His mouth crooked. "And you give my pecker far too much credit."

I would have laughed, but the grim circumstances came flooding back. "I told the girls the truth about Orion. That I'm not sure what to say about the person I met last night. All I know is that . . . he could easily have hurt me, kidnapped me, or threatened me. But he didn't."

Rhymer handed me a fragrant cup of tea, then sat back in his chair. His face hardened. "I'm not sure who you met last night on the river, but I'm betting it wasn't Orion."

"*What?*"

"I believe you'd be dead now, if it was him. The evidence says he's violent and merciless. What you've described isn't like him."

"But you've never met him. How can you be sure?"

"He killed a roomful of scientists on a UniWorld ship. Slashed them to pieces. Women as well as men. He took my sister's corpse. He's never made himself known to his own daughters, but now he's tracking them like a hunter. No, Moll, whoever you met, she or he doesn't fit Orion's profile."

"But I felt . . . nobility. I felt grief. I felt questions."

"You felt what you always want to feel in other people, because you're a sweet soul. Orion kills first and asks questions later. He wouldn't play cat and mouse games. He'd want you to be afraid. He'd force answers out of you. Do you think he'd come this close to tracking his daughters down only to stop and chat?"

"But you've said—"

"Yes, the girls are able to hide from him. I told them to shut him out, not to listen if he spoke to them, not to sing out, and they've mostly done it. Healers are powerful. One alone isn't a match for a Swimmer, but three together, linked by his own bloodline, can put up a shield even he can't break through. Unless *they sing*. So he knows he has to find them through others, such as *you*. And I'm betting he'd be willing to do whatever it took to get information from you." Rhymer grimaced. "Including hurt you, if you wouldn't talk."

"Isn't it possible that he's not a monster? Maybe he simply wants to be sure his daughters are safe. Maybe he wants to know why you've taken them from him. And how you intend to raise them."

"Are you willing to gamble the girls' lives on such hopes?"

After a long moment, I sighed. "No."

"Good. Now, let's talk. Just to be on the safe side, I want you where I can keep an eye on you from now on. I want you to move in here. Agreed?'

I nodded solemnly. Live with Rhymer? Oh, yes. "Agreed."

"And I want your word that you won't encourage the

girls to think kindly of their father. If they drop their defenses—"

"I won't encourage them. You have my word."

"And you'll stay on dry land. No more marathon swims."

"One if by land. Two if by sea. It's true."

"I'm begging your pardon?"

"I'm not alone in the water. You're with me. I know that now. But no more solo swims. I promise." I set the teacup on a nightstand. The comforter slid dangerously low on my breasts. His eyes followed the movement. "Rhymer," I said quietly, "If I'm going to stay here, I need Heathcliff."

"Never fear. I've already sent Jordan to fetch him."

"Thank you."

"Your puss is safe with me."

I arched a brow. "Prove it."

He got up, went to the door, and locked it.

Then he came back to the bed. The briefest pleasure is the most intense.

⚭ ⚭ ⚭

"The bastard's out there," I told Jordan grimly. "I don't know what his game is, but he's close by, and he's planning something."

We stood on the island's beach, watching the water. Moll was on my mind, inside my body, inside my heart.

Jordan crossed his arms over his chest. "If you really believe that Orion is nearby, why did you tell Molly and the girls you don't believe he showed up in Savannah the other night?"

"Because I think he senses fear most of all. I don't want him to feel their fear. To be led here by their fear."

"Let's be frank, cousin — you and I aren't exactly *not* afraid."

"Yes, but we can keep it to ourselves." Always the macho military Mer, that was me. Stiff upper fin, and all that.

Jordan coughed. "Maybe *you* can. But I'm worried. Maybe we should load everyone on a fast ship and get out of here."

"No. On the water we'd be an easier target."

"Then let's move inland. If the legends about Swimmers are true, they can't travel inland too far."

"But neither can Healers. The girls need to be near the ocean, or they'll get sick. So we'll stay here, we'll stay on guard, and we'll hope I'm wrong about him finding us."

Jordan put a hand on my shoulder. "He's found us already. It's just a matter of time before he shows up."

☙ ☙ ☙

I was a *made* Mer woman. I'd made love underwater, breathed underwater, mated underwater. I could see through even the darkest water clearly now, and I saw that Rhymer was lying to me. And me to him. We both knew that Orion was out there beyond our sight, that I had met him. That we were only waiting for him to show himself at Sainte's Point. Waiting to find out what he wanted. I hoped for the best; Rhymer expected the worst.

We made a good team that way.

And Now, a Visit from a Stranger

☙ ☙ ☙ ☙ ☙ ☙ ☙ **18** ☙ ☙ ☙ ☙ ☙ ☙ ☙

I woke up in the not-so-private massage tub of my suite at Casa de Prison Araiza. Godzilla stood over me. I looked up at her in drowsy disgust through the water. Given the rippled effect, it wasn't so bad.

Oh, it's just you, Aphrodite. I sat up, naked, shedding water and salty bath soap. My inflated bath pillow floated away on a riptide of high-powered jets. With nothing better to do in confinement, I'd become addicted to the tub. Particularly the underwater jets at crotch level.

"Get up, Juna Lee," she ordered. "You're going home."

I leapt from the tub like a Sea World porpoise. "Jordan's here?"

"No, but he sent a boat."

"He can't *stand* to be without me. I knew it!" I dressed in a rush, donning something slinky and winding my wet hair up in a decorative bun. Meanwhile, Aphrodite watched me with a stony expression. Odd. She'd never been a cold, dark-eyed bitch before, just a regular bitch. Tonight she gave me the creeps. A first.

"Aw, I ruined your fun," I taunted. "Mamsie-whamsie is pouty-whouty because she won't have Scarlett-wolett to kick around anymore."

No reaction. Not even a disgusted eye-roll. I frowned. Where was the wicked Araiza wit? The Spanish-tinged arrogance? Aphrodite just pointed toward the door. "Follow me."

She led me out of the quiet, sleeping hotel into a sultry

Caribbean night. I strode after her to the hotel's marina, then out onto one of many long docks. She stopped before a nice little yacht. "Go. Goodbye."

"Great. Hey, don't forget to write. Assuming you're actually literate." I flounced aboard, then sang out, "Captain? Oh, Captain! Set a course for Sainte's Point Island, Georgia, in the fabulous United States of America. Full speed ahead! And fetch me a 3 a.m. martini. Let's celebrate! The Oprah Winfrey of Hispanic Mers can't keep me here anymore!" I turned to stick my tongue out at Aphrodite. My tongue froze in midair. She'd vanished. I stared at the long, empty dock, looked up and down, then shrugged. Who said whales couldn't move fast?

Charley stepped out of the main cabin.

"Charley!" I'd never been so happy to see my big, sweet-dumb, steroid-enhanced cousin in my life. "I should have known Jordan would send you to escort me back in style!"

"Come inside the cabin."

Good-natured Charley looked strangely serious. There was something weird about his eyes. "Charley? Give me a smile?"

"We've got a long trip ahead. Come inside."

"Charley?" I followed him into the cabin. He shut the hatch door. And locked it. I frowned back at him. "You're not still mad about that little kidnapping incident involving Molly Revere, are you? I mean, you aren't in any trouble with the Council over it, are you? I'll sweet-talk them for you—"

A knife-sharp vibration stabbed me between the eyes. I sank onto a couch, holding my head and eeking. The pain faded away. Breathing hard, I stared up at Charley. "Charley?"

Only it wasn't Charley. And it hadn't been Aphrodite, either. Whoever lived behind those dark eyes looked down at me with the power to turn my brain cells into quacamole.

"You'll stay in this cabin during the trip to Sainte's Point," he said in a deep, non-Charley voice, "and you won't try to escape. If you do try, I'll hurt you. I'll know when you sleep, when you wake, and I'll know when you think of diving overboard. You won't get far from me, and I'll make you wish you'd never wanted to. What I did just now is only a pale demonstration of my talents. Don't make me do worse."

"You're putting some kind of sonic handcuffs on me? What — I'm a prisoner? You'll keep me under 24/7 sonic/psychic surveillance? You'll see me when I'm sleeping. You'll know when I'm awake. Who are you — Santa Claus?"

"The name's Orion. And you're not here as a prisoner." He paused. Charley's face almost smiled. It was terrifying. "You're here as bait."

Trouble Starts

෴ ෴ ෴ ෴ ෴ ෴ **19** ෴ ෴ ෴ ෴ ෴ ෴ ෴

"Tell me what Hyacinth finds in the underwater cave of the Cyclops," I said, my fingers posed over the keyboard of my laptop. The girls and I were spending the summer afternoon in Lilith Bonavendier's exquisite sunroom. I pretended that we weren't, essentially, living in the mansion as if it were a fortress. Rhymer had given them strict instructions to stay inside me and Heathcliff.

Behind me, Stella solemnly unveiled the magnificent portrait of Melasine. The legendary Mer-Mother looked down on us with her sea-green eyes. *Molly Martha*, she seemed to say, *you're where you belong at last. Now all you have to do is keep these girls and Rhymer alive.*

"Hyacinth finds killer lobsters the size of army tanks in the cave of the Cyclops," Isis suggested. She curled up on a velvet settee, hugging her knees. "When Hyacinth orders them to attack, they snip people's heads off."

"Ahah," I said, trying not to frown at her cynicism. "Gangsta lobsters. Doing drive-by snippings."

"No, I know!" Venus said excitedly. "Hyacinth finds giant, beautiful conch shells in the cave, with talking snails inside!" She sprawled on her stomach atop a Turkish rug, her chin on her webbed hands. "Snails are very friendly. I talk to them all the time."

"What do they say back?"

"They say, 'Where's your slime trail? Where's your shell?'"

I smiled as I typed: "Slinky, slithering slugs like to socialize and snoop."

Venus burst into giggles. Even sour Isis couldn't hide a grin.

Stella sighed at her sisters' fancies. "I say Hyacinth finds a magical amulet. Capable of turning back time and reversing all the terrible things that make us sad."

I looked at her gently. "Wouldn't that be wonderful?"

She nodded. "I vote for a magical amulet."

"I'll put all that in my notes along with talking snails and vindictive lobsters, and we'll see what develops."

I typed a list of plot points, all the time feeling the weight of the girls' pensive scrutiny. No doubt they sensed their father was closing in. Yet I could not believe the . . . the *being* I'd met in Savannah was bent on harming these children. His own daughters. *Dear God, please let me be right.*

Footsteps tapped smartly on the stone floor of the main hall. Sharp heels. Long, urgent strides. The girls looked up. "It's Tula," I said somberly. She'd forgiven me for shutting her out after the Orion incident. She understood my fear that he'd listen and follow me.

Tula halted in the doorway. Picture Julia Roberts with webbed toes and stunned eyes. Her fear hit me, and when she spoke, I understood why.

"Orion's kidnapped Juna Lee," she said.

❦ ❦ ❦

Some Peacekeeper you are, Rhymer McEvers, I told myself. *Some uncle. Protect the girls. That was your only charge. Now Moll's in the mix, and Jordan, and Tula, and last but not least, Juna Lee.*

Jordan was crazed with worry over her.

"I'll call in the other Peacekeepers to aid the search," I told Jordan. "They'll help you find her." He shook his head as he climbed into a small, fast boat at Sainte's Point. Jordan slung an Uzi over one shoulder and nodded to me and Moll. He slid a key into the boat's ignition. "He outwitted Aphrodite Araiza and all her family to steal Juna Lee, so no doubt he'd outwit any Peacekeepers who tried to catch him."

I nodded but stared grimly at the small boat. "Taking such a plaything for a trip through open seas to the Caribbean is risky, even for a pair of Mers."

Tula stoically checked the lashings on the boat's canvas canopy, which she'd lowered for better speed. "Juna Lee is my cousin. Even if she's an annoying diva, she's also my best friend. I expect to find Orion completely in her thrall and serving her martinis while she hypnotizes him with showbiz gossip. But just on the off chance she's really in trouble, I'm going along with Jordan."

"If it's any comfort to you, Orion went to some trouble to take Juna Lee without hurting her. Could be he's hoping to trade her for the girls." I paused. "But he probably senses that I'd never go for that."

Jordan nodded. "I'd never ask you to make that kind of trade."

Tula waved from the stern, where she stood like an elegant warrior woman, holding a rifle. She looked up the knoll behind me, to Moll. "Do I look dangerous enough?" she called.

Moll called back, "Yes! Just like a villainess in a Bond movie."

"A villainess? Isn't that someone who owns a villa?" Tula gave a shaky laugh, then waved goodbye.

Jordan gunned the engine, backed the boat from its coquina and timber berth, then sped across the cove toward open ocean. Two dozen dolphins raised their heads from the cove's surface and sang a silent charm of farewell.

My heart sank. What was Orion up to? Drawing Jordan away from the island to leave me without a lieutenant? I pivoted to find Moll gazing worriedly at the departing boat, then at me. *What would you do if some unknown entity such as Orion took me?*

I'd turn the waters upside down until I found you and res-cued you and killed the bastard who'd stolen you, that's what.

She gently put a hand over her heart, then gave it to me on her open palm.

I'd do the same for you, she sang.

Dancing with the Creature

ᘛ ᘛ ᘛ ᘛ ᘛ ᘛ ᘛ **20** ᘛ ᘛ ᘛ ᘛ ᘛ ᘛ ᘛ

Dear Diary:

I'm not really able to write at this time, trapped on a boat with a shapeshifting murderer, you know, but let's pretend. I don't dare call out psychically to Jordan or anyone else, because *He Who Must Be Obeyed* will dice my brains with his sonic *Ginsu* knife if I do. But worse, I can feel Jordan calling out to me — feel it, but not really catch what he's saying. It's as if Orion has dropped a wall around me. I can't get out, and no one else can get in. I just feel muffled vibes. It's driving me crazy. Let's talk about something else.

"Juna Lee, stay out of the sewer," my mother used to say when I was a child.Not that it did any good. A decorative iron grate covered the opening to a storm drain in the courtyard garden at our historic Charleston villa. One day, when a workman had pried the grate off, I wrapped a silk sheet around myself (always protect your pearl-embroidered playsuit from sewage) and hopped into the open hole. After a thrilling half-hour water ride through a pitch-black brick tunnel that had been dug by slaves when "Charles Town" was still a dot on England's map of the Colonies, I floated to the surface of Charleston Bay, near the rocky hummock crowned by the preserved battlements of Fort Sumter. The first shots of the Civil War had been fired there. Heedless of historic sacraments, I crawled onto a low wall, dried myself in the sun, and took a nap. Unfortunately, a fishing boat full of Landers spotted me, and everyone on board freaked out.

A child. A poor helpless child. Oh, please. But at least I made the local newspaper.

First Grader Continues Poinfax Tradition, the headline said drolly. Charlestonians (who sport a high percentage of Mers — glamorous, elitist, and old money, the historic city is such a perfect Mer habitat) anyway, Charlestonians are nothing if not blasé when it comes to Mer antics. I wasn't the first Poinfax heir to do a nonchalant slalom down a city sewer tunnel.

But if Mama had her way, I'd have been the last. "Augustus," she said to Dad, waving an herbal cigarette with a hand jeweled in onyx to match her evening gown and his tuxedo (they were always on their way to some coordinated gala or other), "Augustus, I know you have fond memories of that storm drain from your own childhood, but I suggest we lock the grate permanently, or else next time our little princess may get flushed all the way to Bermuda."

"No, she'll be fine. She's a dollop of caviar off the old cracker," Dad said proudly, meaning I was a chip off the old block. Besides, Mama and Dad were never seriously concerned about my safety in the world. Like most Mer parents, they understood that even the riskiest Mer child is far more savvy than your average Lander ankle biter. Mers aren't like Landers, who go lily-livered at the thought of dark, mysterious places far below terra firma. We have our sonar, so we can see in the dark underwater, or least *feel* shapes in the dark. We don't mind the cold, we don't mind the damp, and we don't mind being submerged in murky water for long periods of time, though I didn't much like sharing the drain's subterranean waterslide with rat carcasses and clumps of garbage.

By the way, Mama and Dad are currently moored somewhere along the fabulous coast of New Zealand. They've lived aboard one of their yachts for years, floating here and yon, welcoming various nomadic Mers aboard, dabbling in extramarital affairs, gambling at highstakes card games, partying with the famous and infamous. I get psychic hellos from them occasionally, and postcards. Hey, I never said they were good role models.

Strange, but decades later, trapped in the cabin of a yacht with Orion at the helm, I thought of that storm drain. Storm drains and mom and dad and vaginas. Birth canals, to be precise. If Orion killed me, I'd never birth a child. My never-born would never get to jump down the Poinfax storm drain. You just *know* any child of mine and Jordan's wouldn't have been able to resist a challenge like that.

I teared up, thinking about mine and Jordan's child never being born, never popping up near Fort Sumter speckled with mud and bits of old candy wrappers.

Charley/Orion stepped into the cabin, gave me yet another chilly, assessing stare, then locked the cabin door behind him. The small yacht purred along the open waters of the Atlantic headed north. Sunshine silhouetted the faux Charley's hulking shoulders. If I forced myself I could half-way believe my sweet lummox of a cousin was really there, until I looked into his eyes. When Orion gazed at me, I felt like a small sea anemone pinned underneath a scientist's microscope. "You think bizarre thoughts," Orion said now. "I don't enjoy keeping track of them."

"Sorry. I can't keep my mind out of the sewer." Pause. Silence. His eyes narrowed. I sighed. "I know you don't have a sense of humor, but that was a joke."

Charley/Orion, who wore nothing but loose khaki shorts over the illusion of Charley's muscle-bound body, dropped to his heels in front of me. Orion's black eyes bored a laser path through my brain. "I don't intend to kill you unless you make it necessary."

"I'll try my best not to." Like any Southern belle trained in the old rituals of chitchat, I chose the encouraging moment to initiate a polite conversation. "So, tell me, Orion, aren't you and I cousins? Doesn't our family tree go back to the same Old One? Hmmm? Melasine? Assuming you believe in fairytales. Mermaids with finned tails, and all that."

His eyes flickered. "Fairytales? Melasine and the other Old Ones are no fairytales." He paused. "Melasine is my mother."

I stared at him. Imagine that someone tells you, straight-faced, that his mother is oh, let's say, Cleopatra? Or maybe Mrs. Santa Claus. What's the polite response? "How very interesting," I finally managed. "Legend has it that she inhabits the waters of the deepest southern hemisphere."

"Legend has it."

"Your father?"

"Ztecahotezumta, a king of the Aztecs around the time of Cortez."

Well, that was original. "You're what, then, hmmm, 500 years old?"

"Something like that."

"Does Melasine have very many children like you?"

"Not many Swimmers like me, no. I'm a throwback."

Thank god, I thought, then gasped when I realized he'd heard, of course.

"I couldn't agree more," he said. "Thank *god* there aren't many like me. I wouldn't wish this existence on any other Mers."

"What do you mean?"

"Caught between worlds. An oddity even among Mers. Outliving Landers and Mers both. Always alone. The Old Ones have a need for isolation that makes them content to spend entire centuries alone in the deepest oceans of the world. Swimmers aren't that lucky. We want to belong. But we can't."

"Obviously, you can't resist trying. How many children do you have?"

"Only three, living."

"What do you mean —"

"The others died of old age. As did their mothers."

"Except for Tara McEvers, obviously," I blurted. "Did you love her? Did you know she was going to bomb a UniWorld research ship and you didn't try to stop her? And what do you intend to do to the daughters she left you?"

I had gone a step too far. A black swarm of warning clouded my mind. Orion's voiceless hum beat against my skull like a million angry bees. I'd never heard anything so ominous before. I hiccupped and scooted back in my seat.

"You don't want to hear the truth," Orion said softly. "You want to play at interrogation."

"Oh? Show yourself," I demanded in a small voice, because, like I've said, I can't resist jumping down dangerous holes. "*Show your real self*. I'm *not* playing a game. I can take it. I've seen Donald Trump's hair up close. I've got a strong stomach."

"How kind of you."

"My mother used to keep me in line by warning that a Swimmer would get me if I swam too far from home. She said Swimmers have horns and claws. Just a fairytale, right?"

He extended a plain, stubby-fingered, Charley-like hand, holding it up to the light as if reality could illuminate him for me. I stared as the illusion fell away. "Oh. My. God."

"No horns," he said. "Only claws."

∞ ∞ ∞

The moon was waning, the sky over the Atlantic filled with stars. Rhymer and I shared guard duty in the window seat of an alcove just off the girls' suite at Sainte's Point. He'd bolted all the mansion's outer doors, and we were fortressed on the second floor; the girls slept in the next room, or pretended to. I sat in the window seat's deep cushions with my legs drawn up and my back fitted to Rhymer's torso. He draped his arms around my shoulders. One of his long legs dangled off the landward side of the broad window seat; the other was angled beside me. I leaned against it, as if it was a bulwark to keep the sea of the world at bay. We both wore soft, loose clothes, made for efficiency and comfort and unfettered for battle, if need be — me in a long shift, him in baggy trousers and an old white T-shirt. Heathcliff lay at my bare feet, sleeping the sleep of the young and confident, a whiskered smile on his face. In the midst of fear, I still felt that miracle. All the miracles of hope in the midst of darkness.

"In one of Lilith's books," I said, "I looked up the name Orion. Its roots are in Greek mythology, of course. Orion was a son of Neptune. He was killed unfairly by an enemy. In sympathy, a goddess placed him in the stars."

"Our Orion is no mere constellation," Rhymer grunted. "And no victim of circumstances, I'll warrant."

"Tell me about UniWorld," I whispered.

Rhymer's arms tensed around me. "Lots of speculation. Wild rumor. There's something evil there, but even I'm not sure what. My sister believed it was no' about the greed for oil, at least no' all. She believed it was about the destruction of Landers, the restoration of pure-blooded Mers as the grand poohbahs of the world, about legacies and prophecies and such. When this is settled, I'll be looking into UniWorld. Finding out more."

"Your sister died when the sophisticated explosives she was planting on the UniWorld research ship went off too soon?"

"Aye. Their security goons chased her with boats and

divers. She dropped the package. The remote malfunctioned. She was killed by the concussion underwater."

"You don't doubt that's what really happened?"

"I've confirmed it with sources."

"Then Orion didn't—"

"Kill her? No. But he abandoned her. She did it for *him*. He led her into a life of conspiracy theories. He's responsible."

"But you agree with her view that UniWorld is probably corrupt and sinister?"

He laughed grimly. "Since their bastards tried to shoot me when I went to claim her body, aye. But other than that, I only know that my sister did no' die by UniWorld's hands. They were trying to take her *alive*. No, I blame Orion for getting her killed. For getting her into the situation in the first place."

We were quiet for a long time, watching the ocean beyond the treetops that fronted the island. I threaded my fingers through his and leaned my head back into the crook of his neck. I worried that he would not give Orion any chance at all. But I also worried that Orion would not give him a chance, either. "You're named after Rhymer Thomas, the Scottish poet."

He chuckled. "Aye. My parents hoped for a thoughtful, sensitive son, but were stuck with me instead. So they made do and gave me a poet's name."

"No. They knew you'd follow your heart."

"Don't tell anyone. You'll harm my reputation."

"Would it be so bad if someone suspected you of tenderness?"

"Indeed. The world needs two kinds of people: the kindhearted to create poetry and the coldhearted to defend them."

"No law says you can't be both."

He raised a hand and looked out at the ocean, listening.

"I'm feeling the low song of Jordan and Tula. Somewhere in the Gulf. Jordan says he heard a whisper from Juna Lee. Just a word or two. Something about storm drains and claws."

"As long as we know where Jordan and Tula are. That they're safe."

"Aye. As long as we hear them, they're safe. The Araizas are helping them search for Juna Lee. But Orion hides. He can hide from all of them. They look on the water, they see naught but a shrimper. Or a sailboat. Not the small yacht carrying him and Juna Lee."

"I'm trying to imagine Juna Lee facing down a . . . a monster. I feel sorry for the monster. I never thought I'd feel sorry for her. But she was the one who forced me to come here. I have to give her credit for that."

"She's unhurt, I can feel it. And she's a fighter. Speaking of which." He reached beneath a pillow, then withdrew an automatic pistol. "This is for you." He pressed it into my astonished hands. "Do no' be afraid. 'Tis not loaded yet. Tomorrow I'll show you how to fire it."

I carefully set the lethal gun aside. "That will be the least of the test."

"Could you shoot Orion if you had to?"

"If I thought he intended to hurt you or the girls, yes."

"Don't go giving him even that much room for doubt."

"Shoot first and ask questions later? How Wild West."

"Hesitating gets people killed, Moll."

"Such as the girl you loved when you were young and hopeful?"

He turned me to face him. "Such as the girl I love now."

∽ ∽ ∽

The next day, not long after noon, Jordan and Tula disappeared. Psychically, that is. The low, steady hum of their presence, which kept Rhymer and me assured that they were safe and progressing in their search for Orion, snapped as if someone had slashed a phone line.

Rhymer and I were on the island's Atlantic beach at the time. At least, *I* was on the beach, holding the pistol Rhymer had given me. Rhymer had vanished into the ocean over a half-hour before. "I need to have a little confab with the dolphins as to what they've heard or sensed lately," he'd explained before he speared the surf, wearing *naught* but loose black trunks and his sheathed sword.

So I was standing there, looking anxiously from the gray-green ocean to the dunes and woods that hid the mansion from my sight, wondering if the girls were keeping their promise to stay locked in their suite upstairs with Heathcliff for company, when a part of my mind, listening for Tula and Jordan, went still. That's how it felt. *Still.* An engine had been turned off. The telegraph wires had been cut. Dodge City had lost the dit-dit-a-dit of the telegraph from Tombstone.

"Tula?" I said aloud, putting a hand to my head as if tapping my skull a few times would clear the line. "Jordan?"

Just beyond the surf, Rhymer popped to the surface. We traded a grim gaze. *He's got them*, Rhymer whispered to me. *Orion. He may have killed them.*

Things Turn Nasty

☠ ☠ ☠ ☠ ☠ ☠ ☠ **21** ☠ ☠ ☠ ☠ ☠ ☠ ☠

Jordan was bleeding all over my slinky little Anne Blegis dress. Not that I minded. The dress could be dry cleaned. Jordan couldn't.

I looked up at Orion. *Help him, please, help him.*

Orion waved a hand. *He'll live. If he does as he's told. Just like you two.* He gazed quietly at me and Tula, his Charley face a blank mask for those place-of-no-return eyes. Tula knelt on the cabin's floor beside me, speckled in Jordan's blood, holding his head in her lap while I pressed my hands onto the ripped, bloody cloth of his white cotton shirt, low on his right side. Blood poured from two deep gashes.

The bleeding suddenly stopped. Orion shrugged. He'd granted me a small favor. Jordan took a deep breath and opened his eyes. "Sorry," he whispered to me. "Some rescuer I am."

I nearly cried. "Sorry? Sorry for letting a shapeshifting psycho onto your boat because he was impersonating *me*? Sorry for hesitating to shoot an apparition you thought might *really* be me? Sorry you were deceived by a deranged mutant outcast who's so freaking ashamed of his freaking, freakish, freak appearance he still hides behind Charley's face and won't even *show* himself to us?" I glared up at Orion.

Jordan coughed. "Maybe you want to be a little more polite, since we seem to be his prisoners."

Orion smiled coldly. "A wise man. Onward to Sainte's Point."

ॐ ॐ ॐ

The breakfast nook at Sainte's Point was a cozy alcove of delicate white furniture, several small, original seascapes by a who's who of famous artists, and a small, sea-nibbled statuette of a web-footed nymph being caressed by an octopus. I'd never seen anything quite like it in collected antiquities; no Greek, Roman, or other ancient Mesopotamian culture had produced such a strangely erotic ode to inter-species dating.

Women and the tentacled marine animals they love, I thought weirdly. *Next on Jerry Springer.*

The girls and I sat in the alcove, eating a breakfast of butter and boiled shrimp. That's right. Butter and boiled shrimp. We each had a small porridge bowl filled with scoops of the creamiest fresh butter, and a small plate of fat, salmon-pink shrimp. A typical Mer breakfast. All my life I'd hidden my fetish for marbled steaks and lard out of the can. I hadn't known I was just a fat-loving Mer, eating what came naturally.

I stared at the statuette again, not really seeing it, lost in thought. Worrying. Jordan and Tula remained silent. Rhymer was out on the seaward beaches, listening for them looking.

"That statue's very ancient, you know," Stella said. She nodded. Her face, on the cusp between childhood and teenage beauty, was pale and haunted.

I felt her trying so hard to be a role model to her sisters. "Oh? Please, tell me about it."

"It's from a Mer civilization that existed long before the earliest ones Landers remember. The girl in the statue was a princess of an ocean clan. She became a great queen and warrior. Long before the age of Landers."

"How fascinating."

"Only if you're stupid enough to believe in fairytales,"

Isis grunted. She scooped shrimp and butter into her mouth. "I like stories about Santa Claus better. At least he brings gifts." Pause. "Unlike our own father. Who's never even met us but is probably headed this way to *murder* us."

"Isis!" Stella hissed.

"Murder us?" Venus moaned.

I drew myself up in my best former-librarian-shushing-people mode. "Eat your butter and shrimp, Isis."

Venus gazed from Isis to Stella woefully, then turned to Heathcliff, who sat on the table beside her, a happy servant to the child who'd given him back his youth. "Heathcliff," she said solemnly, "When you were a wee kitty, did you know your papa? I bet you did. I'm sure he loved you. Because all papas love their children and mean them no harm, don't they?"

"Yes, yes that's true," I answered for Heathcliff.

Venus looked at me tearfully, trying to believe, and managed a small, hopeful smile.

Later, on the beach, I hooked a hand through Rhymer's arm as he exited the surf. His eyes were tired. "Any news?" I asked.

He shook his head. "They're either dead or Orion's keeping them quiet."

"They're alive. I insist on hoping for the best."

He smiled wearily. "Good. That's your job, Moll. But *my* job is to plan for the *worst*."

"What do you think Orion will do next?"

"I'm betting his next move is to come here and offer Jordan and the others as a trade for the girls."

"But if he makes an offer such as that, you won't accept it."

He nodded, his face agonized. "At which point, he'll slaughter them for sure."

ᗝᗝᗝ

Tula and I helped Jordan onto the long, cushioned bench that served as a sofa across from the yacht's small galley. I covered him with a blanket and put a pillow under his head, smoothed his sun-streaked hair from his forehead, stroked his chin. "I've missed your touch," he mumbled.

"You must be delirious," I countered tearfully.

He sweated and dozed. I watched him without blinking, terrified. Even the best tan this side of a GQ model couldn't hide the pallor of his face. The rise and fall of his chest riveted me. I counted the seconds between inhalations. The slow seep of blood from the clot on his side made me want to wring my hands and moan. Yep, the situation had sunk to the melodramatic level of bad reality TV. Jordan was a contestant on a one-man *Survivor Island*.

Tula sat beside me on the floor. She stared upwards grimly, listening to the rumble of the engines and occasional footsteps as Orion moved about the pilot house above us.

"When he walks," she whispered, "he sounds heavier than any human being could possibly be. He can't disguise *that*."

"He's not really human. You should see his claws."

"I did." She hugged herself. "For just a second. When he leapt aboard our boat and slashed Jordan. I caught just a glimpse of this . . . this huge, knobby, muscular, veined, webbed hand with . . . with claws *like a giant cat's*." She took a deep breath, then looked at me. "And his hand was silver."

I nodded. "And *iridescent*. Like a fish."

Tula nodded wildly. "We're *related* to that creature. We've got *violent fish blood*. This proves it. It's disturbing."

"Oh, please. We're no more related to him than your average Lander is related to a gorilla at the zoo."

"Orion makes gorillas look *civilized*."

The engines stopped. Orion's feet creaked on the top deck as he descended to the cabin.

Tula and I traded a wide-eyed look. "What do you think his *feet* look like?" she whispered.

"Big. Silver. Webbed," I grunted. "But no claws — or he'd sound like a dog clicking across a tile floor."

The door burst open. Charley/Orion thrust his head inside. "Juna Lee. On deck. Now."

I raised one of Jordan's sweaty hands to my mouth, kissed it, then headed outside.

The sun was setting. A hot breeze tossed my hair. Somewhere on the other side of the planet a budding hurricane sent the remnants of its mood our way, rocking the small yacht on shallow, rolling swells. I lurched after 'Charley,' grimacing. "I'm *not* paying for this sunset dinner cruise. It sucks."

He grabbed me by one arm and unceremoniously hauled me to the yacht's bow, then pointed toward the faint hint of a coastline, just a haze on the horizon. "We're only fifty miles from Sainte's Point. We'll arrive there tonight. It's time for you to do your job."

"My job?"

"Sing out. Call Rhymer McEvers. I want him to know you're alive. Tell him I'll hand the three of you to him safely after he meets me at moonrise, alone, at a place called Echo Marsh."

"What? You're going to ambush Rhymer, kill him, then track your daughters down on Sainte's Point and kill them, too? No way am I helping you do that!"

He drew me close to his face. His five-hundred year old eyes burned into me. "I have lived too long and seen too much," he whispered, "to mourn the deaths that necessity demands. To put it bluntly, you pampered child, either you do as I tell you, or I'll rip your friends to pieces while you watch."

I gulped air. "I want your word that you won't hurt Jordan and Tula if I send a message to Rhymer for you. And I want your word that—"

My voice ended in a yip as the razor points of his hidden claws dug into my forearm. "Do you *really* want to see who you're dealing with?" He bent closer to me, and Charley's features vanished. My blood froze. I stared up into the thick-boned face of a silver sphinx, a beautiful horror, like something out of a science fiction comic book. No. Comic books portrayed mermen as sleek, fish-faced people.

They'd gotten it all wrong.

This offshoot of the Mer family tree had a human face covered in silver scales so tiny they formed a glistening, smooth skin. Black hair as coarse as seaweed cascaded down his back in thick braids like dread locks. Large, dark, browless eyes lasered me above a hooked nose and a wide mouth with pale, full lips. Those lips pulled back to reveal broad, white, human teeth, except for the little matter of the top and bottom canines, of which there were four on top and four on the bottom, a pair on each side, all an inch long, sharply pointed, and curved inward like white talons.

"Sing," he ordered in a voice like the rumble of a dark tide.

I sang.

※ ※ ※

Rhymer stood on the beach as if struck by lightning. The ocean stretched to a blood-red sunset. Somewhere out there, Orion waited. I gripped Rhymer's arm. Deep in my mind I felt, or heard, the distant hum of the Mer voice that was speaking to him. *Juna Lee.* I'd know that snarky, sophisticated, Southern Belle drawl, anywhere.

He's making me say all this, Rhymer. The mutant asshole

will kill Jordan and Tula if I don't play along. Let me tell you, I've known some aggressive mermen in my life, but this Orion takes the cake. Not to mention he's seriously in need of a laser peel to remove his freakin' facial scales, and he could use some good cosmetic dentistry to fix —

Silence. Orion had cut her voice off as if punching a button on a CD player.

Rhymer turned to me. "I'm to meet Orion tonight at midnight, alone, at a place near the mainland called Echo Marsh."

I froze. "What else did he tell her to say?"

"That's all. I could feel her fear. I could feel her anger. She's protecting Jordan and Tula. Orion forced her to be his messenger."

"What is Orion trying to accomplish? Why didn't he even offer a trade?"

"Because I was wrong. He's after something else. I'm not sure what."

"Whatever it is, you *can't* meet him alone. You can't. It's a trap."

Rhymer looked at me sadly. "Aye, probably, but better that than have him come here. I do no' want to fight him in front of the girls. They do no' need to see their father's blood."

"*Or yours.*" I reeled. "You can't fight him alone. He's more powerful than any normal Mer, even you."

"Moll, I have to try. I have no choice."

"Please, please let me go with —"

"*No.* I want you to take the girls away from here. Put them in that bus of yours and head up the coast toward your own home state. Don't stop, don't look back, and don't sing out, no matter what becomes of me."

"I can't. I can't just *leave* you. It took me all these years to *find* you."

"You'll never leave me." He put his hand to his heart. I cried.

⚭ ⚭ ⚭

You floated down a sewer when you were a kid, I told myself. *You can surely keep your shit together now and think of a way out of this situation.*

"No, you can't," Orion said aloud.

He threw the yacht's anchor overboard. In front of us the ocean made a black, rolling seascape. Above us, the stars looked like white pin points. I pointed to the night sky. "There's your constellation. The one that looks warped."

Orion laughed, grasped me by the wrist and dragged me into the cabin, then slammed the door behind us. Tula stood up anxiously. Jordan half-lay, half-sat on the cabin's couch, woozy but furious as Orion continued to manacle me by one wrist. *"Let go of her."*

Oh, how I wanted to wrap my legs around Jordan and kiss him, right then.

Orion released my wrist and nodded. "You're a brave man—" he paused "—for caring about her. I salute you."

"Well, how rude —" I began.

Jordan cut me off. "Orion, if you kill my cousin Rhymer or hurt his nieces, I'll hunt you down no matter where you go."

"Don't waste your efforts. As for tonight . . . I've disabled the engine and the radio. You'll get nowhere, even if you escape from this locked cabin. Sing out, and no one will hear. Try to swim, and you'll regret it. Look out the port windows at my pet."

Tula and I sidled over to the windows and peered out. In the starlight, a silvery fin cut the ocean's surface. It glided through our field of vision, then sank out of sight. I pivoted toward Orion. "Your pet is a Great White. Isn't he a little out of his territory?"

"Yes. But I called him specifically with you in mind. The big sharks *like* it when their prey nags and threatens. They enjoy the high-pitched *shriek* of a human voice while they're eating the voice's owner. To them, it's the equivalent of a dinner show. I've told him you'll be particularly entertaining."

"Listen, you shark whisperer, you won't get away with this. You can't trap us here while you go out to Echo Marsh and murder Rhymer McEvers. He's a Mer. He's your . . . your *brother-in-law.*"

"*He stole my children.*"

"*Your children?* You don't *care* about those girls. You've never even *met* them."

"I've visited them many times, I assure you. I've *watched* them for years. They just didn't know it was me."

After a stunned moment I blurted, "So what? They don't know you, they don't *want* to know you, and they're *terrified.* *Leave them alone.* You can't kill Rhymer and just *take* them. He's their *uncle.* Doesn't that mean *anything* to you?"

"To be blunt, *No.* I've killed hundreds of people in my lifetime. From Spanish conquistadors to UniWorld scientists. Mer or Lander, it makes no difference to me. Family ties mean nothing either."

Tula stepped up beside me. "Explain what you mean by that. Until now, most Singers — myself included — believed Mers such as you were just a fairytale. Or maybe a nightmare. You could have dispelled our prejudices. If you wanted to be part of the Mer community, you *could* be. Tell me why you've rejected our society. Tell me why you reject your own children."

"Because I've watched my children and their mothers grow old and die, time and again. Lander or Mer, they always die. Loyalty to a family is a curse, not a blessing."

Tula held out her hands in supplication. "But your own *daughters*—"

"Are of no importance to me except as property."

She stared at him. "You can't mean that."

"I always mean what I say."

I jabbed a forefinger at him. "Bullshit. You just need a good therapist."

Orion stared at me as if I were a lame video game in a theater lobby. I was only worth a couple of quarters before the feature started. "It will be a shame," he said finally, "if you're eaten by the shark. You'll give him indigestion." He left the cabin. We heard the rumble and click of the hatch's lock being secured, then the quick, heavy thud of his footsteps striding across the upper deck, and, finally, the precise *swoosh* as he dived into the water.

Silence. The yacht rocked gently. Tula and I traded worried looks. Jordan struggled off the couch. I quickly slid an arm under his shoulders as he stood. He dripped blood on the floor. "We've got to find some way to get out of this cabin," he said.

"Unfortunately, jimmying locks is one of the rare, nefarious skills I don't have."

"I do," Tula said. When we looked at her incredulously, she sighed. "The Lander I loved — the one whose memory of me I erased? I never told you much about him, Juna Lee, because it's painful to discuss him, but he grew up on the streets of Los Angeles. Long before he became rich and notorious, he was poor and notorious. He led a street gang. Once, for fun, during a long, romantic weekend in the south of France, he taught me to pick locks and hack into the computer systems of major governments." She paused. "He was multi-talented."

"Your mysterious Lander was a streetwise super-hacker? Was his name 'Neo' and did the Matrix finally suck him back into cyberspace?"

"I knew you wouldn't understand," she muttered, then headed for the galley's utensil drawer to search for breaking-and-exiting tools.

Clash of the Titans

☙ ☙ ☙ ☙ ☙ ☙ ☙ **22** ☙ ☙ ☙ ☙ ☙ ☙ ☙

Moll looked a little frail and lost in the driver's seat of her big bus, but her face was set in determination. She hung her mermaid cane from the back of the seat. Behind her, their faces shadowy in the light over a dining table, the girls huddled like unhappy doves, watching us. I stood beside the four of them, my throat closed and aching.

'Tis no small thing for a man trained in fighting to give himself over to the peacefulness of love.

"You do as Moll says," I told the girls. "She's the commander of this operation now."

They nodded. Moll's throat worked. "I'll hold the fort until your return."

"Aye. I'll see you soon."

Probably a lie. I didn't expect to survive a fight with Orion. I tried to hide that thought from Moll, but her eyes squinted in pain. "We'll be waiting."

I caught her behind the head, wound my fingers through her soft brown hair as if tasting silk through my skin, and kissed her quickly, twice, on the mouth. She raised her hands and dragged them down my cheeks and neck. I pulled back for both our sakes and looked at the girls. "Never doubt I'm proud to be your uncle, such as I am."

I turned to go.

Venus launched herself and grabbed me 'round the legs. Stella and Isis crowded in behind her. The three looked up at me. "We love you, Uncle," Stella said.

Moll and I traded a look. Her eyes tearful, she spoke to me privately, inside my mind. *We all love you. Say it back.*

I nodded. "I love the lot of you," I said to her and the girls hoarsely. "You're what makes the oceans rise and fall to me."

Then I turned, stepped down from the bus, headed for Bellemeade Bay without a backward glance that might undo me, and dived into the water.

∞ ∞ ∞

"Nice night to be eaten by a shark," I said grimly. Tula and I sat cross-legged on the yacht's deck. The small cruiser rode the summer swells in silence except for the erotic, rhythmic slurp of the ocean against the bow. I kept a hand on Jordan's shoulder. He was stretched out beside us, his forehead sweaty and eyes half-shut in pain.

Tula got up and looked over the side. A silver fin slithered through the starlit water. The deep, primitive hum of a shark voice — imagine a big dog growling underwater — filled our heads. Tula snorted. "Go away, you oversized minnow. We're not afraid of you."

Just your teeth, I thought. Normally, Mers swim in the company of dolphins. The dolphins are like pet guard dogs, fending off jelly fish and small sharks. Loyal dolphins will even attack a Great White and drive him away. But we couldn't wait for a dolphin cavalry to come to the rescue tonight. Sharks don't converse with us the way dolphins do; like most fish, they're nearly as primitive in their thought process as some professional football players. Speaking to one is like pleading with a big, dumb, hungry linebacker.

Tula sat down beside me. "You try talking to him."

I got up and went to the rail. "Hey, you. Howz about I call up a nice little school of fish for you to eat? Hmmm? I'll do that for you if you'll promise to leave after you clean your plate." Our finned prison guard raised his snout from the water, opened his mouth, and displayed a maw large enough to swallow me whole, outlined with sharp teeth. It was easy to guess what he was thinking.

I don't want an appetizer. I want a main course. Jump in.

"Eat this," I said, and flipped him a bird. I stomped back over to Tula.

"What did the shark say?" Tula asked grimly.

"He's auditioning for a remake of *Jaws*. He wants me to play the part called Naked Swimming Girl Who Gets Eaten in the Opening Scene."

"We're screwed."

"Orion said if we sang out, no one would hear us. But that's not true. Mers all over this part of the coast *will hear us*. The problem is, there's a ninety-nine percent chance none of them can get here in time to help us."

Tula frowned at me. "When I was a little girl and I'd come spend the summer with you in Charleston, I always admired you for jumping down that storm drain in your parents' back yard, even if I was too afraid to jump with you. You never calculated the odds. You never hesitated."

I looked at her, my throat burning with emotion. She was right. "Let's work on that *one* percent."

We sang.

೧೧ ೧೧ ೧೧

Echo Marsh. Where the dead can speak.

Aye, just superstition; a spooky tale told by African slaves and coastal planters I'd read in a local history book from Lilith's library. *If the dead could really speak, my sister would be here, telling me whether I should fight the father of her children to his death or mine.*

Yet as I swam through black, narrow channels into the marsh I felt the ghosts, the dark slip of large shapes in the water. Out in the ocean some miles away I sensed a military submarine cruising silently in the deep. Probably nuclear, hopefully American. During my time in the British service I had worked in a unit controlled by Mers — passing ourselves off as Landers, naturally — quietly going about the job of tracking the Russian subs, and others, that creep beneath the seas with all the subtlety of submerged junkyards. I'd thought only the *man-made* monsters of the deep threatened the rest of us.

Now I had naught but my own kind about me, those monsters. Those shadows. A small, lost whale navigating the salt-marsh rivers? A sea turtle? Orion? Perhaps only *he* was there, casting his illusions. Speaking as the dead.

My arms brushed the milky surface of rotting grasses. As I swam downward in a shallow channel my fingertips dug into the soft bottom, stirring up shrimp. They tickled my palms. Reading them sonically, I watched them dance in front of me in the murky black like large, invisible fireflies. This watery world that Landers dismissed as if it were naught but the dank basement of their house was no' a basement at all; 'twas a whole other dimension, a universe atop which Landers only floated, thanks to their dry boat of an island, unaware that the ocean was big and they were small.

We Mers know the difference. We see the much greater side of the world when we swim. Most of it is noble. Most is breathtaking.

But this marsh, this bloody, black, muddy, haunted marsh, was no better than a maze of dirty alleys in some dangerous slum.

Help us. Help. We're stranded. Danger. Help. That message filled my head, strong and feminine, a duet. I halted, listening, as I anchored myself with a fist around the corroded flute of some long-lost ship's anchor, sunk deep in the muck. Danger. *Help. Come and find us. Help.*

My skin prickled. Tula's voice. And the notorious Juna Lee. *Where are you?* I began, then cut myself off with a silent curse. If I sang back I'd give away my position to Orion. I couldn't risk him cornering me in one of these narrow marsh channels. He'd tear me apart before I could even free my sword from its scabbard.

Help us. Any Mers who hear us. We're trapped. We have a wounded man. Help us. There's no time to lose.

Wounded? They must mean Jordan. What the hell had Orion done to the good cousin who was like a brother to me? I pounded a fist on the anchor's rough surface. I couldn't help them. I had to face Orion here in this marsh, or *none* of us stood a chance. There were hundreds of Mers scattered along this section of the Georgia coast. With any luck, one of them would find Tula, Jordan, and Juna Lee.

Giving a low groan of frustration, I headed toward a stretch of open water at the marsh's heart. When I speared the surface I saw the starlit outline of a small, flat island — just a sandy hummock speckled with clumps of tall grass. I had been drawn there, baited and lured, by Orion. And now he spoke to me from somewhere in the water.

Welcome. Stand on the land and fight.

Dripping mud and saltwater, I climbed onto the tiny spit of sand. A quick pivot revealed naught around me but miles of black ocean on one side and miles of black marsh on the other. Behind the marsh, Bellemeade was just a cluster of tiny lights, winking like the stars overhead. I took a deep breath and slid the ancient blade of Mer tradition from its scabbard.

Come along, you bastard. The fight is waiting.

Across the hummock — no more than two dozen paces from one end to the other — the black nightwater rippled as if some great beast swirled below the surface. A dark shape rose from the water. A large, thick head and massive shoulders narrowed into a sharp V atop long legs with powerful thighs. Heavy arms unfurled and flexed against the starry sky. Broad hands spread, showing the silhouettes of webbing and curving, hooked tips. Claws.

Yet he had the shape of a man. My sister had loved this . . . man. My head tilted back as he straightened to his full height. He towered against the sky, more than an arm's length taller than me, a Goliath. No Mer was this tall, and no Lander either. I tightened my hand on my sword. This freak of our kind had seduced my sister for years on end, fathered daughters he didn't want, then lured their mother into danger, deserted her, and finally had the cold-blooded cruelty to steal the only thing left of her — her body.

In the darkness, his eyes settled on me. He heard me hating him.

Give up, he whispered. *There's no way you can win this fight. You're ordinary. Just a Singer. I can kill you with one sweep of my hand.*

Let's see how serious you are about trying.

Tell me where my daughters are, and I'll let you live.

Don't waste my time.

What, no gun? His voice, even inside my head, was streaked with odd lilts and forgotten accents. He was old; he'd spoken lost languages, lived in cities that were archaeological rubble now. He circled me, a giant, a throwback to some past when our kind was more of the ocean than the land.

Since it's just you and me, I decided to forgo the pleasure of shooting you.

Sentimental, I see. You're not sure what I am, so you give me the benefit of a doubt. She convinced you to do that. The writer. Molly. She has faith. Perhaps foolish faith.

You met her in Savannah. You could have killed her that night, or you could have kidnapped her. But something about her stopped you from harming her. If there's anything decent about you, she brought it out.

I let her live. A trade. Now give me my daughters.

So you can betray them the way you betrayed their mother? You're going to wish you'd brought a gun.

I want your daughters to know I gave you every chance to surrender.

Tara always said you would be the last man standing in any battle. She said you never gave up. You'll have to prove it.

Do no' quote my sister's words to me, when you've done nothing honorable by her.

On that point, you may be right. Regardless, I want my daughters.

To hell with you.

I will kill you slowly.

I raised the sword. *You're welcome to try.*

We began.

ᘰ ᘰ ᘰ

Help us! Hey, aren't any Mers listening? It's me, Juna Lee Poinfax, of the Charleston Poinfax's. Knock knock, who's there? Ivana. Ivana who? Ivana get some freakin' help out here!

The screeching, drawling, sarcastic voice skittered along the inside of my skull like fingernails on a chalk board. I pulled the bus off onto the road's sandy shoulder, cut the engine, and clutched my head. "Juna Lee," I said aloud. "I'd know that caterwaul anywhere."

Please, someone, a kinder voice hummed. *We need assistance. Send a boat. We have a wounded man aboard.*

I dropped my hands. *Tula.*

The girls gathered around my driver's seat. "Jordan is

bleeding," Venus moaned. "I can feel him hurting."

I pivoted in the seat and stared at them miserably. They gazed back the same way. Stella nodded. "It's true, Aunt Molly. Jordan's *hurt*."

"I'm sorry, but I can't go back —"

Isis frowned. "Then we're just running away? And they need us! Just like Uncle Rhymer needs us! Would Hyacinth just run away? No!"

"Hyacinth isn't in charge, here. It's out of the question. I'm sorry. It wouldn't be safe to go back—"

Pain ripped across my right shoulder. I bent over, gasping. The girls huddled around me, patting me with anxious hands. "Molly! Molly!" Heathcliff, perched atop the headrest of my plush seat, meowed worriedly.

I raised a trembling hand to the arm of my white sundress, convinced there should be blood and gashes — but all I felt was undamaged cotton and skin. "I don't know what just happened to me."

"Uncle Rhymer's been hurt," Stella said. "Our father just injured him. You love Uncle Rhymer, so you felt it as if you'd been hurt yourself. Aunt Molly, you have no choice. You're meant to go help Rhymer. He's your mate. Mers don't just love, Aunt Molly. They *breathe* together."

Oh, Rhymer. Shaking, I forced myself to face forward, then put my hands on the wheel. "I promised him. We have to keep moving. He's doing his job, and I have to do mine—"

The girls shrieked as I clutched the wheel and bent over it again. Pain flashed across my back, just below my shoulder blades. The girls stroked my hair. "Molly," Stella cried, "Uncle Rhymer's going to die if we don't try to help him!"

"I have to protect you girls—"

Stella knelt beside me. "Do you think our father won't find us, no matter what? If he kills Uncle Rhymer, then there'll be no one to stop him at all! And Molly, maybe we can talk to him. Maybe he doesn't want to hurt us! Our mother loved him. She couldn't be so wrong. If you don't let us try to meet him, he'll keep hunting for us until he finds us. In all your books, Hyacinth has faith that her parents want her to find them on the other side of the abyss. You believe our father may not be an evil person. Give us the chance to have faith, too!"

I groaned. The pain faded away — for the moment, at least. I pushed a button on the dash. The bus's door folded back with a hydraulic *whoosh*. I slung the holster of Rhymer's pistol around one shoulder then grabbed my cane. "Out of my way, please." The girls stepped away. I went down the bus's deep steps and stumbled onto the sandy roadside in the dark. We were a few miles east of Bellemeade, on a deserted stretch of bay road lined with pine woodland and small marinas. Bellemeade Bay lapped at the pilings of ramshackle docks where a dozen small fishing boats were tied.

The girls crept down beside me. "We can help you steal a boat," Isis whispered. "We know how to start an engine by just *thinking* about it."

"And how to *stop* one," Stella said quietly. "Aunt Molly, please don't be mad, but you can't keep driving. We've . . . we've told this bus not to crank again."

"Don't crank, bus," Venus said to the bus for emphasis.

I turned slowly and stared at them. They looked apologetic but stubborn. *Rhymer, forgive me, but I can't bear to desert you, and neither can they.* "I want your solemn vows, your most sacred promises," I said, "that when we get near Echo Marsh, you'll stay in the boat and let me go on, *alone*, to find Rhymer and your father. *Promise*."

They nodded and crossed their hearts with webbed fingers.

∞ ∞ ∞

I dripped blood, but so did Orion. Not as much as me but still, I'd wounded him. He'd slashed my shoulder and then my back; I'd sliced a ten-inch stripe across his hairless, silver chest. When I cut him, he didn't even flinch.

"Where are my daughters?" he said, as we circled each other. That was his chant. "Where are my daughters?"

"You can't find them because they don't *want* you to find them. Leave them be."

"Where are my daughters?"

"Not where you'll ever find them, as long as I live and breathe."

"*Where are my daughters?*"

"Safe and alive, which is more than I can say for their mother, thanks to you."

He lunged. I stabbed at him with the sword, nicking his side. He danced back, yet he had such broad reach with his long arms that, quick as a whip, he swatted me. The blow caught me alongside the head. The tips of his claws sliced like razor blades, and the force of the strike knocked me off my feet. I landed at the water's edge, rolled, got my footing in the muck, and sprang upright. A neat recovery, except for the roar of pain in my face, the ringing in my ears, and the way my lungs grabbed for air.

Orion could have charged at that moment and won, but he stood back, flicking the tension from his webbed hands, observing me with what seemed to be casual loathing. "Where are my daughters?"

"You might as well change your question. There'll be no answer from me."

He made a guttural sound, something like a laugh. "I'll rip it out of you eventually."

He lunged again.

Another round.

∽∽∽

"Someone heard us!" Tula sang out.

I touched Jordan's sweaty forehead. "It's about time."

We rushed to the rail as a fast little cruiser approached. It was just a black blob in the night, except for the running lights. Suddenly, someone turned a searchlight on us. Tula and I shaded our eyes from the blinding glare. "Turn that down!" I yelled. "I'm getting a sunburn!"

"*Mi dios*, I see you haven't learned any gratitude." The voice was female, Spanish-tinged, and sardonic. "And here I was, worried that Orion would be wearing your skin by now." The deck lights came on. Instantly I recognized the tall, dark and voluptuous woman standing on the bow with the attitude of a smirking dogcatcher.

Aphrodite Araiza.

Mounds of braided black hair swung to her waist. She looked tough in booty-hugging black leggings, which she had topped with a booby-cradling red tank top. She held a deadly looking rifle in her hands. Stroking the gunstock, she looked me up and down — I was sweaty and speckled with Jordan's blood — then feigned disappointment, as if she'd like to take a potshot, but I wasn't worth the trouble. Her cruiser slid next to our anchored yacht.

"Juna Lee, you look the worse for wear. Isn't it time you shed your skin for the summer?"

"Oh, spare me," I snarled at her. "You should be *embarrassed*. No self-respecting kidnapper lets the Creature from the Black Lagoon steal the *kidnappee*. But I have to admit, Orion *does* do a good impersonation of you. His ass is smaller than yours, though."

"Juna Lee!" Charley — the real one — bounded down the steps from the pilot house, grinning.

"Charley!"

"I *told* your parents I'd find you!"

"No thanks to Queen Latifah here."

Aphrodite curled one hand near the rifle's trigger. "Listen, you anorexic *puta*—"

"We have to help Rhymer," Jordan said weakly.

He pushed himself up from the deck, swaying a little. I grabbed him and slid an arm around his back. "You're right, Jordan. I'm sorry." He leaned heavily on me. I patted his cheek apologetically, then glared at Aphrodite. "No more bickering," I ordered. "Jordan's hurt, and we have to follow Orion pronto, okay? Throw us a line. We'll pull you close and climb aboard."

"Jordan!" Charley exclaimed. "I'll carry you, buddy!" He headed for the cruiser's railing, posing to dive in.

"Don't do that!" I yelled. "Orion left us the main homeboy from his entourage." I pointed down between the boats. Charley gaped as a huge dorsal fin pierced the surface. An enormous marine body swirled beneath the dark water.

Aphrodite clasped her big-boobed heart. "What a beauty! Oh, *mi querido, mi amor*, come here!" She set her rifle aside and leaned over the bow rail. To my astonishment, she began talking baby talk — in Spanish — to the shark. Even creepier, I could feel him *listening*. After about a minute of her Latin goo-goo-ga-ga he uttered a soft sonic hum, like a purring cat.

And then *he swam away*.

"Amazing," Tula whispered to me. "She's a *shark soother*. I've never met one before. Did you see that? How the shark responded to her?"

"One shark to another," I muttered, as I helped Jordan move toward the rail. "He was just showing her some professional courtesy."

Molly to the Rescue

❧ ❧ ❧ ❧ ❧ ❧ ❧ **23** ❧ ❧ ❧ ❧ ❧ ❧ ❧

Use the force, Molly Skywalker. Or maybe it's Molly *Oceanwalker?* Either way, I felt like a bumbling, apprentice Jedi as I steered a stolen speedboat across the starlit Atlantic. I estimated our position at a few miles off the coast, somewhere west of Bellemeade. The girls stood close beside me, their long dark hair whipping in the wind, their arms twined around me and each other. "Turn a little bit that way," Stella directed, pointing. "Slow down to a wee crawl now. Quick!"

I reversed the engine and brought the boat to a slow pace. "What's wrong?"

"Nothing, Aunt Molly. But there are two small whales off the bow, only about twenty meters long, just yearlings. They're calling *hello* to us. Hear them?"

Molly Oceanwalker was too rattled to eavesdrop on whale conversation. "I'm distracted. Interpret for me."

"They're Right whales, Aunt Molly. Right whales are very polite. I'm going to ask them directions." Stella was silent for a moment. "They say the marsh is just a wee minute away." She pointed, again. "There. In that direction."

"Are Right whales ever *wrong?*"

Isis harrumphed. "Not like tuna. Tuna are just plain, sneaky *liars*." Venus tugged at my sundress and looked up at me worriedly in the pale light of the boat's console. "Hurry, Aunt Molly. I feel . . . I feel *blood* in the water."

I looked from her agonized expression to those of Stella and Isis. They nodded.

I gunned the engine and headed for the marsh at top speed.

∞ ∞ ∞

Orion knocked my ribs to my backbone. 'Twas how bad it hurt, anyway. I fell into the black marsh water and sank to the bottom, dazed and gulping water, then spitting it out and gulping more. Even to a Mer, a mouthful of saltwater is no treat, though our throats are better than Landers' when it comes to shutting off our windpipes. Worse, the saltwater tasted of my own blood. I gagged. I'd have liked nothing better than to rest on the marsh bottoms a few days or so, or at least until the strangling pain eased from my left side.

Up. Get up and out of here, I ordered myself. *Or else Orion will be on you like a piranha.*

Gripping my sword in one fist, I kicked off and shot to the surface. Before I so much as anchored my feet in firm muck of our tiny island battleground, Orion had me by one arm. "McEvers, only a fool would swim back to the surface so quickly," he said.

"Scared you, eh?"

He slung me about twenty paces. I landed on the hummock's opposite end, sinking into the shoreline mud with a splash and a great mashing of marsh grasses.

I felt another rib crack. Fire spread through my right side. Well, at least I was symmetrical now.

"I'm out of patience," Orion said. He advanced on me, his huge hands spread, his claws flexed and ready. "Tell me where to find my daughters, or I'll rip your throat out."

I staggered to my feet and managed a nasty, bleeding smile. He'd cracked my lower lip with an earlier fist. I swung my sword. It caught the underside of his right arm. I felt the blade connect with bone. Blood spurted. He roared but backed away, clamping a hand to the wound. I braced my legs, put both hands around the sword's handle, and held it up in a hacking pose. Starlight glinted off the crimson-stained blade. "I'm out of patience, too," I said, wheezing. "But I'll give you one last chance to turn tail and swim off."

The bastard threw back his big, silver head and smiled at the stars. Then, his eyes black, he headed for me with his teeth bared.

This time would be the end.

◈ ◈ ◈

Molly Martha Oceanwalker, you're lost. I felt like a minnow trapped in the tentacles of an octopus. Swimming through Echo Marsh was like trying to find my way inside a maze of tiny veins full of black blood. I couldn't see, and whatever underwater prowess the average Mer had — meaning their mystical sonar — eluded me. My bum leg kept veering me off-center. I bumped into mushy banks covered with submerged, rotting grass. Small fish and shrimp bumped into *me.* Larger fish slithered by, flicking me with their sharp tail fins. I felt naked in nothing but panties and a bra. The handgun Rhymer had given me, safely encased in a waterproof bag, was a ton of bricks strapped to my waist. I'd left the girls on the boat, bound by their vow to stay put, but I had no guarantee they'd actually do so. What if they followed me and got hurt? I'd promised Rhymer I'd take them away from danger, not bring them back. I wasn't quite terrified, but I was desperate. And lost.

You still think of yourself as separate from the water, a soft, milky voice whispered inside my head. *But, no. Be part of it. Be who you are, and you'll find your way.*

I froze. The most amazing sensation filled me. Warm and ancient, comforting and wise. An image shimmered inside my eyes, not quite clear. *Who's there? Who's speaking?*

I'm part of you. Believe in me. I'm the essence of the waters of the world. So are you.

The internal image shimmered again, then came into soft focus. In my mind's eye, I glimpsed the portrait in Lilith's sunroom. *Melasine.* A legend, an illusion, a kind of angel?

No. She was real. Out there in the deepest waters of memory and myth, she was speaking to me.

Believe in me, she whispered. *Believe in the waters of the world. Believe in yourself.*

I'll try, I whispered back.

Her image faded away but left a pearl of confidence. I quieted my desperate thoughts, relaxed my squint-shut eyelids, and concentrated on a memory of Rhymer's voice in my ear when we made love.

And suddenly the water came alive.

I sensed the shapes around me, like neon outlines inside my mind. Shrimp, fish, oysters burrowed in the muck, crabs clinging to the floating roots of the marsh grass, the grass itself, and the soft breasts of earth, the ripe islands peeking from the tidal waters. I could even feel the vast shape of the continent a few miles away, and the endless ocean behind me, as deep as outer space, filled with canyons and mountains, ancient river beds and vast, lost lakes, surrounding the bones of Mers and Landers among the ruins of cities older than any ordinary historian had ever dreamed possible.

All I have to do to be part of all that, all I have to do to find Rhymer is go with the flow of the water.

I went.

A few minutes later, a tremor led me down a long channel that began to widen. More tremors, like distant miniature earthquakes, jarred the water. I sank deeper beneath the surface, creeping along the muddy bottom, tracking the ripples of each violent vibration. The clash and struggle of bodies. Rhymer and Orion. I was close. Suddenly, a wrenching pain went through my neck. I flailed, sucking down water, gagging. A powerful grip closed around my throat.

I was being strangled.

And so was Rhymer.

∞ ∞ ∞

Orion had beaten me, and we both knew it. He had me by the throat. I was on my back, my ribs broken, gashes draining blood from my shoulder and back, my mouth bleeding. My sword lay in the edge of the water, where he'd slung it. His hand — a huge, thick killer of a hand, webbed and clawed — encircled my throat. Kneeling beside me, he held me down with just that grip. He bent over me, his eyes like the black abyss, his skin gleaming like a dolphin's silver sides in the star light.

"Rhymer McEvers, you brave fool," he growled. His claws pinched the arteries on either side of my neck. With one flex of his fingers, all my blood would gush into the marsh. "Tell me *now*, Rhymer, or die. *Where are my daughters?*"

I'd always thought I'd die in some battle like this, some war, fighting for a good cause. And I'd always understood that the cause, all along, would be those nearest to my heart, from the girl I'd loved decades ago, to my family — Tara, the older sister who'd been my dearest friend — to her web-handed daughters — to Moll. Moll. We had barely had time to find each other, much less find out how to make a life together. Yet I loved the fragile, bookish, warrior of a woman with my last breath. Her and the girls. They would survive, even if I did not.

"My sister's daughters," I rasped to Orion, as his talons dug into my neck, "are safely hidden from you. 'Tis all that matters. So kill me."

He uttered a long, low roar of a sound, deep in his throat. His hand convulsed around my throat. I arched upwards on the sand, grabbing at his hand, fighting to the end.

Abruptly, he released me.

I fell back, coughing, gulping air, tasting my own blood in my throat. I never took my eyes off him. What game was this? He stared down at me, bending lower, looking through the dark night into my eyes. His hand still rested on my throat, but it relaxed. "You passed my test," he whispered. "I only needed to know that you were willing to die for them."

୭ ୭ ୭

Molly Martha Revere, action-thriller heroine. The new me. I burst from the water with Rhymer's gun in my shaking hands. In the dim light I saw a horrible tableau — Orion, a monstrously oversized human figure — lurking over a downed Rhymer.

I pointed the gun. *"Get away from him."* Orion straightened. I could just make out the dark silhouette of his massive head, turning my way. I shook the pistol in a menacing way. Was Rhymer dead? Was I too late? "I mean it. Back away from him, or I'm going to shoot you!"

"You have too much faith to shoot me. Your hope for me outshines your distrust. Or you'd already have fired."

"I *will* shoot if I have to."

"Moll, *no.*" Rhymer's voice, coming from the darkness, hoarse and coughing.

I nearly fell over. "Rhymer?"

"Yes. Do no' shoot. It's not what it seems."

"Rhymer! I don't understand —"

"Molly Revere," Orion intoned. His voice was like the rumble inside some ancient sphinx. He straightened to his full height, a dizzying eight feet, at least. It tilted my head back and made my knees quiver. "You and Rhymer have proven that you'll defend my daughters against all enemies," he said. "That's all I wanted to know."

"What kind of ruse is this? Rhymer?"

Rhymer pushed himself upright, swaying. "Bit of confusion here," Rhymer managed to say. "But I think it's all right, Moll. Do no' shoot."

"Rhymer!" I clambered out of the water's edge and headed for him, demurely (always the prudent librarian type) placing the loaded pistol on the ground. As I limped past Orion I tripped in the churned, boggy soil. He caught me under the elbow with a hand the size of a baseball mitt. I shrank back and stared up at him. With the gallant aplomb of a knight, he held me steady as I slowly knelt beside Rhymer. I wrapped my arms around Rhymer's bloody shoulders as if I could shield him from an eight-foot-tall humanoid with claws. Orion looked down at me with his head tilted, as if I fascinated him. "You're a remarkable person. I mean you no harm, Molly Revere. Nor him, either. He's the uncle of my children."

"You certainly have a strange way of showing your family loyalty!"

"I had to know what the two of you were willing to risk for my daughters' sake. They'll need strong guardians on their side. Guardians who will never stop fighting for them. I'm satisfied that you're both worthy. I'll leave you for now. I've been out of the water and undisguised more than long enough for my tastes."

He turned away.

"Wait," Rhymer rasped. "I have questions—"

"Not now."

Orion pivoted gracefully toward the water, a startling man-shape in the starlight, huge and terrifying and beautiful, silver sheened, blood dripping from the claw tip of one webbed hand. I glimpsed a powerful back and thick, muscled haunches; he was naked except for a thin, leather-like loin cloth of some kind. I saw feet more aquatic than any traditional Mers', impossible to hide inside a human shoe, broad at the toes, webbed. Yet he moved with the power of a being who lived between water and shore. A missing link. He was about to vanish into the water as easily as a dream evaporates.

Two explosions slapped him backwards. Gunshots. They burst in our ears. Rhymer pushed me down and covered me with his body. I screamed and looked wildly toward my pistol, as if it had jumped up and begun firing on its own. Orion staggered, put a hand to his chest, then slowly sank to the sand. "Oh, no," I whispered.

A boat roared up between the marsh grasses, as if gliding on watery ground. Someone turned a light our way. It flooded the island with an intense white glow. "Keep your head down," Rhymer ordered. He lifted his and looked into the light. "Stop your shooting, you bloody idiot! He's no' the threat that we thought he was. Dammit to hell, don't shoot him again!"

After a second, a tart female voice called out, "How was I supposed to know that you and he had . . . had bonded? What is this — some kind of blood-brotherhood ritual? Should we build a campfire for you Boy Scouts and sing a song? Okay, so maybe I made a bad judgment call. So sue me."

"Juna Lee," I hissed. Rhymer shifted enough to let me squirm from beneath him. I squinted into the bright light. On the deck of the boat stood a horrified Tula, a slack-jawed Charley, a scowling, beautiful, chocolate-skinned stranger, a wounded Jordan — who was leaning on the boat's bow rail, pale and frowning — and finally, Juna Lee. She cradled a massive rifle in her hands and gazed at us with pouty chagrin, an *uh-oh* of dismay on her face. The dark-skinned stranger snatched the rifle from Juna Lee's arms and launched into a sinister harangue at her in Spanish. Juna Lee put her hands on her hips and began arguing back in Spanish with a sarcastic Southern accent attached.

Orion groaned.

Rhymer crawled to him. I crept up close beside and reached out, slowly, to place my hand on Orion's arm. It was cold and smooth, the fine silver scales as soft as silk. He opened his eyes. In the center of his chest, two bullet holes gurgled crimson blood. The heart's blood had already flooded his hard silver belly and was pooling in the muscular, concave indentations of his groin. Rhymer pressed his fingers to the wounds. "Steady now. A figure of our imagination can't be this easy to kill."

Orion smiled, showing a glimpse of blood-tinged teeth, his smile so like any man's expression it could break a woman's heart, despite the dual sets of fangs. "Even Swimmers are capable of dying."

"We'll get you onto the boat. There's help to be had—"

"Where would you seek a doctor for a monster who can't possibly exist? Even my ability to create illusions couldn't manage to overcome that."

"I'll think of something."

"No. I've done what I came to do. That's all that matters. I've made sure the girls are safe. I've kept a vow I made to Tara." His voice gurgled with blood. "Listen quickly. Remember this name: Leviathan. He's a Swimmer. The most powerful Swimmer in the world. He and his cabal at UniWorld intend to capture every Mer and Lander who can be of value to their cause. They have already enlisted several Swimmers. It was a Swimmer who drew me away from Tara that day at the UniWorld ship. I fought him, but it was a ruse, a trap. Tara was killed because I was distracted." He paused, struggling for breath, his eyes icy and black. "I killed that Swimmer, but there are others. They want to catch me for Leviathan. *And they want my daughters.*"

"Tell me where to hide the girls," Rhymer whispered. "Where will they be safe?"

Blood bubbled from his lips. "Many places. You'll learn." His eyes began to dim.

"Orion, please try to fight," I said brokenly. "Your daughters need you. They need to meet you."

"They did not need to see . . . the monster . . . who fathered them. Do not let them . . . see . . . my corpse."

His eyes closed. His chest slowed its rhythm. Rhymer cursed and pressed his hands harder on the pulsing bullet wounds. "Come on, you bastard," he said hoarsely. "You did no' come down through all the centuries to die like an ordinary soul. Fight."

"Please don't give up," I echoed, squeezing Orion's arm.

"Move aside and let us see him," a small voice said.

Rhymer and I turned quickly.

Stella, Isis, and Venus stood there, their sundresses plastered to them, their long hair streaming water and bits of grass. I should have known they wouldn't stay on the boat. They stared with horror at the strange and broken figure of the creature — the man — their mother had loved. The man who had been trying, all this time, to ensure their future. Their father.

"Slide back," Rhymer whispered. "Let them have a look at him."

"Yes," I whispered.

We eased out of the way. The three girls never took their eyes off Orion. They inched toward him, holding hands tightly. The movement of his chest was just a flutter, now. They took one last step that put their bare feet close enough to nudge one of his massive arms. Venus lifted one small, trembling foot, then touched it to his skin.

All three girls gasped as if an electric jolt had hit them. It was an invitation, a recognition, a connection. "Papa," Isis whispered. "You're *real*. And you're *good*."

They threw themselves down on him, hugging him, clutching him, burrowing their heads into either side of his neck, murmuring incoherent sounds of fervent joy.

I gripped Rhymer's hand. "Can they save him?"

"I don't know. He's shot in the heart. It may be too late."

We waited with agonizing uncertainty. For several minutes he didn't move. His arms, ending in those massive hands, remained unfurled by his side. But then, suddenly, his hands flexed. Slowly they rose. The deadly arms closed gently around the delicate bodies of his daughters. The girls stroked his face and smiled at him. I could hear them singing inside my mind. The most beautiful, healing symphony. His eyes opened. He took a deep, reviving breath.

And he smiled back.

☙☙☙

All right, so I, Juna Lee Poinfax, shot and nearly killed Orion. *Mea freakin' culpa.* How was I supposed to know he was a good guy hiding behind some secret agenda? Besides, *anybody* who hurt Jordan deserved to be blasted. And anyhow, Orion didn't *die* from the shooting. His daughters rescued him. In the process, they bonded with their big silver daddy like ducklings to a duck. May I point out that him getting plugged by yours truly led directly to a beautiful *Fathers Knows Best* moment? And that, in fact, he *smiled*? Mr. Fangs. He *smiled*.

I mean, give me *some* credit.

Not that anyone noticed. Orion got up, sang something in private to his girls, then dived into the marsh without so much as a thank you. Apparently, Swimmers are loners with a capital *Lone*. After that there was a lot of somber hugging between Molly and the girls, and Molly and Rhymer, and Molly and Tula, and Tula and the girls, and Charley and the girls. Then the little sweeties performed a laying on of hands to heal Rhymer, who looked like shit, and Jordan, who looked like very *handsome* shit. I cried when I touched my hand to the smooth, tanned spot on his side, where several deep gashes had been. I bawled with happiness.

"He's lucky, no thanks to you," Aphrodite jabbed. She was still pissed about me grabbing her rifle. "Oh, sure, *now*, after you nearly ruin everything, you boo-hoo. *Muchacha del idiota.*"

"Shut up. I'm only crying because Healers can't heal an Ann Blegis dress. I'll never get Jordan's bloodstains out."

We were a disheveled, traumatized group, to say the least. Jordan tossed his ripped and bloodied shirt aside then, bare-chested, grabbed me for a long kiss. Rhymer's clothes looked like an ad for a slasher movie, but Molly didn't seem to mind when he swooped her into his arms.

By the way, Molly had turned into some kind of muddy, kick-ass sociopath. Suddenly, she picked up Rhymer's pistol and pointed it at me. I shrieked. Rhymer drolly clamped a hand around the little ingrate's wrist. "Now, Moll, my brave beauty. What's the challenge in battling Juna Lee after you've already proved you can face a Swimmer? Bit of a letdown, hmmm?"

"I'm just going to *wing* her."

Laughing, he took the pistol. I put a fluttering hand to my chest and pretended to swoon in Jordan's arms. Tula rolled her eyes at us all. Charley guffawed, and even Aphrodite smiled. I guess seeing me get threatened by a geeky, gun-waving Ali McBeal was a big treat.

Standing at the edge of the little island, looking out at the dark waters where their daddy had disappeared, Stella,

Isis, and Venus weren't having such a high ol' time. Looking wistful, they kissed their hands and held them out, letting the ocean wind carry their love after Orion.

Transformation

❧ ❧ ❧ ❧ ❧ ❧ ❧ **24** ❧ ❧ ❧ ❧ ❧ ❧ ❧

Aunt Molly, the girls hummed inside my dreams. *Wake up. We have a surprise for you.*

I resisted. The mansion at Sainte's Point felt like a wonderful cocoon, and I didn't want to lose the sensation. My back was warmly snuggled to Rhymer's front, and I liked the weight of his arm draped over me. When we'd returned from Echo Marsh long after midnight we'd crawled, fully dressed, into one of the big downstairs bedsteads, along with the exhausted girls and Heathcliff. Rhymer had put his arms around me, and I'd put my arms around the girls. All piled up together, a family. Juna Lee, Jordan, Tula, Charley, and Aphrodite were asleep elsewhere in the mansion.

The morning sunshine warmed my face. An open window let the ocean breeze curl through the suite. I sighed and tried to drift back into the heady relaxation of sleep. *Aunt Molly, wake up. It's important.*

Rhymer stirred. Something urgent in their voices opened his eyes. He propped himself on an elbow. I could feel him looking from them to me. "Problem, girls?"

"No problem, Uncle Rhymer," Stella said. "We just want Molly to see what we've done. We hope she likes it. If she doesn't, well, we don't know how to change her back to the way she was."

That popped my eyelids open. "Hmmm?" I rose to my elbows, squinting. The huge bed, draped in soft, luxurious white linens, was a cozy mess. The top sheet was wadded under mine and Rhymer's arms. The girls, with Heathcliff beside them, sat cross-legged alongside us, looking at me somberly.

Rhymer pointed a stern finger at his nieces. "What is it you've done to Moll?"

Venus went wide-eyed and covered her mouth. Isis looked at the ceiling. But Stella met my eyes with a serene nod. "Look at your legs, Aunt Molly."

I shoved myself upright and pawed at the sheet. Rhymer helped me push it aside. The wide skirt of my sundress — a ruined, wrinkled accordion of saltwater-crusted linen — was twisted around me from thighs to ankles. My hands shook as I tugged the stiff material up to my knees.

I gave a soft moan of delight and amazement.

I had two perfect, unscarred legs.

And feet with the most beautiful webbed toes.

∞ ∞ ∞

I was whole now. I walked beside Rhymer on the beaches of Sainte's Point without my cane, without limping. I swam beside him in the Atlantic and in Bellemeade Bay the way a man and woman were meant to swim together — as a beautifully matched pair. We made love without any wounds between us. With such a foundation, I could handle any future.

The water was an elixir on my skin. Sainte's Point anchored us with dark, mysterious allure, but there was a wide world waiting beneath the seas. Sometimes, the girls walked with us. "I believe Melasine may have spoken to me in the marsh," I told them.

"Oh, yes, she's nearby," Stella said. "This is her favorite place in all the world. Most of her favorite children — the Bonavendiers — were born here. That's why this is a safe place. She must have known our father wouldn't hurt us. We can feel him near here, with her. Our father. He's very old. Hundreds of years. Mother said he was born of Melasine and an Aztec Lander king."

"I expect you'll get to see him again some day."

Stella just looked at me sweetly and shook her head. "Not for real. Only the picture he wants us to see. But that's all right. Underneath, we'll recognize him."

Rhymer and I were on the beach one day, quietly discussing our plans to set sail and where we would take the girls when a man spoke behind us. "There are other things I need to tell you."

We turned, startled. A tall, black-haired man stood there, barefoot, dressed in loose trousers and a white shirt open down his muscled chest. The tidal breezes barely seemed to touch him; the seagulls quit their petty squawking and landed on the sand around him like pet canaries. Out beyond the surf, more than two-dozen dolphins lifted their bottle-nosed faces from the water and chorused a sweet, whistling hello. The stranger's effect was so potent that Rhymer began to push me behind him for protection. But then we recognized something familiar in the man's dark, endless eyes.

"Orion," Rhymer said.

He nodded. "I prefer my disguises. One of my endless mirages."

"Is this how my sister saw you?"

"At first. I tried to hide behind this image for her sake. But she always saw through me. And loved me, regardless."

I stepped up beside Rhymer. "Your daughters love you, too. They talk about you all the time since that night at the marsh. They've insisted that you were still nearby."

"I'll always be nearby. Just out of sight."

"What would it hurt for you to be a part of their lives? To show yourself to them? You know they aren't afraid of who you really are. And other Mers would accept you, too."

Something hard shimmered in his expression. "No. Swimmers outlive all but their own caste. It's not wise for one of us to love or be loved by other Mers, or Landers. We've learned through hard experience."

"How many other Swimmers do you know?"

"Only two dozen or so exist. We are . . . *aware* of each other."

"And some of them have allied with this Swimmer, Leviathan, who owns UniWorld?"

"Yes. So our own kind and Landers altered to serve Leviathan are already in Leviathan's grasp."

After a chilling second, Rhymer asked quietly, "What do you mean, 'Landers altered to serve Leviathan?'"

"They swim as Mers do; they are controlled underwater, like leashed dogs; if Landers knew what was being done to enslave their own kind, there would be war on Mers beyond imagining. As powerful as our kind is, we could not survive the sheer numbers of a Lander war. Leviathan knows this. He intends to conquer the Lander world through stealth."

"What can we do?"

"Stay free of him for now. Learn what you can. Pick your battles carefully. But above all, keep silent. The more we talk about Leviathan, the easier it is for him to find us. He senses it. Lilith Bonavendier understands his tactics. That's why she is drawing Mers together in more subtle ways, never mentioning her true purpose. She doesn't want Leviathan to suspect. It is a fight of silence and loneliness, of secrecy and unknown allies and enemies. Most Mers don't know or don't say, if they do know. But you can tell by their allegiances. Actions speak."

"What is this all really about?" I asked, stunned.

"Power. Heritage. Vanity. A belief that we have forfeited the world to Landers against our will, and that we should rule that world openly."

"How?"

"Within this century the world's known sources of oil will be depleted. The world as Landers know it will change forever. If Leviathan is successful in controlling the last of the oil — the oil hidden under the deepest oceans — the world will either be our world again, or no one's.

"Tara was trying to protect me from capture. That UniWorld ship was there to find me. Even Mers can't explore the depths as I can. I am valuable. We Swimmers, a small group. Valuable in the coming age. The age of war and water. Of water and oil. Of Mer and Lander. Because there are vast resources beneath the sea, but only Mers can access them. In the coming age, we can control the world as we did in ancient times. That's how Leviathan and his cabal see it."

"Why did you take Tara's body?"

"Leviathan's people intended to dissect it. They use Mer organs for research. They're working on genetic programs to enhance our traits. Whether we want them enhanced or not."

Rhymer's face tightened. "You did the right thing then. Where did you bury my sister?"

"Loch Larken, near your ancestral home. There is a tomb there, in the deepest channel of that ancient lake. A tomb of Mer ancestors so ancient even Leviathan has no knowledge of it. I put her body there. Her tomb is guarded by . . . creatures. They exist, like me, in the darkness of illusion."

I couldn't help myself. "You mean there really is an unknown species in the lochs of Scotland? There really *are* Loch Ness Monsters?"

He smiled thinly. "They prefer to think of themselves as Scotsmen with gills." He looked at Rhymer somberly. "Someday, I'll show you and the girls how to find the tomb. You have my word."

"But for now Moll and I have no choice but to take the girls on the lam?"

"Yes. They can hear the oil moving beneath the ocean floor. They hear the gurgle and hiss of gases, they sense the lava of hidden volcanoes and the flow of underground rivers. That's why Leviathan wants them. They feel wounds in the earth just as they feel wounds in flesh."

"We'll find sanctuaries."

"Go to the farthest islands, the deepest waters. Molly can tell you where it's safe."

I blinked. "Me?"

"Yes. You will know instinctively. You're a Storyteller."

"Well, yes, I write books for children, but—"

"No, you write books that tell of ancient Mer places. You come from a line that carries the ancient memories. You are an oracle, a source. Your imagination is a living map of cities long submerged, of glories and marvels long forgotten. Civilizations that existed long before any of record in the Lander world. The places you consider to be simply fanciful creations, Molly, are actually memories. You are meant to pass along their history."

"The Abyss of Forever? The deep sea Castle of the Mariner Seahorse? The Magical City under the Tides? You're saying the images I have in my mind of those fabulous places are inherited *memories*?"

"Yes. And if you seek their ruins, you will find them. Take my daughters where your Storyteller's memory tells you they will be safe."

"The Magical City under the Tides."

"Yes."

Rhymer said quietly, "Then that's where we'll head. But what of you? Will we see you again?"

"I'll protect my daughters from beneath the water." He looked at us respectfully. "And you two will protect them from above the shore."

He strode past us, toward the surf. I blinked, heard a splash, and he was gone. Vanished.

I released a long, shaky breath. Beside me, Rhymer stood in subdued thought. "Moll, I don't know what lies ahead, but if you come with me and the girls it'll be the end of your life as you've known it."

"No," I answered. "It will be the start of my life as I've *dreamed* it."

His eyes gleamed. He took my outstretched hand.

We and the girls, along with Heathcliff, boarded a handsome sailboat provided by Jordan. After some thought we christened it *Wanderer*. Jordan, Tula, and the loathsome Juna Lee came to the dock at Sainte's Point, to see us off. Tula smiled and cried as she hugged me. I looked positively alluring in a tossed-back white blouse over a black maillot and slim white shorts. I loved gazing at my pretty legs. So did Rhymer. Tula applauded my svelte new appearance. "You're the most beautiful Mer babe in the world," she said.

"Thank you for your friendship." I hugged her back, and whispered in her ear, "Go and find your forgotten man. Make him remember you."

She smiled sadly. "Maybe someday. Miracles are possible. You've proven that."

"Excuse me. Excuse me!" Juna Lee interrupted, exasperated. "I have something to say."

"Please, let me control my excitement," I deadpanned.

She planted herself on the dock with her hands on her hips, gorgeous and arrogant in gauzy gaucho pants and a fruit-colored blouse, which I suspected was some sort of sarcastic gift forced on her by Aphrodite Araiza, who had recently left for home with Charley in tow. Jordan watched

Juna Lee affectionately but with an arched brow.

"First of all, Molly," Juna Lee said, "I applaud your transformation. Why, you're practically *non-boring*."

"Thank you *so* much."

"Admit it. I did you a *favor* by kidnapping you."

"All right, you did. I'm grateful. Thank you."

Juna Lee puffed out her perky chest as she gave Tula and Jordan a queenly look. "See? There! I'm vindicated."

"I forgive you for everything," I went on. "In fact, I'm sending you a goodbye gift. A little something from the Peabody Hotel in Memphis, to commemorate the day you and I met."

"Why, how sweet of you. Do tell. What is it?"

"Oh, you'll see."

Rhymer touched my arm gently. "Time to go, Moll."

I nodded. With the girls clustered around us and Heathcliff seated nobly on the bow like a small feline masthead, we sailed slowly from the cove at Sainte's Point, headed southward. A phalanx of dolphins escorted us. The girls and I cried a little. We were leaving more than just the island behind. We were leaving our old lives. It was a bittersweet victory, but when I met Rhymer's loving gray eyes I smiled. *No regrets, my love.*

None, my love, he echoed quietly.

ༀ ༀ ༀ

Ducks. Real ones. Quacking, pooping, waddling ducks. Molly's parting gift to me turned out to be a dozen damned mallard ducks, just like the quackers who live in the Peabody Hotel's lobby fountain. Jordan and Tula nearly laughed themselves silly. I sputtered for awhile, then shrugged off the insult. After all, I could afford to be magnanimous. I had come out of the whole Orion drama smelling like a rose, in my opinion. Jordan told everyone who would listen about my self-sacrificing heroics. Now, he was my love slave. I could do no wrong in his eyes.

A man in love is forced to admit that mermaids are women the way women are *meant* to be. Not nicey-nice, not prissy-prissy, not consumed with the fear that someone (particularly of the male variety) won't like us, and someone (particularly of the female peer group variety) won't approve of us. Mermaids understand the right of the Feminine to exist on its own terms, not bound up in girdles or squeezed into some grotesque imitation of The Way Men Do Things. And not apologetic in the least.

The enforced niceness of women is all a great scheme to keep us girls clamped up like nervous oysters. All those hidden, dangerous pearls! Lander girls are brainwashed early on to think they have no real power beyond their boobs, butts, and sweetie-pie submissiveness.

Landers, don't even *try* to tell me you're not submissive — yes, you work at an important job, and pay your own bills, and aren't afraid to tweak a male buttock strolling past you at the local fern bar, but you know, deep in your dusty little Lander heart, that the show of independence can't clobber generations of social conditioning.

You *want* to be submissive and devalued. Admit it. It's much more noble and safe that way. You can't float easily because you weigh yourselves down with like-me-please-like-me worries. *Oh, puh-leeze.* Even if you're the nicest little peach in the pie you're eventually going to realize that the Grand Brainwash was primarily intended to control women so they don't run amok doing all the things they naturally want to do. Since they're not encouraged to do much besides be pleasant and attractive, they're just waiting for some hairy masculine hand to clamp them into a marriage contract for baby-making.

News flash: Being nice and sweet and pleasant and demure and polite and go-along-get-along cooperative is not going to stop the fact that you'll eventually stop being that cute little kitten everyone wants to adopt. Whether you like it or not, you'll turn into a grown cat, and then either you'll the use claws Mother Nature gave you to make the world respect you or you'll sit around in a furry little Lander-cat puddle of your own niceness, getting your tail stepped upon but only whispering *meow, oh, meowowow*, in response, because God forbid you offend anyone or demand to be noticed.

You poor cat-fish.

Thus, I am thrilled to be your role model for change. Please pay no attention to the following scene. It in no way compromises my lecture on not compromising your values in order to please men.

Jordan and I lounged next to his pool at Hilton Head. The ducks quacked contentedly as they paddled around the pool's faux-mountain setting. Maybe they thought they'd escaped to a summer resort in Aspen. I draped a lazy hand over Jordan's naked body. "What's all this nutty talk about UniWorld trying to become the evil empire? I own several million dollars' worth of UniWorld stock. It's solid. I'm not selling."

Jordan grunted. "Don't worry about it. Just stick with me."

"How condescending. Don't worry my pretty little head?"

He trailed a hand down my bare stomach. "Or other parts."

I grumbled. "Don't change the subject. Now, listen, be sensible — world crises, secret plots, hidden undersea oil reserves, conspiracies — you've spent far too much time reading conspiracy theories on the Internet. And watching Nostradamus specials on the *Discovery Channel*. I want you to stop filling *your* pretty little head with all those quirky ideas."

"My sweet, darling, annoying periwinkle."

"Periwinkle?"

"Hiding in the sand."

"You seriously believe all that mumbo jumbo about UniWorld trying to enslave us all?"

"Yes. And so does Lilith. Lilith knows it's time to pull our kind together. That's why she's searching out the Floaters. Spreading the word. Why she didn't object to your diary. She knows battles are coming. So does Riyad. He has connections in the oil world who tell him everything. There's going to be trouble in the years to come, and Mers will be at the center of it."

"So what to do we do right now? Besides drink a stiff tonic and vodka and try not to panic?"

"Well, first, we . . . merge our talents. We . . . merge our interests. We merge our strengths."

I leaned toward him, cleavage to the forefront, chin up, lips slightly parted. My heart fluttered like a hyperventilating romance heroine hoping for a ripped bodice. "Mergers are for CEOs. How boring."

"Agreed. Let's put it in terms you can wrap your little finger around. *We get married.*"

Rip. There went the first button on my inner bodice. I sat up on my lounge chair, fanning myself lightly, eyes narrowing to slits, voice dropping to a soulful drawl. "Why, that is the most *preposterous* idea I've ever heard. Presented with no more aplomb or charm than a request for sliced salmon at the deli. Certainly you're just teasing little ol' me, because a gentleman would never, *nevah*, pledge his troth in such a base manner."

Jordan got up lazily. He arched one brow. He placed one hand over his bare heart. Then he dropped to one knee and wrestled my fanning hand into his. "My darling Juna Lee," he said in a sardonic, syrupy accent, "you have given my very life meaning beyond all hope of hopes, beyond all deserving. Please look down upon my crude, simple, but heartfelt plea for mercy. Please, please my darling, make me the happiest man in the world. Honor me, my darling. My darling Juna Lee, will you marry me?"

"Now *that's* a marriage proposal. I'll think about it and get back to you—"

He pulled me to my feet, then swooped me over one shoulder and slapped me on the bare ass. "I'll take that as a *Yes*," he growled.

"Yes," I said, upside down.

He dumped us both in the pool, scattering ducks everywhere. We wrapped ourselves up in each other and stayed under so long that the mallards stuck their heads underwater to stare.

I've got Jordan just where I want him, I told them. *Inside me.*

Not So Fast . . .

〰 〰 〰 〰 〰 〰 〰 **25** 〰 〰 〰 〰 〰 〰 〰

Dear Diary:

Just when I thought I was free, I'm being thrown back in the clink. I got this note from Lilith today. She's back at Sainte's Point. Just read this, and you'll feel sorry for me:

My dear Juna Lee,

No, you have *not been* cleared of all charges by the Council. You *kidnapped* Molly Revere. You *shot* Orion. Even though you had the best intentions at the time, your impulsiveness once again makes you less than a solid citizen, in the eyes of the Council. Thus, you're still on probation, and I'm still your probation officer. So I have another job for you to do regarding your community service. Since you've demonstrated a certain, ahem, talent as a guidance counselor for your fellow Mers, I'm assigning you to do a makeover on a Peacekeeper who needs to fit discreetly into Southern society.

She'll arrive in Charleston from Brooklyn, New York, in late summer. She's been assigned as an undercover bodyguard to one of the coast's most important Mers, whose name you would recognize if I mentioned it, which I don't intend to do outside the privacy of a face-to-face meeting with you. In today's world, discretion cannot be overemphasized.

Suffice to say, this man is no helpless choir boy, and he is *not* happy to be assigned a babysitter.

Since you'll be spending considerable time on this case in Charleston, you might want to take up residence in the old Poinfax mansion again. You should consider blocking off that storm drain in the backyard. Yes, I know you see it as a quick portal to the ocean, but it's also a quick portal *from* the ocean to your back door. Trust me, given the nature of the Peacekeeper you'll be meeting, and the enemies she's dealing with, you may not want to encourage strangers to pop up among your azaleas.

Call the island and schedule a meeting with me soon. We'll go over the details. Oh, and bring back the sapphire necklace you borrowed from your Great-Aunt Mara's collection while we were on the cruise. If you don't, Mara has spoken to Aphrodite Araiza about having your fingers broken.

Love, Lilith

I sighed at my continuing servitude, then typed in return:

All right. I'll do my duty. Don't worry about me. As long as I have credit cards and a makeup kit, I can handle anything.

∞ ∞ ∞

Dear Diary:

I'm off to Charleston with Jordan by my side, to see what the ocean burps up. A tough New York Mer cop, trying to fit into Charleston society as a Southern belle while doing kick-ass undercover work as a bodyguard for a Mer VIP who qualifies as King of the Untamed Horndogs? Oh, please. Just wait until I get my French-tipped nails into *that* messy pile of pearls.

It'll be so much *fun.*

POPULI AQUARUM

An Appendum of Facts & Fables Regarding the Mer People

Sanctioned for release by the World Council, this date.

Visit the Council's official website,
courtesy of W ebmistress Juna Lee Poinfax:

<u>www.deborahsmith-mermaids.com</u>

Beyond The Ordinary Shore, or Whatever

Interesting facts and
snarky pseudo-scientific gossip about Mers

by Juna Lee Poinfax

Okay, Mer afficianados, listen up:

The three primary oceans — Pacific, Atlantic, and Indian, combined with their junior buds such as the Mediterranean, Arctic, Antartic oceans, and others, aka Oceanus to Mers, cover 70 percent of the Earth's surface and fill the vast majority of the globe's spherical surface volume. In other words, land-based critters are like the Hindu cashier in the corner convenience store outside Shreveport. Not exactly a majority, you dig? Over 90 percent of the planet's recorded species live in Oceanus. Only about one percent of this vast World Ocean has been mapped and explored by human eyes.

Well, by Lander eyes, at any rate. Mers can tell you things about the Deep that would curl your butt hairs. Just consider the possibilities that things you never suspected can exist out yonder in the briny deep. The average ocean depth worldwide is two miles. The deepest known ocean depth on Earth is a canyon in the Mariana Trench, Pacific Ocean, near Guam, where the ocean floor is over seven miles below the surface. If you sank Mount Everest into the Mariana Trench, the Trench would pat it on the head and say, "What a cute little hill."

It is estimated by Lander scientists that vast numbers of unknown marine species are yet to be discovered in the oceans. An understatement. Landers don't even know they're not the only kind of humans on the planet.

The average Lander can only hold his/her breath underwater for a few minutes; Mers can remain submerged for a minimum of an hour. How do Mers do this? Various physiological processes are involved, but in lay terms, it boils down to this: just like whales and other marine mammals, Mers hoard oxygen. Mers are the Federal Reserve of oxygen bankers. We also conserve heat and take to cold temps like a, well, a fish to water. Cross-section our subcutaneous fat and you'll find a layer of cellulite so dense not even a bulimic sorority girl could puke it out of her system. We are *insulated*, baby. As long as the water's not frozen, we're happy and chillin'.

Mer people can't really exist. It's genetically impossible, you say? Oh right, Darwin breath. Considering the huge gaps in scientific documentation of humanoid stepping stones in the staircase of homo sapiens, and the sparse theories based on bits and pieces of primate and hominid fossils scattered over thousands of years, for all Landers know they could have ancient cousins who are bunny-eared mutant *rabbit* people. Alternative theories abound about the possibilities of semi-aquatic homo sapiens (casually described under the pseudo scientific name, home aquaticus.) So why haven't archaeologists found evidence of a single web-toed aquatic humanoid? *Because the evidence is all underwater.* Like, duh.

Using compressed air (scuba tanks) Landers can only descend at most 500 feet below the surface (and that's stretching it). After about a hundred feet most Lander scuba divers go into a rapturous death trance because their blood gases are in deep sea-doo. Mers, on the other flipper, often comfortably explore the waters at depths of a half mile or more, with the record being set by British Mer Sir Phineas Argo Bonswith, who dived down at least 5,000 feet in the icy North Atlantic to retrieve a fumbled champagne bottle on a dare. When he surfaced, triumphant, his luxury ride, the R.M.S. Titantic, had sailed on without him. Sir Bonswith disgustedly swam back to England. In 2003 his daughter, Lady Penelope Bonswith Sirgade, sold the empty champagne bottle on eBay to a Mer collector for 30,000 dollars.

Why can't Mers fly in airplanes easily — i.e. what's the deal with Mer altitude sickness? It's all about handling the pressure, baby. Oh, not the pressure of picking out the perfect Jimmy Wongo slingbacks to match a new summer frock — that's a given, natch, but *air* pressure, you know (yawn-from-lack-of-oxygen). Landers get the bends when they dive too deep below sea level. Mers, who could happily survive in a (well-decorated) cave at the ass-bottom of the briny deep, get their own version of the bends when forced into the skies. I mean, if God had meant for Mers to fly he'd have given us webbed armpits instead of toes, right? Anyway, put us in your average commercial jet and we'll be lying in the aisle moaning. Not just because the airline's showing yet another Jennifer Lopez movie, but because every joint in our body hurts and we want to upchuck our dinner lobster into the nearest carry-on tote.

Mers who insist on flying do so in specially pressurized jets. Put a Lander on such an aeronautical high-pressure ride and he'd curl up in a gasping, fetal ball. Like my reaction to an Emenem CD. Excruciating.

So what's the deal with this "psychic illusion" card trick by which Landers only see whatever Mers tell them to see? Look, it's simple: Landers are gullible. Evidence: they believe celebrities are innocent and politicians are honest. Let Simon Cowell (a Mer on his father's side), tell them a scrawny nobody who sings like one of the Bee Gees on helium deserves to be the next American Idol and they'll believe it. Tell them the A tickets at Disney World are worth the price and they'll believe it. Tell them electronic voting machines can't possibly jerry-rig elections faster than a Haitian poll officer with a pack of number two pencils and they'll believe it.

Landers: Gullible with a capital Gull.

Famous Mers. Now, look, if I *out* every major Mer singer, actor, aristocrat, politician, and business tycoon in the world, the Council will fine me for blabbing and, worse, Elton John will never invite me to another of his Tinseltown Oscar bashes again. But I *can* name-drop a *few* names. I'm not saying the following were or currently are hiding a set of webbed toes, I'm just, hmmm, saying that they, hmmm, *could* be. That is, they fit the typical Mer profile: gorgeous, rich, talented, charismatic, etc. If you believe some celebrities are *born* able to tread water even in a hurricane, doesn't it explain a lot?

Jacqueline Kennedy Onassis, Barbara Streisand, Grace Kelly, Katherine Hepburn, Cary Grant, Rock Hudson, Clark Gable, Gwynneth Paltrow, Paris Hilton, Oprah Winfrey, Steven Spielberg, Bill Gates, Tyra Banks, Diana Ross, Beyonce, Puff Daddy, Keanu Reeves, Princess Diana, Amelia Earhart, Tiger Woods, Merlin (of King Arthur fame), Cleopatra, Shakespeare, and the entire cast of that 1960s fave TV show of Mer kids everywhere: Flipper.

I could name dozens more. But not without a Mer lawyer to fend off the complaints.

Science versus Mythology; Facts of Ancient Mer History

by Acarathena Bonavendier, PhD
Founder, Archaeological Research Consortium (ARC)
Mobile, Alabama

Like my elder cousin (and, in the spirit of disclosure, ARC's largest financial donor) Lilith Bonavendier, I fully support the idea that Mers and Landers share extensive genetic, sociological, cultural, and historical roots, in essence, being separate branches off the same family tree. However, unlike (but with all due respect to) Lilith, I prefer hard science to fanciful mythology when it comes to the ancient origins of Mer culture. Fables of Atlantis-like kingdoms, of half-human, fish-tailed beings, et cetera, are simply that: fables. Without going into volumes of detail about the artifacts and fossils gathered by Mer scientists for hundreds of years, I will sum up the indisputable conclusions briefly:

Mers and Landers diverged from a common ancestor at least six million years ago. Mer scientists excavating submerged sites off the coast of Africa in the late 1970s recovered the bones of numerous aquatic hominids, known in the research vernacular as "aquatic apes" (i.e. chimp-like head and torso, broadly splayed feet with fossil imprints of webbed toes).

According to Lander archaeologists and ancient Lander historians, Sumeria was the site of the first advanced human civilization, existing 6,000 years ago on the coast of modern-day Iraq. Yet Sumerian mythology speaks of earlier civilizations that predate that time by thousands of years and insists that half-man, half-fish "gods" came out of the ocean after a catastrophic worldwide flood that wiped out most of mankind (i.e. Landers). According to Sumerian texts, these gods were mentors and teachers from the lost cities. They restored civilization.

Yet Landers insist that no evidence of pre-Sumerian civilization exists. Why haven't Lander researchers found such evidence? Because it is now hidden on the ocean floor.

Without dispute, all scientists, both Mer and Landers, agree that the last ice age ended approximately 15,000 to 20,000 years ago. At that time, the melting of the glaciers raised ocean levels worldwide. It is accepted fact that the modern day Persian Gulf was once a vast, fertile plain fed by the Tigris and Euphrates rivers. According to Sumerian legend, this veritable real-life paradise was home to an advanced civilization with numerous great cities along the ancient Mesopotamian coast.

Until the waters rose.

Geological evidence indicates that while this gradual flooding of each section of the continental coastlines worldwide, occurred over thousands of years, research also indicates that turbulent climatic changes also may have caused sudden, catastrophic increases in ocean level. In league with evidence of massive volcano eruptions, such as those suspected in the ancient Greek islands, one can easily picture shocking floods and enormous, deadly tsunamis. Indeed, since virtually every ancient culture on Earth — on every continent — includes legends of a "great flood" that destroyed most of mankind, it is accurate to believe that such legends date to specific, real, cataclysmic events associated with glacier melting.

How does this prove that Mer civilizations pre-date all known Lander civilizations, or at the very least, openly co-existed alongside Lander civilizations at one time?

The lost cities have been found.

While a few Lander scientists and curious sport divers have long reported finding mysterious, megalithic ruins in waters off the coasts of the world, their contention that those ruins represent human civilizations lost to glacier flooding, therefore pre-dating the earliest known civilizations by 10,000 years or more, have been laughed off by mainstream Lander archaeologists as bizarre conjecture.

Mer scientists, however, are under no such narrow presumptions. Working in deep waters, guided by ancient Mer texts, Mer researchers have gathered a treasure trove of extraordinary fossils, artifacts, and engraved writings from Mer and/or Lander civilizations at more than thirty major sites worldwide.

How then, if Mers once ruled empires of both Mer and Lander, may we explain the current state of affairs — i.e. that the end of the last ice age began a swift period of decline in Mer influence and population, so that our entire branch of the human race dwindled to a tiny, elite minority lost to legend and cloaked in secrecy?

Sadly, it has taken until recent decades for science to develop the tools that could answer that question definitively — i.e. the combination of forensics and genetic testing that have identified heretofore unsuspected clues.

Unfortunately, at this point in time, due to investigations and allegations being pursued by the Council in regards to the UniWorld situation, I'm constrained from elaborating on the details of those clues.

The Legend Of Water People

Excerpted From Fables of the Water People

Compiled and Edited by Lilith Bonavendier

In some ancient time of great honor and noble deeds, some millenium thousands of years before our own — once upon a time, as they say in fairytales — Melasine and the other Old Ones, male and female, ruled a great empire of extraordinary beings such as themselves, wholly human but also wholly aquatic.

Whether this mythical empire existed in the blue waters of the Aegean, as is usually coined by fervent fans of the Atlantis legends, or in some totally unconsidered ocean realm, is unknown. Certain scientists among our kind have quietly removed incredible statues of the Old Ones from sunken ports in every ancient coastal city of the world.

Their findings suggest that an amazing civilization existed long before the first Greeks erected temples to sea gods and goddesses. It is quite likely the fabulous worlds of Melasine and her kind had been in ruins for millennia when Neptune began paddling around Grecian male fantasies with his nubile nymphs and phallic trident.

Water is life, water is love, water is the womb. All the great religions believe so. Water People say the earth formed as an afterthought inside the glorious depths of great seas, hardening like the dull, dry pit of a luscious fruit. At the risk of insulting those Water People who believe Landers cannot possibly share our legacy, I must point out that if the sea is the mother of us all, then we must all be, at heart, both Water People and Land People. Do not all children float first in the womb as female beings? Thus all men begin in fluid, as women. Similarly, all Landers began as Water People. And all Water People began as the Old Ones.

Mermaids.

I rarely use that cartoonish term, but it does prove convenient for first impressions. Whether fact or fancy, the portrait of Melasine at Sainte's Point indicates she is far more surreal and complex than a simple, popular name can surmise. I have no doubt she exists — an ancient, ageless, female being, isolated and reclusive, lonely and yet seductive.

When Melasine and the others like her — both male and female — were young, they called themselves Tamerians, after their greatest city. The Tamerians openly ruled the coasts of the ancient world, creating amazing palaces in the waters, traveling across land via rivers and inlets and fantastically engineered channels which connected the great seas and freshwater lakes. Landers — pathetic, two-legged, short-lived humans — were deemed inferior and treated as servants or were driven to the wild interiors of the continents, where their shuffling, land-trapped ways could be ignored by the elegant and handsomely finned Tamerians.

Ta-Mera was built more in the water than on the land, with submerged temples and fluid passageways, fine promontories of marble for sunning in the warm air, and broad canals of the most beautiful stonework, allowing Melasine and her kind to travel throughout their empire without ever leaving the water. (Dear Readers: You might want to look for an article from the magazine *Strange Science*, circa May of 1997, titled "The Mysterious Lost Alleys of the Ancient Coasts." It's inaccurate but fascinating, especially to those of us who know why those "alleys" truly existed.) The Tamerians were a far older race than the plodding Landers. They considered themselves a far more brilliant kind, far more talented, far more *evolved*.

There is always a "pride goeth before the fall" theme in mythology, and the Ta-Mera story may be just such an instructional tale. Perhaps the Tamerians abused their hold over the Landers, treating them as a lesser tributary of the familial sea, and the Landers finally rebelled. Or the Tamerians worshiped inconstant gods who smote them for frivolous injustices. Or they were doomed by the ordinary afflictions of both Land and Water Kind — greed, envy, lust, and jealousy.

Whatever the curse that descended upon them, it inspired all the great fables of the world since. Is it not true that in the storytelling traditions of every major culture we find tales of unthinkable disasters, which cleansed the world and restored order? Of course, among Water People these tales have a certain irony. For example, in our version of Noah's Ark, the world was destroyed by a great drought.

Be that as it may, some terrible cataclysm abruptly destroyed Ta-Mera and the vast empire it anchored, along with all the Landers — except three young men — and the Tamerians — except Melasine and two others — young mermaids named Acarinth and Leirdrela.

In some accounts the three surviving Landers are described by Water People as barbaric and low (typical Landers, some insist) and are assigned names commiserate with such an unpleasant portrayal. A web-footed priest writing in fourteenth century England named the Landers Gumaldin, Fray Daval, and Altenhop — names from the classic storytellers' lexicon of bumbling demons and clownish villains.

Even modern Water People coax their children to sleep with disparaging comic tales about the three Landers. In many bedtime stories the trio become drooling lechers named Squat, Frag, and Goop, and children are assured that our finned foremothers nobly consorted with them only for purposes of repopulating the ocean with Water People.

Most Water People, however, prefer a more romantic and sympathetic image of the three legendary Landers — who are, after all, our mythological ancestors. They call the threesome by handsome names that were assigned to them in a classic eighteenth century narrative written by a Bonavendier relative, the infamous Victorian singer and poetess Emilene Merrimac Revere (Molly's great-grandmother), of Boston, Massachusetts. To quote a verse:

> Stalwart and true, by Ta-Mera's princesses enslaved
>
> Devoted lovers, bound to earth yet fulfilled in water,
>
> We shall whisper their mortal names on shores kissed by eternal tides,
>
> And forget them not in fluid rhyme:
>
> *Beckrith, Padrian, and Salasime.*

Beckrith, Padrian, and Salasime. The mates of the three Tamerians and the mythological founding fathers of all Water People. They were pureblooded, two-legged, ordinary Landers. After the great cataclysm nothing was left of either Land People or Water People except those three gentlemen and our three ladies. A classic dilemma.

Even if you were the only man left on Earth . . .

Melasine, Acarinth, and Leirdrela fell in love with the men. The Tamerians were not yet creatures of determined solitude. That came later, during centuries of loneliness and loss. But after many years their devoted Landers died, and also their halfling children and grandchildren and great-grandchildren — all mortal.

As the centuries passed, every lover and every child left them. The three Tamerians realized it would always be so. Thus they began to harden their hearts against Landers and even halflings, to stay alone, until some rare man lures them into love again or some descendent earns their sympathy.

So they cannot resist loving us. In their souls they cherish their mingled descendents, neither Lander nor Tamerian, neither earth nor water, but the best of both.

And that is a truth I believe.

◆◆◆

Popular modern myths say Melasine, Acarinth, and Leirdrela continue to take lovers among the men of the earth and to birth new generations of extraordinary descendents. The more pragmatic among Water People insist that no such finned ancestors ever existed and certainly don't exist now, and that variations in our skills and physiology are mere vagaries, easily explained by random intermingling among our kind. (Dear Readers: I will not get into any wilder claims here, but do please read my addendum about clans.)

Many Water People claim (as, in fact, we Bonavendiers do) to be only a few generations removed from either Melasine, Acarinth, or Leirdrela. We engage in endless debates over reported sightings and encounters with the three. A certain snobbery demands that one not only claim a member of the trio as near kin but also show proof that the link actually exists.

That proof is always suspect, however. The portrait of Melasine at Sainte's Point has generated spirited controversy among Water People for two hundred years. Some fervently accuse us of fraud. Did she actually pose for the artist, or was her image merely conjured up by social climbing eighteenth century Bonavendiers? I assure you, dear readers, she posed.

Regardless, let us all be proud of whatever talents we have inherited, however and whenever, at every level of clan and kinship. I fully admit that my native Southern fascination with family history is as strong as my devotion to my kind. And thus I am calling, as I said to begin with, for pride and unity.

I do believe in legends.

And I do believe, Dear Readers, that we are all One People, separated only by fluid degrees.

Land People fight and struggle and yearn to find magic in their lives. Water People hide behind that magic but realize the loneliness of it. As for Bonavendiers, add to our psyche the spoiled attitudes of a silver-spoon upbringing in the deep, coastal South, and you have that most dangerous of all combinations (and here I stoop to use two common stereotypes).

Southern belles who are also mermaids.

Gilding the magnolia, to say the least.

Now you know.

Clans of the Water People

Introduction

As I have already stated, both Land and Water People are descended from three couples in ancient mythology: Melasine and Beckrith, Acarinth and Padrian, Leirdrela and Salasime. Most of the world's Lander population is so far removed from those origins that they have no hint of the fabulous traits left in them. But because Melasine, Acarinth, and Leirdrela still exist, still occasionally fall in love with men, and still bear children, we Water People are only a few generations removed from their original ancestry, and our talents are strong.

A more scientific explanation? Historically, some clans of Water People have shunned Landers and intermarried only with other Water People, thus re-enforcing certain special traits. Some of our kind are even so strong in bloodline that very, very amazing talents are reported. Most such reports are suspect and very hard to believe, however.

The terms I've listed below to categorize our clans are, at best, fluid and capricious, often leading to prejudices and foolish judgments among Water People, who can be quite smug. As I said earlier, we Bonavendiers are Singers. One of the more highly evolved clans.

But enough discussion or I shall digress into vanities. Here, in simple terms, are our clans and their most basic descriptions, in descending order.

Clan Designations

The Old Ones

Melasine, Acarinth, and Leirdrela. Our real or imagined half-human, half-aquatic progenitors, also known as the Tamerians, who, according to legend, mated with three Landers after the ruin of Ta-Mera. They have continued to mate with men in all the centuries since. They are assumed to be immortal and extremely reclusive, yet also extremely seductive. No absolute proof of their existence has ever been produced.

Swimmers

Swimmers are either first-generation halflings (the immediate descendents of a Tamerian mermaid and a Lander), or simply Water People of extraordinary and rare abilities. Claims of encounters and matings between Swimmers and other Mers abound, but may simply be a fanciful way to cover up reckless romances or to further gild the reputations of children with unusual abilities. Example: A pregnant woman with no husband may insist she was seduced by a Swimmer — who, of course, left the scene immediately afterward. Swimmers are variously described as predatory, irresistible, incorrigible loners, and terrifyingly possessive shapeshifters. They cannot or will not live among either Landers or Mers.

Swimmers are said to be acutely psychic (much more than other Mers) and possess extraordinary powers in the use of sonar and sonic vibration, which can be used as a weapon. Their lifespans are impossible to calculate, but according to anecdote and speculation they may live for hundreds of years.

Healers

Healers are a small population among us. Some are born with lightly webbed hands as well as feet and other unusual physical traits, which makes them avoid Lander society, but nonetheless they tend to be moderate souls, and, as their caste name suggests, they exhibit a marked talent for healing others. Some scientists among the Mers believe their healing abilities are related to our prevalent talent for sonar and sonic vibration, which has been shown to have a marked effect on cellular regeneration.

One might say that if Swimmers represent the dark side of Mer-dom, then Healers are the light.

Singers

Singers represent the largest caste of Mers and are by far the most successful at coexisting in the Lander world. Singers are categorized by webbed feet, remarkable swimming abilities, and an average lifespan of ninety to one-hundred-ten years, among other traits. Our prevailing talent is indicated by our clan name: we are psychic "singers," with the ability to lure, enthrall, and communicate in wordless vibratros of emotion. Virtually all of us also have extraordinary singing voices in the more conventional sense of "singing." In fact, a notable percentage of the world's popular singers and operatic stars are Mers.

Good manners and common sense prevent me, unlike Juna Lee Poinfax, from naming celebrity names.

Floaters

Many of you, dear readers, are Floaters, though you don't know it and probably think of yourself as just a Lander. Your Mer ancestry is hidden at least a few generations past, and your feet, I'm sorry to say, are indeed the feet of a plain

Lander. But you have a marked love for the waters of the world, whether fresh or salt, and you can often be found on some sunny coast or shady lakeside. You may be a sea captain or an oceanographer, or simply a land-bound devotee of the water. Regardless, you revel in fluid whimsy and daydreams, you are drawn to the great marine mammals and the colorful fish, and you are quite elegant in style, in purpose, and in thought. You sense something different about yourself, something that sets you apart from the Landers — an urge, perhaps, to take a long ocean voyage and settle in some exotic cove, or to swim beneath the surface of life's illusions and breathe against all odds.

I firmly believe that most of the great sailors and ocean adventurers of the world are, at the very least, Floaters.

Landers

Land people. They make up the vast bulk of the earth's population, good and decent and special in their own way, yet so far removed from their glorious beginnings in the seas that they fear the water and try to conquer it. They are to be treated kindly and welcomed into our midst and, dare I insist, respected for their love of the earth, no matter how stubborn they are in their dominance. I intend to reform them.

There is no more to say about them than that.

A Primer Of Mer Wisdom and Quotations

by Lilith Bonavendier

The more pragmatic among Water People insist that no finned ancestors ever existed and certainly don't exist now, and that variations in our skills and physiology are mere vagaries, easily explained by random intermingling among our kind. I will not get into any wilder claims, here.

∞ ∞ ∞

They say there are tragic water spirits who sing to passing boatmen. Yet as anyone who has heard one of us singing can tell you, there is nothing tragic about the music of the water. It is the singing, not the silence, that matters.

∞ ∞ ∞

Almost all the stories of Water People are preposterous and insulting. They say we lure people into the sea and steal their souls. What a terrible stereotype. Our souls are in the water, not theirs.

∞ ∞ ∞

It is quite likely the fabulous worlds of Melasine and her kind had been in ruins for millennia when Neptune began paddling around Grecian male fantasies with his nubile nymphs and phallic trident.

∞ ∞ ∞

To sing is to charm the soul with illicit lures, said the churchmen of old. And so the songs of Water People, male and female, were designated a form of witchcraft. How sad, to turn love into darkness.

≈ ≈ ≈

Stalwart and true, by Ta-Mera's princesses enslaved
Devoted lovers, bound to earth yet fulfilled in water,
We shall whisper their mortal names on shores
Kissed by eternal tides,
And forget them not in fluid rhyme:
Beckrith, Padrian, and Salasime.

Ode To Mermaids And Men
Emilene Merrimac Revere
Victorian poetess and singer

≈ ≈ ≈

At the risk of insulting those Water People who believe Landers cannot possibly share our legacy, I must point out that if the sea is the mother of us all, then we must all be, at heart, both Water People and Land People.

≈ ≈ ≈

The fantastic abilities of Water People are rooted in the physical laws of nature, not fairytales. I say that quite seriously.

≈ ≈ ≈

Land People fight and struggle and yearn to find magic in their lives. Water People hide behind that magic but realize the loneliness of it.

❧ ❧ ❧

Some Water People use the word *halfling* as a slur when someone exhibits Lander-like traits. That usage, however, is generally considered both inaccurate and ill-mannered.

❧ ❧ ❧

The Celts called him the Waterman and said he was once a sea-god named Dewi. In Christian times, he became Saint David. By any name, he was reported to be irresistible when playing the harp and singing. No doubt, since he was one of us.

❧ ❧ ❧

A notable percentage of the world's popular singers and operatic stars are Water People. Good manners and common sense prevent me, of course, from naming celebrity names.

❧ ❧ ❧

The world is a very narrow stream for most people. They never realize how many other streams flow to the same ocean.

❧ ❧ ❧

Often we read the hoary old tale of dangerous sirens luring ships to their doom and men to damnation: The Cyrenes of Homer's *Odysseus*, beckoning ordinary men and their possessions. The truth, dear readers, is far more sentimental; our kind tends to rescue hapless travelers and take only a small commission in return. It is the travelers who steal from *us*.

∽∽∽

As for Bonavendiers, add to our psyche the spoiled attitudes of a silver-spoon upbringing in the deep, coastal South, and you have that most dangerous of all combinations (and here I stoop to use two common stereotypes.) Southern Belles who are also mermaids. Gilding the magnolia, to say the least.

∽∽∽

The term "mermaid" is literally translated as "virgin of the sea." And thus I have never considered that popular term a particularly apt or complimentary name for our kind. To celebrate the water is to celebrate the consummation between water and earth, female and male. To have never experienced that unity is to be half-lived.

∽∽∽

In our version of Noah's Ark, the world was destroyed by a great drought.

∽∽∽

The Nagas of India were matriarchal tribes named for the mythological serpent children of the Goddess Kadru. They were said to host fantastic undersea mansions and keep mystic books of wisdom and in return, the goddess granted them long lives. What a beautiful story. All true.

∽∽∽

Water People say the earth formed as an afterthought inside the glorious depths of great seas, hardening like the dull, dry pit of a luscious fruit.

THE WATER HYACINTH SERIES

BY M. M. REVERE

(Available only at Finsters' Books, somewhere under the sea)

Book 1 — *Hyacinth and the Mermaid's Torch*
Book 2 — *Hyacinth and the Temple of Neptune*
Book 3 — *Hyacinth and the Curse of Poseidon*
Book 4 — *Hyacinth and the Siren's Ghost*
Book 5 — *Hyacinth and the Cave of the Argonauts**

*Currently unfinished. This book's completion date is uncertain, since Molly's writing schedule has been interrupted by recent events. She's now traveling to unspecified locales with Rhymer and the girls. But Molly does expect to finish the book as soon as possible and will send it immediately to her publisher in New York.

ABOUT THE WATER HYACINTH SERIES

In a shameless homage to the success of the Harry Potter series, the *Water Hyacinth* series by M.M. Revere features some basic similarities to the J.K. Rowling novels: a lonely child, unaware that he/she is special, discovers a separate world of magic and adventure, complete with loyal friends, strange and wondrous pets, lovable mentors, and evil villains.

But in other respects, *Water Hyacinth* is very much unique.

Introduced in the series' blockbuster first installment, *Hyacinth and the Mermaid's Torch*, twelve-year-old Hyacinth Meridian, who has never known her parents, lives a lonely, shy life at a drab orphanage in Victorian-era Boston, Massa-chusetts, until a magical pendant lures her to the harbor docks, where she's benignly "kidnapped" by dolphins.

The dolphins take her to the fantastic undersea world of Finsters Academy, a school for elite mer children. The lov-ably irascible headmistress, Artemisia Coral, explains that Hyacinth is the lost princess of "a small sea kingdom" and that she was hidden for her own protection in the world of "dry people" as a baby, after her parents mysteriously disap-peared in the sinister Disappearing Sea.

But now she's been found, and it's time for her to learn all the magic — and responsibilities — of a well-schooled Mer princess. Including the spoken charm that transforms scruffy, two-legged Hyacinth into a beautiful twelve-year-old mermaid (and back again, when she wants.)

Thus Hyacinth embarks on a fantastic adventure of dis-covery, making friends such as Barnabus T. Tradvorius, adopt-ing a pet stingray she names Tickle, and yet also coming to realize that the dark forces behind her parents' disappear-ance may also be lurking in the abyss, waiting to capture her.

The plots of the books that follow expand on the mys-tery of Hyacinth's parents and put Hyacinth face-to-face with a growing list of villains and allies, some comical, some deadly serious. In the meantime, she solves mysteries, visits amaz-ing places beneath the waters, and embarks on numerous escapades both at Finsters' and back on dry land in Boston, where Hyacinth is determined to rescue friends she left be-hind at the orphanage.

A Brief Overview of the
Mer Council System

The World Council was first established in its modern form in Venice, Italy, 1432. Prior to that the Algamedum, as it was known, consisted of a loose network of Mer clan patriarchs and/or matriarchs convening in tribal fashion during annual pilgrimmages to beacons — i.e., areas of enhanced energies scattered around the world, where it was believed that communication was bolstered by natural forces. from these ancient gathering spots the five major coalitions of clans ruled in democratic consensus on matters of importance to Mer society, worldwide.

When the Venetian council was established it codified lesser councils at the five beacon sites, giving them specific powers to rule on matters within their clan coalitions. Thus when a modern Mer speaks of the Council, he/she is usually referring to a sub-Council, not the supreme Council. When being specific, a Mer may say World Council, which indicates the worldwide body. In addition, Mers often designate the sub-Councils by their beacon sites. I.E. Impatha Council (India), Brittany Council (France), Pacific Council (Easter Island), Arctic Council (Greenland), and Atlantic Council (Georgia, USA).

Sub-Councils rule on all mundane controversies of Mer life: territorial disputes, personal grievances, and relations with local Landers. The World Council rules on far more serious and far-reaching issues, including war and murder.

Famous edicts of the World Council in modern times include the Call to Arms of 1940, which directed Mers to aid the Allies in WWII; and the UniWorld Edict of 2002, which condemned and ostracized the Mer leadership of the massive conglomerate on grounds of multiple assaults against

Mers and extreme violations of the legendary Terra Firma Harmonium Edict of the founding Venetian Council in 1432. This edict established tolerance, goodwill, and respect as the cornerstones of Mer treatment of Landers, who were (and are) considered inferiors and thus deserving of noblesse oblige.

For more information on Mers, the WaterLilies series, and additional books by official Mer chronicler Deborah Smith, visit the following websites:

www.bellebooks.com

www.deborahsmith.com

www.deborahsmith-solomonsseal.com

www.deborahsmith-mermaids.com

Everyone's special
in their own way.

KASEYBELLE
The Tiniest Fairy in the Kingdom
by Sandra Chastain

Book One in the Everyone's Special
Southern children's series

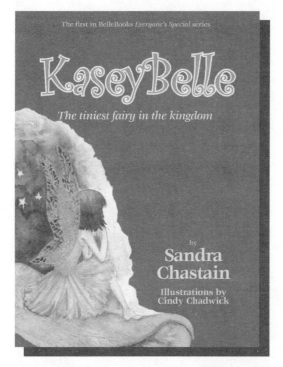

KaseyBelle
saves her
friends from
an angry
giant and
learns that it's
not the size of
her wings
that makes
her special,
but the size of
her heart.

The Mossy Creek

MOSSY CREEK

Book One

The first book in the series introduces a mayor who sees breaking the law as her civic duty and a by-the-books police chief trying to live up to his father's legend. We've got a bittersweet feud at the coffee shop and heartwarming battles on the softball field. We've got a world-weary Santa with a poignant dream and a flying Chihuahua with a streak of bad luck. You'll meet Millicent, who believes in stealing joy, and the outrageous patrons of O'Day's Pub, who believe there's no such thing as an honest game of darts. You'll want to tune your radio to the Bereavement Report and prop your feet up at Mama's All You Can Eat Café. While you're there, say hello to our local gossip columnist, Katie Bell. She'll make you feel like one of the family and tell you a story that will make you laugh — or smile through your tears.

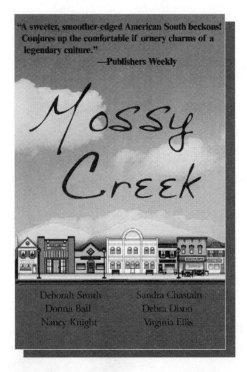

"A sweeter, smoother-edged American South beckons! Conjures up the comfortable if ornery charms of a legendary culture."
—Publishers Weekly

Mossy Creek

Deborah Smith   Sandra Chastain
Donna Ball   Debra Dixon
Nancy Knight   Virginia Ellis

Hometown Series

REUNION AT MOSSY CREEK

Book Two

This time they've got the added drama of the big town reunion commemorating the twenty-year-old mystery of the late, great Mossy Creek High School, which burned to the ground amid quirky rumors and dark secrets. In the meantime, sassy 100-year-old Eula Mae Whit is convinced Williard Scott has put a death curse on her, and Mossy Creek Police Chief Amos Royden is still fighting his reputation as the town's most eligible bachelor. There's the new bad girl in town, Jasmine, and more adventures from the old bad girl in town, Mayor Ida Hamilton. And last but not least, Bob the flying Chihuahua finds himself stalked by an amorous lady poodle.

The Mossy Creek

SUMMER IN MOSSY CREEK

Book Three

It's a typical summer in the good-hearted mountain town of Mossy Creek, Georgia, where love, laughter and friendship make nostalgia a way of life. Creekites are always ready for a sultry romance, a funny feud or a sincere celebration, and this summer is no different. Get ready for a comical battle over pickled beets and a spy mission to recover hijacked chow-chow peppers. Meet an unforgettable parakeet named Tweedle Dee and a lovable dog named Dog. Watch Amos and Ida sidestep the usual rumors and follow Katie Bell's usual snooping. In the meantime, old-timer Opal Suggs and her long-dead sisters share a lesson on living, and apple farmer Hope Bailey faces poignant choices when an old flame returns to claim her.

Hometown Series

BLESSINGS OF MOSSY CREEK

Book Four

The good-hearted citizens of Mossy Creek, Georgia are in a mood to count their blessings. Maybe it's the influence of the new minister in town, who keeps his sense of humor while battling a stern church treasurer. Maybe it's the afterglow of Josie McClure's incredibly romantic wedding to the local "Bigfoot." Or maybe it's the new baby in Hank and Casey Blackshear's home. As autumn gilds the mountains, town gossip columnist, Katie Bell, has persuaded Creekites to confess their joys, troubles, and gratitudes. As always, that includes a heapin' helping of laughter, wisdom, and good old-fashioned scandal.

Look for Book Five of the Mossy Creek Hometown series
coming in June 2005

A DAY IN MOSSY CREEK

Coming soon from BelleBooks...

All God's Creatures
by Carolyn McSparren

The story of a Memphis Cotton Carnival Princess who gave up her debutante throne to become a large animal veterinarian.

Mother's reaction to my announcement that I was changing my name and planning to become a veterinarian was typical.

"Don't be ridiculous, Margaret," she said. "Nice girls do not become veterinarians. And Maggie sounds like an Irish washerwoman."

In my previous attempts to break out of the mold she kept trying to force me into, I had meekly gone back to being a nice obedient daughter and relinquished my goals.

Not this time. Mother took to sighing deeply and casting her eyes to heaven every time I mentioned anything about Dr. Parmenter or vet school.

She even enlisted a couple of her Junior League buddies to 'counsel' me.

I never answered back or argued. I simply smiled and signed up for more chemistry classes. Now, that really infuriated her.

By the end of that August I had endured summer courses in biology and chemistry in un-air-conditioned classrooms, and nearly died of asphyxiation. The straight A's kept Mother's disapproval at bay, but only barely. She had retrenched, and was now suggesting that I become a nurse. Then I could marry a doctor.

Dr. Parmenter never questioned me about my plans, although I was up to working four afternoons a week and all day Saturday for him. I had also graduated to doing most of his anesthesia and was learning how to stitch up wounds on old innertubes.

One hot afternoon as he finished neutering a tabby cat, he looked over those glasses at me and asked, "Well, do you really want to do it?"

I nodded. I knew what he was talking about although we had never actually discussed my becoming a veterinarian.

"They won't like it," he said, and clipped the last suture.

"If you mean my parents, they already don't like it."

He pulled off his gloves, balled them up and tossed them overhanded like a basketball into the waste receptacle in the corner. "Goal." Then he turned to me and sighed. "Assuming you get into vet school, and that's a mighty tall assumption, your professors won't like it, your colleagues won't like it, and if you should graduate, a great many potential clients won't like it."

These days more than half the graduating veterinarians in this country are women. I truly think that when the men discovered the pay was lousy, the hours and conditions frequently frightful, and nobody appreciated them, they fled to more lucrative pastures like people medicine and left the field open for the girls. They have dashed through joyfully.

But not then. There were women vets, of course, but more up north than in the mid-south. Tennessee didn't yet have its own vet school, so that meant I'd have to vie for a place at Auburn or Alabama or Mississippi State. Against all their native good ole boys.

"Why should they care?" I asked. Because I spent twelve years in a girls' school environment, I had never worried about competition with males, and Southwestern at that time demanded good brains from both genders that attended.

He lifted one scrawny hip onto the edge of the examining table and clicked off the reasons on his fingers.

"Your professors will not wish to waste their time teaching you as you will undoubtedly get married, quit the profession and raise babies."

I snorted.

"Your male colleagues will dislike you because you are taking a place that should have gone to a man. Your female colleagues will resent you because they wish to be queen bees. Finally, your potential clients will think you're incapable of being as good a vet as a man, particularly if you should decide to treat large animals as well as small."

"So I'm doomed?"

He shook his head. "Indeed not. I saw the lust in your eyes five minutes after you walked into my surgery with your pup. I have since discovered you have an excellent brain, good manual dexterity, a complete lack of fear of animals—which will get you into trouble one day if you don't watch it—and a considerable amount of brawn for a woman. If you continue to be serious and to make the grade both in school and here, then when the time comes, I will get you into Mississippi State."

"Right. You and what army, Dr. Parmenter?"

"I, Miss Maggie, am an army." With that he turned around and walked out.

He was, too.

I have never known exactly how he cajoled and browbeat Mississippi State. I suspect there was an element of blackmail. He's the reason I can add D. V. M. to my name. I can never repay him.

But every life I save, every cripple I mend, even the animals in pain that I release from suffering, are tiny installments on the debt.